CAPTIVITY

By Jonathan Gillman

Acknowledgements:

Cover, Bryan Swormstedt
Assistance, Meghan Evans and Gail Fresia
Landscape photo, Jonathan Gillman
Author photo, Pamela Nomura

Captivity
A novel by Jonathan Gillman
Second Print Edition

ISBN: 9781098503666

For Pam

C'est mon témoignage à toi

I

Chapter One

Word spread quickly that morning: savages were sighted nearby; an attack was imminent.

Carrie took Hannah to the compound, as Gideon instructed.

She was to remain there, inside its high wooden fence, until he gave permission for her to leave, no matter how peaceful it seemed. "You saw what happened last time, how they lulled us into thinking we were safe and then, when we were least expecting it, they attacked. And they will do it again. I know."

And no, he would not leave her with a musket. It wasn't seemly.

Who, she wanted to protest, would see her?

His raised hand silenced her.

Carrie knew that gesture. "This is what I say," it told her. "This is what you will do."

She was quiet, waiting for him to go on.

Her brother, the good Minister Isaac, would protect her.

Only Isaac wasn't there. He set off shortly after she arrived, taking Gideon and the other men toward the north, muskets in hand, to intercept the heathens. "I can see them, sister, lurking behind trees; the Lord God has shown me the way. I cannot rest until every last one of them is dead."

The only ones there were Carrie, with her daughter Hannah, and Isaac's wife, Rebecca. That was all. No men. No weapons.

"And nothing to defend ourselves with," she complained to him, "in case the heathens do attack, except the fence around the compound and the safety of your house."

"And your belief in the Lord God Almighty," Isaac reminded her, "which is stronger than a dozen muskets or a row of cannons. Nothing to defend yourselves with? I am leaving you with the best defense there is. Even if it is just the two of you women here, and you are surrounded by a hundred screaming savages, each with a musket in one hand and a tomahawk in the other, and yelling blood-curdling oaths, your faith in a just and righteous God will protect you. But if you doubt, if in your faith you waver even one iota, a regiment of soldiers will not protect you." Isaac stopped in his preparations, looked directly at her. "You do not doubt this, do you?"

"No, brother," she answered, staring back at him, "I do not doubt it."

Carrie stayed there half the day, as she was instructed. It was a sunny day in late September, a good day to be at home, working.

Rebecca did her usual chores—cooking, cleaning, baking. Carrie felt useless. She helped the little that she could. She picked the broom up. Rebecca snatched it from her.

She reached to take the bread from the oven to test it.

"It is not yet ready." Rebecca's icy tone stopped her as if she had been slapped.

Carrie tried talking. "Have you covered the parsnips yet for spring harvest? Gideon says we should plant more early crops now and hope they winter over. After two cold winters, he says, we are due for a mild one. What do you think?"

Her eyes lit on a spider, spinning down on its line in the corner. She tensed, waited until it landed, brought her shoe down on it, ground back and forth until she was sure it was dead. "And all these spiders, everywhere. You kill one and it seems two more appear. We will never be rid of these demons." She ground her shoe over it once more.

Rebecca swept the dead spider into the fireplace. She

was never one for idle conversation. Today she seemed burdened to have Carrie and her little one around, as if she wanted nothing more than to be left alone.

Hannah was restless. She fidgeted. She whined. Every time she made a noise, Carrie glanced at Rebecca, to see if her daughter had offended. She couldn't tell. Her sister-in-law's face seemed frozen in a frown.

She remembered Hannah one day turning down her mouth, furrowing her brow. "Look, Mommy, Auntie Becky. Look."

"Auntie has her reasons to be sad," Carrie had explained. But now she started to laugh at the memory, had to clamp her mouth shut. Rebecca's look told her she had done something terribly wrong, like yawning during one of Isaac's interminable sermons.

"Go outside and play, Mommy. Go outside." Hannah tugged at Carrie's dress.

"Shh." Carrie put her finger to her lip.

"I want to."

"We have to stay in here," she whispered.

"Why?" Hannah screeched.

A hand struck the bread board.

"Shh!" Carrie did not need to look to know Rebecca's response.

"Play patty-cake, Mommy." Hannah pulled at her mother's arm, wanting her to knead dough, as Rebecca was doing with the second batch of bread, as Carrie did at home, pushing it down, sliding it forward, stopping to slap doughy hands together.

"Not now," Carrie whispered.

"Please, Mommy."

Behind her Carrie heard Rebecca's kneading slow, stop, pause, continue faster, harder—punch, slap, punch. Her own stomach knotted, feeling Rebecca's disapproval.

"Here, Mommy. Let's play with Auntie." Hannah reached her hand toward the dough.

Carrie grabbed her arm, pulled it away just before Rebecca's open palm descended on it. "It is not our house.

Come. Let's go outside."

Outside Carrie sighed. She felt as if a rope which circled her chest, pulled tighter and tighter, had been loosened.

She looked up at the sun and blue sky. It was a beautiful day.

Kneeling while her daughter stood smiling, the dimple showing on her check, Carrie played patty-cake with Hannah—patty-cake, patty-cake, baker's man—over and over, their hands patting their own, each other's, faster and faster until Hannah burst into squeals of laughter, flung herself into her mother's arms, grew calm, then pushed away, demanding, "Again, Mommy, again," clapping her hands together until Carrie played again. Their Gideon-isn't-home-and-no-one-else-is-watching game.

Carrie glanced over her shoulder. Rebecca had stayed inside.

After the seventh time, Hannah remained nestled against her. Carrie slipped her arm around her daughter, her pale cheek and sparkling hair against her mother's knee. Carrie leaned over, sang softly into Hannah's ear, songs and nursery rhymes her mother had taught her. "Where is Thumbkin? Where is Thumbkin?" Hannah sat up, alert, holding her hands out. "Here I am!" She wiggled her thumbs, hid her hands behind her.

Carrie didn't respond. Hannah poked her with her fingers. "Play Thumbkin, Mommy." Carrie shook her head. She wondered if Rebecca might hear them, who she would mention it to, these songs and games of hers that both Isaac and Gideon thought unseemly.

Hannah kept prodding with her hands.

Carrie relented. "Just once."

After the fifth time she said, "Enough for now, sweetheart," kissed Hannah on the cheek. In her mind Gideon stood behind her, his silence reproaching her. "You spoil her with these games."

A noise startled her. Carrie jerked around, expecting an attack, ready to stand, grab Hannah, and rush for the house.

A boy burst into the compound, shooting an imaginary musket. Another, looking identical, yelled out, clutched his shoulder, fell to the ground, lay still.

"Paul!" Carrie started to call, thinking it was Rebecca and Isaac's son. The word had not left her mouth when she realized it couldn't be him. He had been shot in a raid the year before, on a day much like this one. She and Rebecca were sitting on the grass, shelling beans.

Paul knelt a few feet away, playing with his new wooden top. It was the only toy his father, the good Minister Isaac, thought appropriate, "for all the lessons it taught." Even that he only approved of reluctantly. Carrie had to argue with him, over and over, "Life can't be all work, boys need to play too," before he relented.

Without warning, shouts and shots filled the air. Paul half cried out, fell to the ground, face down.

Carrie grabbed Hannah, wrapped her in her arms.

Isaac and Gideon ran out from the barn, aimed their muskets toward the heathen attackers, already retreating into the woods at the bottom of the hill, fired, reloaded, ran down after them. At the bottom, Gideon stopped, but Isaac, calling out, "Cowards. Godless cowards!" disappeared into the woods.

For a long while they heard nothing but yelling, a shot, another shot, another yell, that might have been the cry of someone wounded or a person shouting, "Godless Cowards!"

Gideon had already rejoined them when Isaac walked out of the woods and trudged up the hill toward them, his musket in his right hand. Without a word he went to where Rebecca sat on the ground, holding Paul's body against her, rocking back and forth. Carrie squatted behind her, trying to comfort her.

Isaac stopped above them, stood looking down, then put his head back and roared, a cry so loud the heathens who did this must have heard, no matter how far away they had gotten. "Death!" he called. "Death to all heathens!" He knelt beside Rebecca, hugged her, gently took his son from her, and wrapped his arms around the body, tears streaming down his face. As he did, Gideon removed the top from the boy's hand, held it behind him in his fist.

For the next twenty-four hours, Isaac did not let go of Paul. While Rebecca sat in a corner by herself and for hours at a time did not move, Isaac carried his son everywhere. Even when he went to bed he did not relax his hold, but lay, eyes open, staring out at nothing, the body on his chest.

The next day Gideon dug a hole, only the second grave for their new cemetery. Would it hold only children? Carrie wondered. Was this the Promised Land? Or a place accursed, with yet another dying young?

Gideon knelt by his brother-in-law. "Isaac, you need to give him up. It is not right in the eyes of the Lord to cling so to the things of this world. As flesh he must pass. You know this. Not to do as is right with him is to tempt the wrath of God."

At the simple ceremony at the gravesite, Isaac and Rebecca stood holding each other while Gideon read scripture. "I may not do this as is right, Lord, but I do it in Thy spirit, as well as I am able," he said, as he commended his nephew's body to the earth and his soul to the Lord. "It is the Lord's will," he counseled the wailing parents. "Not to accept it is to grieve Him, to question Him, to anger Him."

A child shouted. It startled Carrie back to the present. It was only Jeremiah. He had no gun but a pretend one, and the person he stood over, peering down at in childish triumph, was his twin brother Joshua. Suddenly Joshua grabbed Jeremiah by the arm, tried to pull him down. The two rolled on the ground, shouting, yelling, raising the dust.

Carrie was about to urge them to be quieter, they didn't want to alert the savages, when Sarah, Gideon's sister, walked around the corner of the barn, holding her daughter's hand.

Carrie smiled. "Here's Susannah," she whispered to Hannah. "You play with her now. Mommy needs to rest."

Sarah sat on the ground beside Carrie. "There is no sign of our attackers?"

Carrie shook her head. "It has been this quiet all

day."

Sarah smiled as Jeremiah and Joshua whooped again. "The savages can hear them half-way to Boston."

Carrie started to lift her arm to silence them.

Sarah's hand caught hers. "Hopefully it's another false alarm."

Carrie nodded, let her hand fall to her lap. You can't be too careful, she thought. Not after what happened with Paul.

She wanted to know where Sarah had been, why it took her so long to get there. She didn't want to sound like Gideon. She ran the phrases over in her head. "Were you delayed in leaving?"

"I had just put the bread in the oven. I didn't want to have to start over."

Carrie nodded again. The uncertainty, the waiting, wore at her. She wished she had started her own baking. But she was wasting time with Hannah.

"It took a long time rising. The whole while I kept thinking, our house is almost in the compound."

Carrie glanced past Sarah in its direction. It sat on the other side of Isaac's, just outside the fence they built after the raid that killed Paul. It was also on the top of the hill, not halfway down like hers and Gideon's.

"It is on the edge. I know Isaac doesn't think so, he said I needed to come too. But it is close."

Carrie nodded. "I wanted to get the parsnips covered." She shrugged. "Let's hope this weather holds."

Sarah smiled. "With our luck, tomorrow will be damp and cold."

"And the next day," Carrie added, "it will snow."

They both laughed.

Carrie wished she saw more of Sarah. There was always so much to do, and the little way past Isaac's that her house was made it seem so much farther.

Carrie watched Hannah playing with Susannah on the ground. Her hands and arms and face and clothes were dirty. Carrie would have to clean her up before Gideon returned.

The sun had moved past overhead, into the west. A few flies buzzed. A breeze stirred, its sharpness reminding her it was no longer summer.

Susannah gathered blades of grass, piled and mounded and patted them together, as if making a nest.

Hannah stopped playing. She got up from where she was, walked over, sat beside Carrie. “Rest time.” She laid her head in her mother’s lap. Carrie leaned over, whispered into her ear. “Now I lay me down to sleep . . .” In a few moments Hannah’s breathing was steady.

Carrie stretched, looked around at the compound. “Isaac’s Godly Settlement,” a haven against the wilderness, consisted of several acres on a hill at the western edge of the Massachusetts Colony. The barn, the house and the church beside them were surrounded in all four directions by a palisades-style fence. Beyond it to the south, part way down the hill, was their log cabin, off by itself; to the north and east sat Sarah’s house, the stream, the dam, the small pond, the mill, the one room cabin they used as a school, the half dozen other houses that made up their community, and the few small fields they had cleared and planted. To the west lay the wilderness, dark and forbidding.

At the top of the hill the two boys squatted on the ground. Joshua, wearing his new hand-me-down leather belt, took turns with Jeremiah, playing with their wooden top.

Seeing it gave Carrie a start. It had been Paul’s. Gideon gave it to them after Paul died. No sense letting it sit idle.

Joshua wound it up, spun it.

Carrie wanted to take a turn herself, watch it swirl around, wobble as it slowed, fall listing to one side, wrap its string around it, spin it again.

She felt drowsy. “It’s making me sleepy,” she said, “this doing nothing.”

Sarah yawned, stretched. “Yes. Me as well.”

Carrie shut her eyes. Sounds of delight from the boys punctuated her sleepiness. She knew they had to be on their guard, but surely the danger had passed for today. She should wake Hannah, take her and go home.

There was so much work at home waiting to be done. Water to draw and heat, soiled clothes to wash, others to mend. Bread to knead and bake. The house to sweep. Supper to fix. All to be finished before Gideon returned, no matter what the excuse.

She would rest a little longer, her hand on Hannah's shoulder, see what Sarah thought. Carrie was sure she would approve. There was no point asking Rebecca. She was home already.

Carrie stirred, dreaming Daisy, their cow, had broken free from her tether, walked crashing into the woods. She started to call out, "Gideon, the cow," put her arm to her side to rouse him.

A second crash sounded, not a cow but part of the waking world. Pandemonium broke loose. Sarah tugged her arm, screamed, "Heathens!"

"Mommy," Joshua called. "Savages!"

Carrie shook sleep and its images off, opened her eyes.

"Get inside!" Sarah cried beside her. "Susannah! Joshua! Jeremiah! Get inside! Hurry."

Carrie heard a shot, a child's voice call, "Oh, Mommy!"

Ten feet of the fence on the compound's western edge lay flat. Heathen warriors raced across it, naked except for loin cloths, leggings, and moccasins. They whooped and cried, holding guns over their heads, rushed up the hill.

At the sight of them, Carrie gasped. Goose bumps rose all over her arms and legs.

She picked up Hannah, hurried to the house, pushed on the door. It didn't move. She pushed again. It seemed sealed shut.

"Rebecca." She banged on the door. "Let me in!" She pushed harder. "Rebecca! Please!" It remained shut.

Carrie heard the pounding of the heathens' feet,

their calls, cries, shouts, even their breathing, getting closer.

She turned, ran toward the top of the hill, looking for a way to escape.

There it was, everything she had ever been warned about. A dozen half-naked savages, larger, louder, more real than she had imagined, were running toward her. She tried to mutter a prayer. "Lord, protect and save us." She couldn't remember how to say it. She tripped over the words, abandoned it part way through. There wasn't time. The heathens were almost to her. She had nothing to defend herself with, not even, when it mattered most, her faith.

She heard a cry, another shot, two more.

Hannah in her arms jerked her limbs straight out. She heard three more shots.

Everything happened in a jumble. Heathens rushed past, running here and there, like figures in a nightmare. Three of them disappeared behind the barn. A cow bellowed. Sarah, holding Susannah, hurried toward the barn, screaming, "Joshua! Jeremiah!" Flames started up one side of the barn.

Carrie heard wood splintering and a loud crash, looked back to see two heathens breaking open the door of the house.

From inside Rebecca shrieked. "Heathens! Devils! Stay away from me!"

Sarah, still carrying Susannah, ran away from the burning barn toward the fence at the top of the compound.

Hannah, limp in Carrie's arms, hadn't stirred.

A child lay face down in the grass, a wooden top clutched in his hand. "Paul," Carrie thought. She took a step in his direction. Everything spun. She tried to take another step. She couldn't move.

Two heathens carried Rebecca, kicking and flailing, from the house. "Filthy savages!" She screeched. "May the wrath of God strike you dead!"

Above them the sky remained blue, silent, still. No lightning flashed out of it.

An animal cried out from the barn, a hideous, agonized sound that wrenched Carrie's heart. Another bellowed.

Carrie smelled singed hair, heard wood crackling. She tried to move toward the child lying on the ground. A hand grabbed her arm, squeezed so hard it hurt. Another pushed her around, started her down the hill.

Chapter Two

Carrie walked where the heathens made her, down the hill, over the flattened portion of the fence, into the woods. Whenever she slowed or hesitated, the one behind her shoved her forward.

They crossed the stream, set off following a path the heathens seemed to know was there. They moved quickly, stepping over rocks she stumbled on. Whenever she lagged, the one behind her trod on her heels, step, kick, step, step, kick.

She had trouble keeping up. She had her baby to carry.

When she could, Carrie leaned over, comforting Hannah in her mind. "Just a little longer, and then we'll rest. We'll play patty-cake again and eat, and I'll sing to you and you'll lie down in your own bed and go to sleep. Not much farther. You are being so good. Even Gideon would be proud of his little girl. He wouldn't call you willful, not today," wouldn't warn she was too headstrong, they had better beware, she had the Devil in her.

The foot of the person behind her grazed her heel. She tried to speed up.

Her arms ached, her shoulders hurt, her legs throbbed, but on Carrie went, step after step.

After what seemed like hours she bumped into the person in front of her. They had stopped. She looked around. They were in a small, grassy clearing, with woods all around, and a stream along one side. Everyone was resting.

Carrie sank down onto the ground, nestled Hannah against her, whispered to her, soothing, "We can rest now. It's not much farther."

Carrie shut her eyes. Her neck throbbed. Her feet hurt, her calves ached. She couldn't remember ever being so tired.

She heard voices near her—a woman talking, a man answering, the woman talking again, all in a harsh language she didn't know. It sounded as if they were arguing.

Something cold touched her shoulder. Carrie opened her eyes. One of the heathens stood looking at her. There were scratches on his face, making hideous shapes on his yellow skin. One of his front teeth was missing. Half his head was shaved. The other half had hair longer than hers, cut above her shoulder in the "city, New World" way Isaac did not approve of. His reached in a braid down over his shoulder.

He kept staring at her.

What was it he wanted? Was this where they killed her? Did they bring her there to do it? Did he have something worse in mind, and this was when it happened?

She clutched Hannah closer.

Behind him an old heathen woman spoke. The savage shook something in front of Carrie.

She looked at it. The little finger of the hand holding it was half missing.

The urge to vomit rose into her throat. She had to clamp her mouth shut to keep it down.

The old woman took what the man was holding, lowered it, moved it a little away from her.

It was a dipper of water.

Carrie started to reach her hand toward it, remembered what Gideon had said. The list of what to do and not do if you ever were captured ran through her mind. One of the first was: Never eat or drink anything a heathen offered you. She shook her head.

The old woman held the dipper closer. Carrie pushed it away. The heathen man still stood there. He looked impatient.

The old woman lifted the dipper to her own lips.

Was she really drinking, Carrie wondered, or only pretending? Hadn't Gideon warned her how cunning they were.

A little water dribbled down the old woman's chin. She lowered the dipper toward Carrie, said something. Carrie didn't understand the words, but the meaning was clear. "Drink."

The heathen man spoke sharply, started to stomp away. The old woman answered even more sharply. He stopped, stood waiting.

The old woman seemed calm, gentle. She took another sip, half smiled at Carrie, held the dipper closer.

Carrie reached out, took hold of it, thought, "I hope, Lord, what I am doing is right", and drank, slowly, until the water was gone. She hadn't realized she was so thirsty.

While Carrie drank, the old woman spoke. Strange, harsh noises came from her mouth. She pointed at Hannah, made indications with her hands, spoke again. "Put her in the earth," she seemed to be saying. The sounds of her language were rough and unpleasant; they were hard to listen to.

"No." Carrie shook her head, let the dipper fall as she held Hannah tighter, waiting for one of them to grab her child and pull.

The old woman only spoke. She turned to the heathen man, made a harsh sound.

"Dead." He said it in English, in the coarse way one would talk who was not used to the language. It took Carrie a moment to realize it was a word she knew.

"No!" She shook her head more vigorously. The heathens were trying to trick her. Hannah was only sleeping. Resting from the—

Carrie leaned over, started singing to her baby, moving in rhythm with the words.

Rock a bye, baby, in the tree top.
When the wind blows, the cradle will rock.
When the bough breaks—

Carrie stopped, kissed Hannah's cheeks. They were cool now. That was good. She wasn't feverish.

When the bough breaks, the cradle will fall,
And down will come baby, cradle, and all.

Carrie kept rocking back and forth, the tune, without words, going on and on in her head. She hoped that soon Gideon would step out of the woods, return from wherever he had gone, and lead her and Hannah back to the safety of their house. Maybe, if she kept thinking it, wanting it, before long it would happen.

"Long path."

The heathen's voice startled her. Again he had spoken in English.

Carrie looked at him.

He pointed the direction they were headed. The next moment he was gone.

All their party rose. The old woman lingered, held her hand down toward Carrie, grasped her elbow. Carrie jerked her arm away, pulled herself to her feet, clutching her daughter to her.

Before she was ready, they were walking again. Off they went, through unbroken woods. The narrow path climbed, leveled out, climbed some more, twisting and turning over rocks and boulders. Carrie struggled to keep up.

Hannah seemed so heavy, weighing her down more and more. Her hands, her arms, her shoulders said, "Hold on, keep going. Don't drop her; don't let her go."

Carrie thought each step would be her last, but on she went.

The climb got steeper. It took all her energy to pick up her right foot, move her left foot forward, following the rhythm of the others. Going downhill was harder; she had to brace herself to keep from lunging forward and falling. If she faltered or slowed down, the heathen behind her pushed his hand into her shoulder, kicked his foot against her heel. Sometimes that happened when she thought she was keeping up. She tried to move faster.

She needed to think about Hannah, what she would do with her when she woke. She wondered why she was sleeping so long. It wasn't like her. Maybe the rhythm of walking lulled her.

It made Carrie think of Mary, her second born.

Something had been wrong with her from the beginning. She wheezed when she breathed, gasping for air. When Carrie gave her the breast, her lips grabbed it eagerly. She started to suck, screamed as the milk hit her throat. Carrie took the nipple from her mouth, patted her, soothed her, tried again. Mary gummed it, sucked, screamed again.

Carrie was desperate. Her baby cried from hunger, cried louder when she tried to eat.

"Gideon," she asked. "What is it? What have I done? Why can't I feed my lamb without her crying out? What must I do? How have I displeased Him?"

Gideon said nothing. He turned away, sat by the candle reading the Bible, his lips moving with its phrases.

By evening Carrie was exhausted. She held the wailing child to her, walking back and forth, trying to soothe her.

The cries sounded strange, like a violin untuned or played off key. The little body got tenser, more rigid.

Carrie almost fell from fatigue. She brought the baby toward the bed with her.

Gideon glared at her. "You are not bringing that child in this bed."

"Gideon, what else can I do?"

"Put her in her cradle and come to bed alone. It isn't seemly."

Rebecca, who had delivered her, looked in to find Carrie pacing the sitting room, holding the screaming child to her chest. "What have you done to her?"

Before Carrie could answer the baby wailed.

"You need to feed her."

"I have tried."

Carrie tried again. She held the baby to her chest, let loose her swollen breast, stuck the nipple in the baby's mouth. Mary gummed it, started sucking, sucked a few moments, opened her mouth, and screamed. White liquid dribbled down her chin.

"Is your milk bile?"

Carrie took her finger, ran it across the liquid, brought it to her mouth. It tasted sweet and sticky.

Rebecca pointed at it. "It is the Devil's drink."

"It is only milk. Taste it." Carrie scraped a drop more onto her finger, held it up toward Rebecca.

Rebecca stepped back, her eyes wide open. "Why do you tempt me? What abomination is this?"

"It is my milk. It was good enough for Hannah."

Rebecca stared at her.

"The fault is not in the milk."

"No," Rebecca responded. "It is in the mother." She pointed at the baby in her arms. "Or in the vessel the Devil has chosen to inhabit."

"She is an innocent babe."

"Who of us is born without sin? Who?"

Carrie looked down at the tense baby, so newly born, and wondered, where could she have acquired sin?

"In Eve's fall we sinned all." Rebecca said as Carrie thought it. "You know that full well. Don't you?"

Carrie nodded. She knew. She needed to put her baby down and let her fuss. How else would she ever learn?

Instead, Carrie lost her temper. She knew it was a sign of weakness, and one of the grievous faults, but she couldn't help it. She spoke harshly to Rebecca and sent her away. "It is easy for you to say that. It is not your child. If it was, I don't think you could follow your own advice, no matter how much Isaac urged you to." Carrie caught herself before she said more. "I thank you for your kind help, sister. But now there is nothing more you can do."

She put the baby down in her cradle, climbed into bed beside Gideon. He already slept. She lay, eyes open, listening to the baby and her strange sounds and muffled cries. Before long Carrie slept, started awake, listened, slept again.

She woke in the middle of the night. Something had changed. She heard it in the silence, the absence of cries and wheezes. She tiptoed to the cradle, peered in. The little body, so tight and contorted when she laid her down, had relaxed, all except the fingers, still clenched in two tiny fists. Carrie picked her up, shut her eyes, and held the child, crying. She stood with the baby Mary a long time, swaying with her bare feet on the cold wooden floor. She wanted to wake Gideon to tell him. She didn't dare. That wouldn't be seemly.

Every time he stirred, or shifted his position, or his breathing changed, she worried. What if he woke? Would he chastise her for being out of bed? Command her to hurry back? She thought of putting Mary in her cradle, waiting until he noticed. "Carrie, come quickly. Something is wrong with our angel." Half the day might pass—his breakfast eaten, chores done, the Bible read—before that happened.

The rest of the night Carrie stood, clutching her child to her.

A little before dawn Gideon stirred. Carrie climbed back under the covers, still holding Mary, waited for him to wake. She didn't know any other way to tell him.

Gideon opened his eyes, looked at her, and sat up. "What do you have there?"

"It's Mary."

He drew away from her. "Put her back in the cradle. Put her back this instant." He pointed. "Didn't I tell you?"

Carrie didn't move.

"Why are you not obeying?"

She thrust the child toward him. "She is dead. See."

"Oh." Gideon was silent.

She let Mary go, giving her into his hands.

Gideon did not take her. He pulled his hands away. The baby fell the short distance to the bed, lay face down between them.

Carrie waited, for him to pick up the baby, or touch her, or soothe and comfort with his voice.

The silence continued.

Gideon put his fingers together, looked off into the distance. "If the Lord has taken her, He must have His reasons."

Carrie started crying. She couldn't help it. She tried to hold it in but the sobs continued.

Gideon frowned. "Why do you weep? We must accept the Lord's way, not cry out in lamentations."

She could not stifle her sobs.

"Do you question what He has done?"

Carrie shook her head. One more heave escaped her. "I'm sorry."

"Rejoice that she is gone."

Carrie turned and looked at him. Her mouth fell open.

"Rejoice. There is one more sinner gone."

"Rejoice?"

Gideon nodded. "The Devil tried to take her, but he failed. She is with the Lord now. Rejoice!"

Later that morning at Sunday service, Carrie sat by Gideon in their usual spot near the front, her jaw tight, staring at the floor, as the others of their parish walked past. Except for Sarah, not one stopped to offer solace or condolences. They seemed to hurry by without looking at her, to leave a space around her, turn their words and glances away, their every gesture saying, this, the first death in their little colony, was her fault. Something was wrong with her, so wrong they couldn't sit by her or talk with her without being contaminated themselves. Even Gideon seemed as if he'd rather be anywhere else than there with her.

And her own brother Isaac, who not that long before would have offered comfort, made his sermon The Devil in Little Children. "We are none of us born without sin," he intoned. "There is no one who is immune," he thundered from the pulpit, "when the Devil has his way," another of his "We must be vigilant" sermons that had the small congregation nodding in agreement.

Carrie felt as alone then as she did now, with

heathen strangers on all sides, hurrying her on, farther and farther from the sanctified ground where Mary was laid to rest.

She longed to be back in England, where even Isaac would have hugged her and said, “Sister, how can I help?” And where there was always her mother, who would not say Carrie was bad, would not imply she had done something wrong. She would maybe have said, “There are things that happen we don’t understand, and that makes them so much harder.” She wouldn’t have said much. Mostly she would have wrapped her arms around her daughter, and held her and rocked her, humming or singing in her ear, the way she did when Carrie was young and skinned her knee, or fell and bruised her arm. She would have stayed that way as long as necessary, hours or even days, until it didn’t hurt and ache so, and Carrie was able to smile again, and go off on her own.

But her mother wasn’t there. She was far away, past inhospitable land, across an ocean. No one had taken her place.

A hand pushed Carrie’s shoulder. She lurched forward.

Mary’s dying hurt so much, but Mary was alive such a short while. She hadn’t become a person yet that Carrie knew and loved and delighted in. Not like Hannah, her sweet, wonderful Hannah.

She should have put her in the earth when the heathens offered.

She knew. She had known from the moment her daughter convulsed without a sound, when the heathens came whooping and rushing up the hill.

The hand shoved her shoulder again. She almost stumbled, caught herself, straightened half-way up, the weight of her daughter dragging her down.

Carrie needed to stop. Her body hurt, her arms ached, her shoes pinched, her feet throbbed. Every step seemed like her last. She needed to do something with Hannah, do something with Hannah, do something with Hannah, her thoughts stuck in the rhythm of walking, one foot in front of the other, in front of the other, in front of the other.

Chapter Three

Hours later they came to a clearing. Everyone stopped walking.

Carrie didn't put Hannah down or flop to the ground herself, but stood, holding her, her feet going up and down, not moving forward, slumping over more and more until Hannah's own dangling feet touched the ground.

Carrie leaned over still farther, slowly let Hannah down. As if putting her in bed when she had fallen asleep in her arms, Carrie laid her gently down to rest, sat on the ground beside her, shut her own eyes. Her arms felt as if they had stretched to twice their length. The back of her neck throbbed. Her heels and toes burned.

When she opened her eyes, it was dusk. Other heathens were gathered there. They were all around. Men, with their sweat. Women, with dresses made of skins. Children, running, playing.

An unpleasant odor hung in the air. It was the people, the scent of their skin, mingled with dirt and sweat. Another smell mixed in, of meat, cooked on a fire.

The heathens sat in small groups, eating.

Carrie's stomach rumbled. She was so hungry, and so tired she couldn't keep her eyes open. Even her thoughts were slow.

She felt on the ground beside her. Hannah was gone!

Didn't they eat children? Wasn't that another of Gideon's admonitions? If you are captured, and you have a child with you, don't ever, ever let the child out of your grasp.

And she in her neglect—

No. Her baby was still there. Carrie's fingers found

her, a little to the side.

An old heathen woman—the one who had given her water, with her short, solid body, high cheek bones, tight lined skin, and a dark braid flecked at the temples with gray—set down beside her a cup of water, a bowl of porridge, started to move away.

Carrie grabbed for her, held the air. "Wait."

The heathen woman stopped, looked down. Carrie pointed at Hannah, tried to duplicate the gestures the woman had made. "Put her in the ground?"

The old woman nodded, said something Carrie didn't understand. She gestured, her hands moving quickly, again and again. Carrie still didn't understand.

The old woman spoke into the dusk. A heathen materialized beside her. It was the same one who had spoken to Carrie earlier, with scratches on his face, and the smallest finger on his left hand ending in a stub, just above the first bend.

"Next sun," he said in English.

Carrie held out her hand as if to say more, tried to indicate "Now".

The heathen shook his head, walked away. The old woman followed.

Carrie's throat ached. The bottom of her mouth wanted to cry. She didn't know how she was going to get through this.

She picked up the bowl. In it was a kind of porridge with nuts, with a strip of meat on top and a few more chunks mixed in. She wasn't going to eat, she remembered. She was going to study everything she was given, the way Gideon told her, to make sure it wasn't poisoned.

Around her the heathens ate what looked like the same food. Carrie was too hungry to wait. She didn't care.

She started pushing the food into her mouth. It was gone quickly. She hardly chewed the meat. In two swallows she gulped down her water.

Carrie wanted more of everything. She looked around. In the middle of the clearing stood a large cauldron. Beside it the carcass of a deer hung from a frame of poles. The skin and meat had been removed. All that remained was its tail and the rounded bones of its ribs, forming a hollow cavity. It seemed as naked and unprotected as she felt. Was that what was going to happen to her?

Her hunger made Carrie bold. She left Hannah on the ground, as if sleeping. Keeping her eyes averted, she approached the cauldron, a large clay pot hanging over the fire. It was almost empty. She dipped in the long-handled spoon, started to serve herself. A hand on her arm stopped her. She looked around.

A man stood there, a large scar on his right cheek; it looked like a jagged bolt of lightning.

His head shook, as if to say, “No more.”

Carrie didn’t let go of the spoon. “For my child,” she said.

The heathen still held her.

“My baby.” With the other hand she imitated the motion of rocking a baby.

The heathen shoved her away. Carrie almost lost her balance, recovered, stared at him. He stared back. Neither spoke.

Without taking her eyes off him, Carrie stepped closer to the cauldron, filled her small bowl, broke off a bone from the bare carcass, picked up one small strip of meat from the ground, brushed it off, filled her cup, went back to Hannah. She spooned food out to her, tried to slip it between her parted lips, as she did when Hannah was being “willful” or wasn’t hungry. A small amount stuck to her cheek, dribbled down her chin.

“You don’t want it?” she said to her child in her head. “We can’t waste it. We don’t have enough.”

When she finished the second bowl, gnawed all she could off the bone, sucked out the marrow, savored the water, Carrie was still hungry.

She made a second trip to the cauldron. The man with the scar watched her. He spit on the ground between them, but didn’t move.

Carrie pretended she didn't see him.

The cauldron was empty. She ran her finger around the edge, licked. There was nothing.

No stray strips lay on the ground. The deer's chest cavity was broken apart. There wasn't a bone left that had any meat on it.

Carrie trudged back to Hannah, sat on the ground beside her, took her hand, held it. Her mouth turned down. She pursed her lips to keep from crying.

In her head she tried to smile. There was still time to play patty-cake if Hannah wanted before she went to bed. If they did it quietly, they wouldn't disturb Gideon, sitting in his chair, reading the Bible. Carrie knew even her finger to her lips couldn't prevent Hannah's squeals, or Gideon looking up over the Good Book and staring at them. "Shhh." She hugged Hannah to quiet her.

Not tonight. Hannah was too tired for that. It had been a long day. She even went to sleep without a song.

Carrie looked down at Hannah, lying still, as if at the end of a long nap. Her sides didn't move, her chest didn't rise or fall with her breathing.

Like Mary, when Carrie woke and realized what the stillness was.

Carrie felt dazed. The day, that had started and progressed like any other, in one moment turned into a bad dream. Couldn't she go back to where it went wrong and have it continue like other days?

Her fingers twined through Hannah's hair, stuck at a snarl. Hannah didn't jerk her head away or squeal, "Ouch, Mommy, you're hurting me." She lay, not moving, not responding.

Carrie wanted to lean down, nuzzle noses with her, turn Hannah's frown to a smile.

She couldn't. It had really happened.

Now what? What was Carrie going to do with her child? How commit her to earth in the name of the Lord? She had no Bible, brought nothing with her but the clothes on her back. She always relied on Gideon and Isaac for strength and wisdom and guidance. How would she manage without them?

Carrie tried to comfort herself with Scripture. What little of it she remembered was jumbled in her head.

She was so tired. Her eyes kept shutting. Her feet hurt. They throbbed from the heel, seared from the small toe.

Something touched her shoulder. She whimpered, thinking of snakes and wolves and blood-sucking beasts. She opened her eyes. A few flares burned. She was chilled. Dew had settled over everything.

A short, squat shape stood beside her in the dark. It was the old woman who had brought her food. She indicated for Carrie to come.

"Beware," a voice inside her said. "She is one of the Devils, no matter how kind she appears. Don't forget your lessons. Turn away. Draw back. Beware!"

Carrie stood, started to follow. The woman stopped, indicated Hannah.

Carrie was so weary. How could she pick her up, much less carry her one foot more? She shut her eyes, tried to summon the strength to do it. She bent half over, opened them. Hannah wasn't there. Carrie looked around. Where could Hannah have gone?

There she was. Carrie saw her: the old woman held her.

Carrie straightened up; the old woman handed Hannah back to her, walked away.

Carrie started after her, hurried to keep up

The old woman led her to a place where people relieved themselves, stepped away.

Two women squatted over a small depression in the ground, their lower bodies exposed. Carrie thought she'd be sick. One of the women wiped herself with leaves, stood up, handed clean leaves to Carrie. Carrie set Hannah on the ground a few feet away, squatted down, exposing as little of herself as possible. She shut her eyes, imagining she was in the back house at home. Her abdomen hurt from having to urinate, and from holding it in. It took a long time to relax enough to relieve herself. Once she started, it didn't seem she would stop.

When Carrie was done, she picked Hannah up. It took her a moment to stand at full height.

Carrie rejoined the old woman. She led her through the dark to the other side of the clearing, stopped in front of a dome-shaped structure. It looked, Carrie realized, like a place where heathens lived.

The old woman pulled a flap of skins aside, beckoned for Carrie to enter. She didn't move.

This was the next temptation.

"Do not, under any circumstances," she heard the drone of Gideon's voice, "sleep in their presence. Ask the Lord for the strength to endure an eight days' march without rest before you set foot in one of their houses, or close your eyes for so much as an instant."

Carrie had decided that if she had to sleep, it would be outside. She would stay safe that way. She would not enter one of their dwellings, and invite herself to be violated.

An owl hooted above her. Carrie jumped, let out an involuntary cry.

It hooted again. Its call trailed away. It sounded as if it was laughing, mocking her. It hooted once more. It seemed close, within sight. She looked up and around. All she saw was darkness.

Carrie looked for its eyes, expecting to see pins of light, like coals from the Devil, searching her out.

She saw nothing.

Where was it hiding? Was it waiting to swoop down, poised to pounce and strike, as if she were a mouse, and carry her off to its nest?

Her mouth was dry. A little urine trickled down the inside of her thigh.

Carrie looked around. There was no cross, beckoning her with faith and hope, no friendly face or familiar house, only Gideon's voice, weak and fading, that the owl's call seemed to drown out, and savage strangers, her deep fatigue, and darkness without end. She didn't know what to do.

Lord, give her the strength to do what was right.

The old woman bent down, stepped inside. Against her better judgment, Carrie stuck her head in, looked around. A dim flare burned from a stand.

Three other people were already inside. On one side a small shape lay, sleeping on the ground, what looked like a boy's head visible from under a skin covering. Near him lay a man, his eyes shut. She thought, from what little she saw of him, it was the same heathen from earlier, the one who spoke in English. On the far side sat an old man. He was heathen too.

It did not look like a place of debauchery, but a home.

Carrie lifted her foot. "If this is a mistake, Lord, protect me in it. I do not know what else to do."

She stepped inside.

The old woman pointed at a skin spread out by itself on the ground, sat down on the far side, next to the old man. When Carrie looked back a minute later, they both were lying down, their eyes shut.

Carrie set Hannah down on the skin, sat on the ground beside her, reached to feel her feet. They each throbbed in new places: both sides of the heel, the outside of the little toe, the big toe, the end of one in the middle. She leaned over to take her shoes off, drew her hand back. Suppose someone attacked her and she had to run? She needed to leave them on. But the way they hurt... She bit her lip. She didn't think she could stand the pain.

An owl hooted above. Carrie jerked her head at the sound. It was closer than before. It sounded as if it was inside, just above her in the darkness, waiting to dive and peck out her eyes. Her heart pounded. She cowered against the side, listening. Was that it, there, that silence? or that, the impenetrable blackness, there?

Gideon, she thought, I need you. Help me. Come for me, now. Please. Before it's too late. I can't be too far away. Half a day's walk, that's all. Follow their path. If you left right after us, you're almost here. If there's blood on the ground from my shoes, follow it. And when you are outside, here, where my head is, underneath the owl, make a noise like a cat or a dog, and I will sneak out and join you, and we can escape this wretched place together.

Carrie waited.

All she heard was silence, and the breathing of the other four—a quiet, steady sound, a whistle, a catch, a snore, silence again.

Now was the greatest danger, she had learned her lesson, now, when it seemed most peaceful.

She kept her eyes open, watching the darkness, trying to stay alert.

Now is when it happens, she thought. Now when the others are asleep comes the crime too horrible to mention.

Carrie breathed evenly until all she heard was silence, the sleeping heathens breathing in and out.

How soundly they slept. Now was her chance to steal away. She rose to her knees.

Above her in the darkness a voice called. “Whoo! Whoo! Whoo!”

Chills ran down her spine. Her breathing came in short, quick gasps.

Carrie sat back down, rearranged her clothes around her, as if to say, See, I am not going anywhere, lay down next to Hannah, covered them both with the skin, her heart still pounding.

She lay still, hoping it would subside.

She thought she heard a noise, there. Was that him, the heathen with scratches on his face and a stub for a finger, approaching in the dark, coming to...?

She shut her eyes, tried to remember Scripture, drifted toward sleep, started herself awake, half sat up. She had to be watchful, vigilant. She looked around, peered into the dark, saw nothing. She lay back down.

She was so tired. Couldn’t she think of Scripture? “Our Father, which art in Heaven—”

She was in the woods, not far from Isaac’s compound. She couldn’t see the fence but she knew it was there through the brambles. It was mid-day. The sun was shining. The woods were dark, seemed to be growing darker. Other people were with her, Hannah, Rebecca, Gideon, Isaac. Carrie couldn't see them anymore. The woods kept getting darker. She couldn't see anyone.

Above she still saw sunlight filtered through the leaves and, beyond that, patches of blue sky. It seemed farther and farther away. The trees kept growing taller, the leaves fuller and darker. Where was everyone? Carrie wanted to get back home. She needed to. The compound was not far. Just over there, she thought. She couldn't see it anymore.

She shut her eyes, tried to go toward where she thought it was. Brambles scratched her face, snagged in her hair, snapped her head back. Grapevines coiled around her ankles, hissing and waving like snakes, their tongues lapping at her. She opened her mouth. It felt as if a hand was clamped over her throat. She couldn't call out. She couldn't move.

Carrie opened her eyes. She couldn't see. Darkness enveloped her.

An owl screeched above her, diving toward her head. She screamed.

Behind her something roared. The earth shook. All the creatures of the woods began calling and bellowing and hissing and roaring. On every side new dangers waited for her.

"Gideon!" she called. Carrie knew he was there, on the other side of the fence, looking for her.

"I'm here, Gideon. Can't you see me? Please look. Look harder. If you find me and bring me home, I will be good in all things. I won't play childish games, or be willful or disobedient or not follow your instructions. I will be the wife you always wanted and I could never seem to be. I promise."

If Carrie ran, maybe she could reach him before one of the wild creatures sprang on her and tore open her flesh. She tried to lift her legs. She couldn't raise them off the ground. Snakes, grapevines, serpents, tigers, bears, wolves, brambles, trees snared and encircled her.

"Gideon, I'm here. Come help me. Gideon! Gideon!"

She opened her mouth, shouted as loud as she could. No sound came out. The darkness of the trees and the vines and the brambles grew darker. Only a little corner of light was visible, high above her. It too disappeared.

She turned, tossed. Her hands twitched, her feet jerked. She opened her eyes, sat up. It was dark. Her heart was pounding. She was sweating, her clothes soaking wet.

Carrie reached beside her to wake Gideon, felt Hannah's cold, stiff arm. She cried out, snatched her hand away.

Chapter Four

"Carrie?"

Carrie heard her name, heard it repeated.

"In a minute, Gideon." She stretched. "You wouldn't believe the dream I was having." She started fashioning it in her head. "I was captured and—"

She rolled over. The ground was harder than any bed. She opened her eyes. It was light. Carrie saw, not her room at home, but the bark and saplings that formed the side of the wigwam. She felt for Hannah. Her daughter was gone!

She sat up. Where was her child? Who had stolen her away?

The leg of a woman stood beside her, wearing moccasins and a deerskin dress. Carrie clutched the animal skin to her, drew back, looked up. It was the old heathen woman. She was holding Hannah.

Before Carrie could reach out for her daughter, the old woman spoke.

"Come," she indicated. She took a step away.

Carrie stared at her. Where was she taking her child?

Around the wigwam the others slept.

The old woman said something else, said it again, more sharply. The shape that was the heathen man stirred.

The old woman spoke again.

"Now," Carrie thought she was saying.

"Now?" The man questioned.

"Yes, come," the old woman said again.

The man sat up, rubbed his eyes, looked at the old

woman. He pointed at Hannah in her arms, said something, started to lie back down.

The old woman spoke harshly to him, repeating the same short phrase over three or four times.

The man said one more thing, lay all the way down, shut his eyes, covered his head with the skin.

The old woman unleashed one more burst at him. The man grunted from under the skin. His head did not emerge.

The old woman turned toward Carrie. “Come!”

Carrie stood up. Her feet throbbed. Her shoes pinched. She wanted to sit back down, take them off, massage her feet.

She put her arms out; the old woman held Hannah toward her. Carrie took her child, sagged from the weight, struggled to follow the old woman outside.

The old woman led Carrie first to the place where people relieved themselves. An older man was there, and a woman. Carrie waited until the old man was done. He took a long time.

When she was finished, she gathered Hannah back into her arms. With great effort she straightened up, set off after the old woman. Before long they came to where the clearing ended and woods began. In they stepped, walking on a worn, narrow path.

On the old woman strode, stronger and faster than Carrie expected.

How much longer? Carrie wondered. Hannah seemed so much heavier than the day before. Carrie’s arms hurt, carrying her; her legs ached; a pain shot through the back of her neck, as if stabbing her just below the base of her skull.

Carrie couldn’t keep going. She would fall in a heap, there in the woods, unable to move. The old woman would leave her there, and all her misery would be over.

Ten feet more was all she could manage, maybe less. She was about to collapse when she saw open space through the trees. The woods ended. Carrie stepped out into a field, half dropped Hannah onto the ground. Her arms, legs, neck, shoulders, everything ached.

Carrie looked up, squinting. The sun, large and bright, angled through the trees.

The old woman touched her elbow, held her arm out. Carrie looked where she pointed. They were at the top of a long field; it sloped down and away, surrounded by woods.

The old woman gestured as she spoke. "Where? Woods or open?"

Carrie walked to a place at the top of the field, against a deeper section of woods. She was afraid to look into them. They reminded her of her dream, dense and dark and dangerous. In the open she felt safe.

The old woman stopped where Carrie indicated, dropped to her knees, started scratching at the earth with her fingers, brought up a few handfuls of grass and dirt. She found a sharp pointed rock, jabbed at the ground with it.

A man's voice startled Carrie. She looked up. The heathen man from their wigwam stood there, a shovel-like object in his hand. The old woman rose, stepped to one side. He leaned forward, started digging a hole where she had been scratching. Brown dirt and rocks mounded up beside it. After a while he stopped. The old woman said something. He shook his head. "Deep enough," he answered in English.

Carrie too tried to show it needed to be deeper. He patted his chest. "Our way." He held his hands apart. Then he opened them to indicate earth, air, sky. "Deeper, just earth." He held the shovel out toward her, as if saying, "You want it deeper, you dig."

Carrie took the shovel, scraped a few times, moved a small amount of dirt. Her muscles were sore. Her whole body hurt. Inside hurt even more. She handed the heathen back the shovel. The hole was deep enough.

The heathen man went back across the top of the field to where Carrie had left her daughter, picked her up, carried her back. He set Hannah down next to the hole, stepped away. Carrie knelt on the ground beside her, touched her face, leaned over, kissed her cheeks, her forehead. She slid her arms under the stiff body, lifted her, held her tightly against her chest. “Oh, Hannah,” she thought. “Oh, Gideon.”

A hand on her elbow startled her. The old woman indicated the hole.

Carrie lowered Hannah into it, removed her arms, held her daughter’s hand, picked up the other one, patted them together, mouthed the words, “Patty cake, patty cake.”

“May you rest in peace,” she muttered. “May you dwell in the spirit of the Lord, and the spirit of the Lord dwell in you, forever. And in His name, may this rough spot—”

She touched the tips of Hannah’s cold fingers together one more time, laid her hands, crossed, onto her chest, leaned over, kissed her on the forehead, said what she whispered to her every night. “Now I lay me down to sleep, I pray the Lord my soul to keep. And if I die before I wake, I pray the Lord my soul to take.”

Her chest filled with sadness and aching pain, as sharp as the raw spot from her shoe, but deep inside, where she couldn’t rub and soothe it. She tried to go on. “May this rough spot—” How was she going to manage? “May this rough spot be as sanctified as any more holy ground. Amen.”

She took a handful of earth, scattered it over the still body. “From dust You have made us. To dust we return.”

Carrie stood, took a step back. It was all she could do to keep from crying out.

The heathen shoveled dirt onto the little body.

Hannah was gone. It wailed inside her: Hannah, her sweet sweet child, her joy, was gone.

The heathen finished covering her. He looked at Carrie, as if to say, What more? She stared back. She didn’t know.

He grabbed two nearby sticks, placed them together in the shape of a cross, laid them on the mound of earth. “Like this?” he indicated. His left eye twitched. He rubbed it with his stubby finger.

Carrie nodded, mouthed, “Thank you,” bit her lip.

She thought her heart would break.

The old woman, standing by the grave, tapped her chest, and the man's too, urged him to speak for her.

"Ours too," he said.

The old woman made a show of shooting.

"In war also." He kept speaking in English.

The old woman tapped her head, then her chest.

"We know," the man said, "how it hurts."

The man and the old woman stared at the mound. They seemed sad.

The old woman spoke. The man nodded, reached into his pouch, pulled something out. The old woman took it from him, held it in front of Carrie.

Carrie gasped. It was the face of a heathen girl, cut from her head in one of their ghastly ceremonies. Her stomach rose. She turned away.

The old woman still stood beside her, holding it out.

Carrie looked back.

It wasn't real, she saw looking again, but a clay mask, done so well it looked real, with ears, eyes, and nose, and her lips parted in a slight smile.

The old woman touched her chest.

The heathen took the mask from the old woman. "Mine," he said. "Wren." He flapped one hand like a bird in flight, made the sound of its song, then kissed its cheek. The old woman kissed it too, coaxed his hand forward. He held the mask toward Carrie.

Carrie reached out, took it from him. On it, she saw a young girl as she must have been alive, as lively, as lovely and as loved as Hannah. Tears ran down her cheeks. She kissed the mask on its cheek, handed it back.

The old woman took it, ran her fingers over both cheeks, gave it back to the man. He shut his eyes, clasped it to his chest.

Carrie heard a strange noise beside her, turned toward the old woman, saw tears in her eyes. "Uunhh." She was making a mournful sound that seemed to come from deep in the earth.

Carrie bit her lip harder, trying to hold her feelings in. In another moment she too was sobbing. Heaves pushed her chest up. Tears streamed down her face. She fell to her knees beside the grave. She opened her mouth and moaned. "Uunhh. Uunhh!" She started pawing and scratching at the fresh mound, slowly at first, then more and more frantically. Dirt flew out behind her. Faster and faster she clawed. Then, just as quickly, she stopped, flung herself forward onto the grave.

The old woman squatted on one side of her, put her arm on Carrie's arm.

Carrie jerked her arm away. "Leave me here."

The old woman spoke quietly. It sounded soothing.

On the other side, the heathen man also squatted beside her. After a moment, he spoke. It too sounded gentle. "In life, you are the mother. Now earth is."

"No." Carrie gripped the grave more tightly.

The old woman on one side and the heathen on the other grasped her arms firmly, pulled her back until she was sitting upright.

The old woman held her there while the man scraped a handful of dirt off the top of the mound. The old woman coaxed Carrie's hand forward, turned it over. Slowly the man poured the dirt into her open palm. Her fingers closed around it. She pressed it to her chest, covered it with her other hand, shut her eyes.

She was quiet, and empty, and sad.

Chapter Five

The camp was bustling when Carrie and the heathens got back. The wigwams were down, the bark piled on horses, the poles lashed to their sides.

The old woman held a bowlful of porridge out toward Carrie, spoke to her firmly. “Eat!”

Carrie stared straight ahead, seeing nothing.

Beside her she heard loud voices. She turned toward them. Two men were arguing. One was the heathen with the stub finger. He pointed at her as he spoke, making first a gesture that looked like shooting, then rocking with his arms, as if holding a small child.

Another heathen stood nose to nose with him. When he talked, the blood vessel in his temple bulged.

Several older heathens were there too, trying, it seemed, to calm them. The old woman stood beside the one with the stub finger. She spoke sharply to the other heathen, pointing at Carrie while she did.

More people gathered around, crowded together. Many talked at once. No one seemed happy.

The other heathen responded with a burst of angry sounding words, gestured toward the others. “Follow me,” turned and limped away. Some of the group walked after him. Others spoke harshly toward them, stayed where they were.

As they moved away, Carrie became aware of a woman in a long woolen dress. It took her a moment to realize it was Rebecca, a Bible in her hand. Carrie’s throat filled up. She started crying. She opened her mouth. No sound came out. She cleared her throat, raised her hand, raised it higher, waved it back and forth. Rebecca stopped, stared at her.

Carrie took a step toward Rebecca, hit her foot on a protruding rock, fell to her knees.

Rebecca looked at her another moment, turned and walked away, following the limping man.

Carrie's mouth stayed half-open. Her crying got stronger. She felt more alone than ever.

She heard a baby cry. Hannah!

No, not Hannah.

Near her a heathen woman rocked a child against her chest, gave it her nipple. The child stopped crying, but Carrie couldn't. All she wanted was to sink down into the ground and hold her little girl.

The heathen with the stub finger spoke, started off in another direction with those who were left.

The old woman waved her arms. "Come," she was saying. She reached down, helped Carrie to stand. Carrie stifled her sobs, bent to carry Hannah, held only air.

"Come," the old woman said again.

"No!" Carrie took a step in the opposite direction.

With one hand the old woman stopped her, with the other held out the bundle she was carrying towards Carrie. "Help me. My back hurts, and my leg." She put her hand on her lower back, limped a few steps, held the bundle out again.

Carrie took it, hugged it to her chest.

"Now," the old woman seemed to say. Gently laying her hand on Carrie's arm, she moved toward the others.

Carrie started after her, the bundle snug in her arms.

They walked all day, left foot, right foot, left foot, right. Carrie's feet hurt. Her clothes chafed. At almost every step the one behind her pushed or kicked.

They stopped by a stream for water and rest. It gurgled and sparkled over rocks. After she drank, Carrie stayed sitting beside it, eyes shut. The old woman had to wake her to go on.

They stopped at mid-day by a small river, had no food, only water.

"Don't you ever eat?" she thought. "You can't walk all day without eating."

No one complained. They seemed used to it.

Carrie's stomach growled. Her head felt light. Every part of her hurt. Her insides were empty, a well that went down into darkness. She wanted to stop right there, climb inside it, where no one could see her, shut her eyes, not move from there, have them go on without her.

She took a step to the side, stopped by a tree. The old woman nudged her back onto the path.

She took a step forward, and then another. On she went—stepping right, stepping left, thinking of Hannah, of playing patty-cake with her, or singing to her, the words and actions disappearing in her fatigue and the rhythm of stepping right, stepping left, stepping right, stepping left.

They stopped again, later, by another stream, for water and rest.

The old woman knelt by her feet.

The heathen with the stub finger stood beside her. He spoke quickly. His words sounded angry. "Leave her alone." He spoke in his own language, but Carrie was sure she understood what he was saying. "She is so foolish to wear this leather on her feet. Let her if that's what she wants."

"She is in pain," the old woman answered as she worked. "She hobbles and can hardly walk. She slows us down."

"Leave her here. It would be better if we never saw her."

"Yes, many things would be better if they never happened. It would be better if you did not take a captive. But that is how it is."

The old woman unlaced Carrie's high shoes. Carrie drew her feet back.

"See. She knows it is wrong. Leave her alone."

The old woman's hand coaxed Carrie's feet forward, removed her shoes, as gently as she could peeled off her worn-through, blood-soaked woolen stockings.

Carrie opened her mouth. It was all she could do to keep from crying out. Her feet were red and raw. Blood oozed from them. They throbbed and seared with pain. But with the shoes off they felt better.

The boy who slept in their wigwam stood watching. The old woman had him dip a cloth in the stream, bring it to her.

Carrie's feet jerked as the cold water touched them, twitched as the old woman washed them. Gradually the cloth and the water soothed them.

Carrie shut her eyes, rested her chin on her chest.

The old woman washed her feet again and dried them. Carrie watched as the woman took leaves from her pouch, rubbed them on the sore places. She set the shoes to the side, wrapped a dry cloth around each foot, had the boy bring a pair of moccasins from her belongings.

Carrie sat up, alert. What was the old woman doing? She couldn't put heathen slippers on her. What happened to the stockings and the shoes? They were hers.

Before she could protest, the heathen stepped forward. He gestured at Carrie's feet. The old woman couldn't do that. Those were the moccasins of someone important, Carrie couldn't tell who, someone gone or dead—his wife, maybe, or sister.

The old woman held her hand up. Yes, they were her daughter's. Now she—indicating Carrie—needs them. There was to be no more argument.

She held a moccasin up. Carrie tightened her foot, held it rigid. No heathen clothing was despoiling her.

The old woman took her foot; stroking it over and over, she repeated phrases in her own language. Whatever she was saying felt as calming as "Rock a bye, baby, in a tree top."

For a moment, it wasn't the old heathen woman holding Carrie's foot, but her own mother, soothing her hurts. Her mother she would never see again. Tears came into her eyes. She fought to hold them back. How different life was in England, though the countryside looked much the same, only gentler, not so rough and harsh and untamed.

While she was thinking of her mother, the old woman slid the right moccasin on, picked up the other foot, pushed that one on as well.

No, Carrie thought. She was ready to kick them off. Before she did, she noticed her feet did not hurt in them, not nearly so much. The sides and bottom were soft and pliant. They felt so much better than her stiff, hard shoes she almost cried with relief.

Carrie shut her eyes. She hoped wearing these Devil's accouterments was no sin. She knew she should have fought harder to keep her shoes, but she was so tired, her feet hurt so much. Couldn't she just stay there and sleep?

She heard movement in front of her, opened her eyes to see the old woman hand the heathen her shoes.

Carrie was about to protest, "Those are my shoes," when the heathen dropped them on the ground. What did he want with these? He leaned over, pushed at Carrie's shoulder. "Time to start walking. We've rested too long."

Carrie looked down at her feet. Like that, with barely a fuss, she had given up her stockings and her shoes, let herself be decked out like a heathen.

That was how they defeated you, when you were worn down and tired. Little by little they changed you from what you were to what they were, and you never knew when, or how to resist.

The heathen pushed her shoulder again.

Carrie stood up, resumed walking. Her feet did not hurt so much.

The heathen started after her. The old woman spoke sharply. The heathen stopped, went back, picked up the shoes.

At the next stream, Carrie noticed him slip away from the group, walk up it until she couldn't see him anymore. When he rejoined them, a few minutes later, he no longer carried her shoes. He had left them, she imagined, against a rock in the water far from the path, where anyone looking for her would never find them and know she had come this way.

She felt alarmed. It made it even less likely she would ever be rescued.

Day after day, it seemed to Carrie, they walked until almost dark, stopped, set up the wigwams, ate or didn't eat, slept, got up at the first light, ate or didn't eat, walked, slept, walked again, always too hungry and tired to know or care where they were, how long they had been gone, or where they were going.

The air grew colder. The wind sliced through her. The old woman threw an animal's skin over her. It smelled vile, but kept her warm. She left it on.

Carrie lost track of the days.

On one, it snowed. Light flakes swirled around, stung her cheeks, stuck to the ground. Walking was slippery. The next day the sun came out, the air was warmer, she took the skin off, the snow all melted.

On another, all she could think of, at every step, was Hannah, how much she missed her, how, at the moment of her capture, she had died. She had lived all her short life among Christians, died among Christians—lived a Christian life, died a Christian death. She did not face the evils and temptations of life among the savages.

It made Carrie wonder. What would happen to her? She was fed when there was food, given a place to sleep, had not been violated. She walked until she could no longer stand, but so did the others.

All she wanted was to be at home, rising with the day, building up the fire, mixing oats and water in a pot, hanging it over the flame, sweeping out the kitchen, airing the bedding, tidying the house, baking bread, kneading and working and pounding the dough, Hannah beside her, kneading and working the air. Patty-cake, patty-cake, baker's man—reaching her doughy hands over, playing patty-cake with Hannah, glancing behind her. There stood Gideon, his silent stare showing he did not approve.

He must be happy now. She wouldn't play these foolish games anymore.

Isaac as well, in his zeal leading them from outpost to outpost, extending the torch of God and the one true faith deeper into the woods, farther into the wilderness. Was that devout belief, as she always thought, or madness? Was this the end he had in mind? Was this why they had come there?

First Mary. Then Paul and Hannah! Now herself as well, forgotten here among the heathens. She might as well have been dead too.

On yet another day, she realized in the middle of walking, she didn't know when the Sabbath was. She couldn't remember when the last one had been at home, or even how long she had been gone. It might have been days. It might have been weeks.

She must have missed it. Carrie stopped walking. The old woman behind her pushed her shoulder, scolded her for moving so slowly.

She had missed the Sabbath! She hadn't thought of it once since her capture.

She was horrified. Surely, she was beyond redemption. She pretended she cared, and she forgot something as important as that.

She needed to hold her own private Sabbath, to quote Scripture to herself, remember the text of Isaac's sermons or his admonitions, that she had heard time and again.

She couldn't recall a single one. Words, phrases started to come to mind, and were as quickly driven away by the pain in her legs, growl of her stomach, the sight and smell of the heathens all around her. If Carrie slowed her walk in her thinking, the old woman stepped on her heel.

Later she would have to think of it, after they stopped, or when she was lying alone, eyes shut, waiting for sleep, hoping for rescue or deliverance. She would start with her evening prayers. She ought to remember them. If she did this every evening, got back in the habit, by the next Sabbath, whenever she decided that was, she should be able to go off by herself, commend herself to the Lord, recall her prayers in a manner even Isaac would approve of.

Every evening when they stopped, and again in the morning before they left, the old woman had Carrie sit on a rock or the trunk of a fallen tree, removed her moccasins and the cloth, examined her feet. They still hurt, but seemed better. There was no fresh blood. The old woman rubbed leaves over both feet. One raw spot stung. Carrie pulled her foot away. The old woman urged it back, rubbing gently, re-wrapped each foot with a cloth, pushed and slid the moccasins on. Carrie nodded her head in thanks.

One morning, not long after they got up, there was a commotion. Everyone stopped what they were doing, hurried toward a tree.

The whole group was gathered there. Two deer, long and solid, hung by the hind legs from low branches, heads inches above the ground. The man with a stub finger stood by one, smiling. Everyone talked at once. They sounded happy. People bustled here and there. A woman built up the fire. Soon it was roaring.

Two men removed the skin from the deer. Another woman took it, started rubbing and pounding and working it, as if it was dough and she was kneading it. Another man cut strips of meat off the carcass, laid them on a frame, placed it near the fire. Carrie smelled the meat cooking. Her stomach rumbled. She was so hungry. They hadn't eaten in days.

People sang. They chanted. They laughed and called. Someone whistled. One beat on a drum. Another played a flute. A fourth one sang. A fifth one danced.

The man with the stub finger laid the liver on a slab. Hands reached in, cut pieces off. He stood with one held out on the tip of his knife toward Carrie. She stared at it, shook her head. What abomination was this?

He still held it there. “Eat. Good.” He bit off a piece, chewed it, swallowed. “The liver,” he said, patting his side. “Gives strength.” He took the piece from the knife, laid it in her hand.

It was still warm. It felt slimy. Not cooked. Were they cannibals too, the way some said? Was she becoming more and more like them?

Lord, give her the strength to endure.

Around her everyone ate, smiled, laughed. Hands reached to take more. The old woman caught her eye, gestured to her to eat.

“Lord, I do not know if I have been reduced to something less than human.” Carrie thought of Gideon, Hannah, Isaac. “But if it is Your will that I survive, it must be in this manner.” She lifted her palm to her face, put the entire piece in her mouth. The taste of blood and of raw meat mixed with her saliva. She began to chew, worked off a small piece, swallowed it. She thought she might vomit. It stayed down. She broke off another, and another, chewed and swallowed them both.

The rack of meat was taken from the fire, leaned against the tree. People gathered around, taking off strips, cutting them in pieces. The old woman handed Carrie several. When she finished one, she started on another.

People ate, took more, ate again. They grabbed the meat with their hands, tore it with their teeth. No one talked. The only noises were the sounds of chewing and belching. When people ate all they could, they slept where they were sitting. Their snores filled the clearing.

Carrie was disgusted, but she kept eating, piece after piece, ripping it with her hands, tearing it with her teeth, chewing loudly, swallowing, taking more.

More finished. Still she ate. She ate until she couldn’t eat any more. She got up, waddled over, sat down against a tree next to the old ones. They were already sleeping. On the other side of her sat the boy from the wigwam; beside him, the man with the stub finger leaned against the trunk, staring at the bare carcass, hanging from another tree.

Carrie shut her eyes. She felt a burp rising, tried to stifle it. Out it came, louder than she expected. It echoed through the clearing. She opened her eyes, looked around. No one had noticed.

Another burp rose. She didn't try to hold it down. Out it came, louder than the first.

She was becoming more and more like them. And she didn't care. She hadn't given thanks to the Lord before she began, but just grabbed and ate like the others.

Her stomach was full, but her soul felt empty.

Wasn't that what Isaac had warned of. "Beware! Don't feed the body but starve the spirit."

Carrie started to protest. She had been so hungry.

"Does that justify becoming little more than one of the beasts?" She heard Isaac's voice in her ear, saw his stern, unwavering blue eyes glaring at her.

She tried to frame her thoughts, to defend herself. She was too tired. She couldn't keep her eyes open.

As she dozed off she felt Hannah lie against her. She reached down to comfort her, rest her hand on her hair or shoulder or the back of her neck. But it wasn't her. It couldn't have been.

Carrie opened one eye, looked. No one was there but the boy, resting beside her. She moved her hand over, brushed the hair from his face. He slid down until his head lay on her leg; her hand settled on his shoulder.

They all five slept.

Chapter Six

Carrie lay still.

Around her in the dark four breathings went in, out, in, out.

She stared up, saw nothing.

She felt something on her arm. She jerked away, tried to brush it off. Felt something on her cheek, slapped at it. Felt something under her dress, thwacked her thigh.

One of the four breathings stopped, exhaled. She lay still. It resumed its rhythm.

Her feet throbbed. Even in their new moccasins, they were sore.

Her legs ached. Her eyes started to close.

No! That was when they attacked you, wasn't that what Gideon had said, when you ceased being vigilant. They hadn't so far, but that didn't mean they wouldn't; they were waiting until she let her guard down, and then—

Carrie lay rigid, staring up toward the Devil she knew was there. She couldn't find him in the dark.

Her eyes started shutting. Her head tipped sideways.

She was at home, kneading dough. She kept hearing voices, the voices of people she loved—Hannah, Gideon, Mary.

"I'm here," she said. "In the kitchen."

"Come find us," they called.

She wiped her hands on her apron, turned around to look.

The small house suddenly opened into a long corridor, with many rooms off either side, the doors to all of them shut. One by one she lifted the latches, pushed them open. The rooms were empty.

She kept hearing the voices, moaning that they missed her, they needed her. They scolded her for not finding them. "If you loved us, you would find us. If you were a good mother, if you were a good wife, you would open the right door."

Isaac was there, preaching from a pulpit. "Faith is not a trivial matter. It is a matter of life and death, not of your body, but of your soul. How do you know if you have the one true belief? You may fool me. You may fool your neighbor. You may even fool yourself. But do you think you can fool the Lord God on high who knows everything?"

Carrie was running, flinging doors open onto empty rooms. The corridor seemed endless. All she saw were more doors, more rooms with no one in them.

Mary's voice stopped. So did Gideon's. Only Hannah's kept calling her. And it was getting fainter.

Carrie lay awake on the ground. She was panting. Her heart was pounding. It was darker than it had been before.

"Hannah." Her mouth moved. No sound came out. "Hannah!"

"Come find me, Mommy." Hannah spoke from the darkness.

If Carrie got up then, no one would notice. She could walk back to where she left her.

They wouldn't mind. She was just going to get her Hannah.

She heard Hannah's voice again, low and distant.

Carrie pushed with her arm, sat up, waited a moment, rolled over on to her knees, started to rise.

An owl shrieked above her, shrieked again. Another answered; it shrieked a third time.

Carrie stopped moving. Her hands turned icy. Her throat jumped into her mouth.

"Shriek!" She held herself even stiller. She knew if she moved it would swoop down and pinion her in its claws.

It was beginning to get light. Carrie looked around,

making out other shapes in the wigwam.

In front of her stood Rebecca, Bible in her hand. Carrie smiled, leaned forward to hug her.

Rebecca turned away. Before she did, she fixed Carrie with a cold stare.

Isaac thundered from the pulpit: “If a person doesn’t follow the one true path, here in church, or alone in the wilderness, where God sees all, she doesn’t deserve to live”.

Gideon took her jaw in his right hand, turned her face toward him. “Why do you think I haven’t tried to rescue you?”

Mary and Hannah stood like angels, side by side. Mary turned away.

Carrie heard Gideon’s stern voice, “You don’t deserve to live.”

Carrie looked back at Hannah, reached out, tried to take her by the hand, held only light and air. “What about you, my baby lamb?”

“Who held me as I died?” the child answered. “Who exposed me to dangers, left me among strangers? You don’t deserve to live.”

Something nudged her.

Carrie pulled her head from under its cover, opened her eyes.

The old woman stood in front of her. She wore a skin over her body, covering her deerskin dress. She held another skin out toward Carrie, indicated for her to throw it over her shoulders.

Carrie did not want to.

The old woman insisted. The boy came beside her, helped her put it in place.

Carrie felt sad and disgusted and lonely. She was becoming less and less civilized, more and more like the heathens every day. Look at how she was dressed. Her woolen stockings and her precious leather shoes she had given up without a struggle. In their place, she wore moccasins, and liked them, how comfortable they were on her feet. Now her Christian garments were covered by a wild beast's skin, and she accepted it without complaint.

If Isaac or Gideon came to rescue her back, would they recognize her? or move on, thinking she was one of the heathens?

The others packed everything, took down the wigwam, loaded it onto a horse. The air was wet, the rain cold, the ground slippery. The old woman gave her a bundle to carry. They started walking.

They walked through woods all day, stopped three times by streams for water and to rest. Carrie was tired. Her body hurt. She wanted to be home, with Hannah and Gideon, doing nothing harder than kneading bread, baking it, sweeping. And she had thought that was difficult.

Before it was dark, they stopped, set up the wigwams in an open space beside a small river. The ground was damp, the air cold.

In the morning Carrie did not want to wake up.

The old woman shook her until she opened her eyes, grunted and prodded until she got up.

Soon the wigwam was taken down, folded up, and they were moving, again without eating.

That day was like the day before, not warm but without rain. Through woods they went, up hill and down. By streams. Across a river, soaking her to the neck, her wet clothes chilling her, and so heavy she could hardly walk. When they stopped to rest, she squeezed them out, handful by handful, as best she could before they moved on.

Again they went to bed hungry.

Carrie woke twice in the night. Once to the feel of her own stomach, rumbling. Once to the image of Hannah, whimpering. "Mommy, when are we going to eat?"

The next day was damp and raw; Carrie slogged along, tired and hungry and cold.

It started snowing. Wet flakes stung her bare skin, piled up an inch or two on the ground, slowed their walking.

In the middle of the day, there was an attack. Cries rang out. Before Carrie could think to call out, "Here, I am here," and show herself, or try to break free and run toward the attackers, the old woman grabbed her, hurried her, the boy and the old man ahead, hid them among boulders. The men with their muskets ducked behind trees, shot off behind them, disappeared into the woods.

Soon it was over. The shots scattered more widely, ended. The men rejoined them. On they walked, squishing through the snow.

Carrie was glad the settlers were still near, sad they didn't find her. She was wet and tired and cold. On she trudged, in the dull gray day, looking neither left nor right, wanting nothing more than for the heat of her movement to warm her.

They walked until it was dark.

Carrie woke in the night. She was warm, her body wet with sweat. She threw off her skin cover, slept, tossed, woke cold, re-covered herself, slept finally what seemed only a few minutes before the old woman shook her.

Carrie opened her eyes to darkness, shut them again. "Leave me be," she thought. "Let me sleep until morning." She shivered, pulled the skin cover tighter around her.

The old woman shook her again. She had to get up.

Carrie heard voices calling, confusion. She sat up, alert. Was it another attack?

They were surprised, it appeared, but not by an attack. It was snowing, as it had the day before, only it was not stopping.

Carrie stood up, stepped outside. Snow was falling heavily; it was already above her ankles.

They had to leave. For where, she did not understand. Now, before the snow was too high and they could not move.

Even under her skin covering, Carrie was cold. Her teeth chattered.

They started walking. She could not see. She put her hand on the boy's shoulder, followed him.

Her mouth was dry. Her throat burned. She scooped up a handful of snow, pushed it into her mouth. It stung her teeth. She sucked on it until it melted. It soothed her throat. When it was gone, she took more.

People were yelling, pushing. It smelled like horses, wet clothing, sweat.

They walked slowly, lifting their feet high.

Her head throbbed. Her ears burned. She took the skin off, carried it, got wet and chilled, put it back on.

She slipped, fell in the snow, rose part way, slipped again, lay, her cheek against the cool wet. Hands lifted her.

They walked on, going down, up, down more steeply. Carrie tripped on a rock, fell again, slid forward on the downward slope, stopped against a tree. She could not get up, did not want to. The snow on her forehead soothed her. She buried her face in it until her cheeks stung and she could not feel her nose.

Heathen voices argued over her. One, she could tell, said, leave her here, she has caused enough trouble. The old woman said no, urged her to get up.

They should go on without her, she answered in her head. She could not make the words come out.

She was still trying to say them as the old woman and the boy, and a hand with a stub finger, lifted her, put her on the back of a horse.

The last thing Carrie remembered was throwing the skin covering off, pulling it back on, while the horse jostled this way and that, and the snow, falling thicker, clung to her, her clothes, its back, the ground, piling up all around.

II

Chapter Seven

Carrie tossed from side to side, twitching and whimpering in her sleep.

Gradually she breathed more evenly. A great calm came over her, a deep peacefulness. She slid into consciousness, lay half awake, eyes shut, becoming aware of an unfamiliar sound.

It took her a moment to realize what she was hearing. It was rain, sheets of it, hitting the house wall, running off the edges of the roof, dripping into puddles.

She could not remember the last time she had heard it.

And then boom, close and loud, and boom again. Carrie started, lay tense, eyes open, waiting. Another boom, louder, closer. She lay there alert, ready to jump up, except, another boom sounded. It was not an attack. It was thunder. It rolled, shaking the house, rolled again.

Carrie sat, still half sleeping, listening. It rained harder. Water dripped faster. Even inside the air was warm and damp.

It was spring.

Carrie stretched, looked around. She was not in the cabin at home, but, it seemed, in a Long House full of heathens. Only she wasn't afraid of them. And they seemed to know her. There was a heathen boy, who waved when she looked at him. An old woman, who grunted and said harsh sounding words that meant, "Come help". Carrie understood this, without knowing how.

She shut her eyes, opened them again. She wasn't dreaming. She was awake.

She looked down at herself. She was still wearing her gray woolen dress, her familiar clothes. What was going on?

The old woman grunted again, more insistently.

Carrie swung her feet out of the narrow bed. There, lying on the floor, were not her hard leather shoes, but moccasins, heathen footwear, waiting for her. She slid them on. Her feet seemed to know them. She was more confused than before.

In a moment, still not fully awake, she stood beside the woman, helping in a task her fingers, hands and arms seemed to know, but she had no recollection of, scraping meat from a bone into a cauldron of soup, stirring it over the fire.

Above the dripping and booming she heard the sound of voices. All through the house heathens were working—folding, shaking, packing.

Carrie wondered how long she had been there. The snow that was deep outside and now was melting, where did it come from? And Hannah and Gideon, where were they?

The old woman, the boy, the man with the stub finger, they all seemed familiar, talking to her as if they knew her. Some of their words she understood. Beside her worked an old man; he said nothing, but she felt she knew him too.

Before long the soup was finished and eaten, everything was packed, taken outside. The rain and thunder had stopped, the sky was clearing, sun breaking through onto a wet world. Carrie was wearing as a covering a skin that also seemed familiar. The heathens were walking, and she was walking with them.

They wound up a path away from the house and a collection of other buildings. The ground was slick and muddy. To the side of the path, snow lay in clumps. The air at her head was pleasant, at her feet, still cold.

They walked in a single line, not speaking, one foot after another.

As she settled into this rhythm, Carrie began to remember walking like this on a warm day in fall, surrounded by heathens, feeling lonely and sad; walking for days. It got colder. Snow piled up. She stumbled along, hardly able to go on, wanting nothing but to lie down in it and be forgotten. Even in the cold, her forehead hot. Falling and not getting up. Someone lifting her out of the snow, bringing her on a horse to the house. Collapsing into bed. Hearing a baby cry, feeling her breasts respond, trying to rise, to find the baby and feed her, quiet her crying. Lapsing back into sleep. A long time of fever and visions, as the snow grew deeper, hoping she would die, they would stop feeding her and leave her outside, or that she had died already and after a long journey would rejoin those she had left behind.

Only, Carrie realized, as the one behind her kicked her heel and she hurried to keep up, she had not died. She was alive. Winter was over. She was the captive of heathens, and had been for a while.

Carrie and the heathens climbed the slippery hill, walked for hours as the land leveled out, went down a little, up, down, up some more. After a long time, they stopped to rest by a stream, its banks on one side still covered with snow, its water so cold her teeth stung.

It made her remember going out with the old woman and the boy, stepping high through deep snow until they came to a stream. She was standing on it, on snow and ice, the water gurgling beneath her. Then pins and needles were sticking into her legs in a thousand places, from her ankles to her thighs, the icy water rushing past her. Carrie struggled to keep her footing. The pain stopped. She felt nothing.

From the bank the old woman and the boy reached their arms out to her. She grabbed them, slipped, was wet up to her nose in water so cold and so fast it was carrying her away. Before she floated away forever, they pulled her back, hauled her to the edge. She stood, slipped again, climbed out of the water, cold to the bone.

Then she was in the house, by the fire, her dress dripping, teeth chattering. The pain was back, stabbing her on every side, and she was in bed again, sick.

Carrie wanted to go back to the stream, to put her

head under it and not come back up, no matter how hard anyone pulled, but she was too weak, could not get herself up.

Now she was beside another stream. Before she could step into it and disappear, they moved on.

There was a commotion behind her. A man rushed forward. As he passed, a jagged scar highlighting his cheek, he seemed to slip on the snow beside the path; he reached toward her for support. She put her hand out toward him to help. He shoved her to the side and kept going. Carrie bent her knees, tensed her legs, caught herself with an arm as one leg slid sideways and her knee hit the ground.

The boy yelled after the man. The man yelled back, kept going without slowing down.

"Is well?" the boy asked, helping her up.

Carrie nodded, looked down at one knee covered with mud.

"He didn't have to do that."

She nodded again. Whenever there was trouble, the one with the jagged scar on his cheek seemed to be part of it.

It reminded Carrie of another time, earlier in the winter. They were already in the Long House but the snow was not yet deep. While everyone slept, the one with the scar on his face nudged her awake. "Come," he gestured. To gather nuts or berries, she thought, and her help was needed.

He led her out into the woods. No one else went with them. She was not too sick to go, but she was not well, coughing and coughing, having to stop and catch her breath while he pushed her forward.

They walked and walked, picking through snow, never stopping to rest or eat.

Going home at last, Carrie hoped.

She wanted to smile, but couldn't. The heathen with the jagged scar kept pushing her forward, making her go faster. She did not recognize any of the path. Maybe they were lost.

A raw wind blew. It hurt her throat. She coughed more.

The sky was dull gray. It started snowing; the flakes stung her cheeks.

It snowed harder. They stopped. The man ran a rope around her waist, pulled it tight, tied her hands behind her back, slung it over the branch of a tree, secured it there, too high for her to reach, muttered a few words in his guttural language, and left.

"Wait here," she thought he said. "They'll be here soon."

Gideon and Isaac were coming to rescue her!

Carrie waited.

The snow lightened, stopped. The wind persisted. Her chest ached. Her hands got cold, and her feet. She could not sit, could move only half a foot this way or that before the rope jerked tight behind her.

It started snowing again, more heavily, with large flakes at first, then smaller, finer ones that landed in her hair, on her shoulders and arms, making her colder.

The light faded. No one came. Maybe they were not coming after all; they had forgotten her, and had left her there to die.

Carrie hoped it would be soon, and not hurt too much. Already the feeling was gone from her feet.

She must have dozed off. She came to as the rope jerked her waist, held her up, half suspended over the ground, her feet she could not feel still on it. She shut her eyes, dreaming of sleep. A voice called, a woman's voice. Her mother!

They were back in England. She had hidden so well at blind man's bluff her mother couldn't find her.

"Here," she called. "I'm here!"

The voice called again, low, harsh, guttural.

"Here," she said. She opened her eyes, saw nothing but snow. She was not in England. "Who is it?" Her bones were cold.

The voice got closer, was only a few feet away before

she finally saw, not her mother, but the old heathen woman, grunting, saying words Carrie did not understand.

No, Carrie thought, as the old woman loosened the rope behind her. Don't take me away. They're coming here for me. They won't find me if you move me.

Once the rope was loose, she collapsed onto the woman's shoulder. The old woman, half a foot shorter than her, didn't sag under the weight but kicked at Carrie's feet, to get them back under her, started walking.

The tree disappeared. All Carrie saw was snow, so thick it made a white wall against the night.

The old woman grunted, urging her to walk; it was not much farther.

Carrie tried to support her own weight, keep her feet on the ground under her. She could not feel when they touched it.

Then they were not moving. Carrie was lying on the ground, on dirt and rocks, in a place cold and dark, but without snow.

She slept, woke under a skin, shivering. The old woman removed Carrie's moccasins, rubbed snow over both her feet. Carrie slept again, woke twitching her feet. They itched and burned. She could hardly stand it.

When she woke again, her feet no longer hurt; they were dry, and her moccasins were back on. There was a small fire between her and the snow, and she was warming, little by little. The old woman poked her awake, held her head up, spooned broth into her mouth, holding it shut as the broth went down, too hot on her lips, tongue, throat, spooning in more until it was gone. Then Carrie was lying back down, sleeping, waking, sleeping, waking—the old woman propping her up, spooning in more broth, the fire smaller. It was daylight, still snowing. She was in a small cave, not high, not deep, the entrance half blocked with snow. Again she was sleeping, waking, sleeping, waking, opening her eyes to find the fire out, the old woman gone, alone, maybe now to die, worried about snakes, bears, rats, wolves, listening, hearing only quiet, the snow higher on the cave, thinking it would go so high it would block the entrance and be her tomb, or like a bear she would sleep all winter. The higher the snow the warmer it was, but Carrie was still cold, the warmth from the fire gone.

Sleeping, waking up shivering, dark again, unless the snow covered the entrance.

Waking again; this time the old woman was there, and a fire with its red flames, warming her, and more broth that she drank, that was also too hot, but she held it in. Then the old woman was pulling her forward, lifting her, speaking to someone outside the cave. Hands, one with one stub finger, reached in, took her, lifted her onto a horse.

The snow was higher than the man's knees. The air, clear and sharp, stung like a knife. Carrie started coughing, could not stop.

The old woman sat on the horse behind her, holding a cloth over her mouth, the man walking beside them.

Then she was lying on a bed in a Long House, drenched in sweat, throwing her covers off. The man with the stub finger stood to one side, listening, while the old woman argued with the one with the jagged scar, wanting to take her somewhere even hotter, to sweat the disease out of her. No, he said, she could not; it was sacred, she was not one of them, it would offend the gods, the boy explained to her later as she lay pushing covers off, pulling them back on, pushing them off again.

The old woman made broths and soups and poultices; nothing helped. Carrie lay for days, she lay for weeks, sleeping in feverish starts, not knowing, when she was awake, where she was or who she was with, thinking it was her mother spooning her soup or applying poultices. She heard Isaac and Gideon castigating her, and preaching, and lecturing, and praying for her and her soul, as she hugged to her what she thought was her dear dear Hannah but may have only been the heathen boy squirming to get free.

On and on it went like this, sickness, sadness, fever, and crying all mixed together, the boy and the old woman, and sometimes the old man, or the one with the stub finger, feeding and caring for her, and she no surer if she wanted to live or die, or maybe she already had died and they did not know it yet.

Carrie's right foot came down on mud, close to where the boy in front of her had stepped; it slid forward. Her legs tensed, she caught herself, but not before her knee again landed on the ground. She stood back up and kept going before anyone could notice, jolted out of her memories.

Carrie was not still sick. She was not fully better yet either. But here she was, on a muddy path with the heathens. It was spring, and they were walking.

Chapter Eight

The next evening, when they went into the wigwam, the boy who walked in front of her pointed up toward the top. “Many Legs is here. See.” Carrie saw a spider, dangling down from a web.

She watched the insect, wary, looked at the boy.

He was like a son to her. That is where the pang was, the emptiness. There was a daughter she had. It was coming back to her. Where was she now, her darling Hannah?

Carrie cried inside, but no tears formed. They were all dried up.

All night she lay, not sleeping, filled with visions of Hannah. Happy ones came back, but more and more of them were sad.

Hannah was gone. And Gideon. And their home. Carrie had been captive for so long, and no one had come to ransom or rescue her. Not a word from anyone.

No one was coming, ever. They had forgotten her. There was no reason to go on.

In the early morning light, Carrie lay on the ground in the wigwam, her sadness overflowing. Out of the corner of her eye she saw movement: from the top of the wigwam, a large spider began its descent. Carrie watched it come part way down, slid along the ground until she lay directly under it, shut her eyes, and waited.

A hand rested on Carrie’s arm. She opened her eyes.

The boy sat on his knees next to her. “Shh. Is well. Is well.”

“What is all this sticky?” Carrie lifted her arm. A spider web was wrapped around her. She tried to push it off. It clung to her fingers. She tried to shake it off. It stayed where it was. “Get it off me. Get it off! Hurry!”

“Is well. Look.” The boy pointed at the spider a few feet above her. “See.”

Carrie’s eyes grew large. “Kill it. Smash it.”

The boy did not move. He sat watching.

“Please!”

“Is well. All is. See.” He slid his hand along under the web that covered her, lifting it up without touching her. “Move this way.” He indicated for her to slide toward him. He held the web up until she was free.

She kept watching the spider, eyes wide.

“That’s Many Legs. She’s our friend. Remember?”

Carrie stared at the boy as he took the web, laid it gently on the ground beside her. “And when she wraps you like that, it means she protects you.”

Does it make this sadness go away? she wondered, as she looked from the heathen boy to the spider, spinning up its thread toward the top, back to the boy. Then, with a sudden movement, she reached out, grabbed the boy, pulled him toward her, wrapped her arms around him. She kept hugging him, harder and tighter, her body convulsing in silent sobs.

After a minute he lifted his arms and wrapped them around her, a little at first, then more and more until he held her as tightly as she held him. They stayed like that a long time. Even after his arms relaxed and slid down her back, she kept holding him.

Carrie woke, hungry. The wigwam seemed quiet. The heathen man and the old couple were gone. Only the boy was there. He looked at her, smiled. “Morning,” he said.

She reached out, hugged him, her long lost friend. He hugged her back. They hugged a long time.

“It is late?” she asked after he disengaged himself.

He nodded. “You are to help with food and cleaning, cooking and baking.”

"We are not walking today?"

"Today is a day for hunting. The men dressed early and took their guns. I went to go with them. The old one said, 'Today you stay here and help.'"

"The 'old one'?"

"The old woman. My grandmama. 'The old one' is what I call her. I told you this before."

Carrie shook her head. She had no recollection of it.

"Her real name is Spotted Turtle. Turtle whose back is speckled with sunlight. No one calls her that."

"You are called—?"

"You don't remember that?"

She shook her head.

"You don't remember anything."

No, she thought, not even who I am, or how I got here.

"I told you this, before the snow came."

"I don't remember before the snow came."

He spoke slowly. "I am called Tiki."

"Tiki." She repeated his name. It seemed she had heard it before; she didn't remember when. "Tiki." She said it again, her mouth getting used to the shape of the word.

"Everyone has boy and girl names. When we grow up we get our real ones, from dreams we have or things we do."

"And the man with the stub finger?"

"I told you that too."

"I don't remember."

The boy nodded. "That is Mohee."

"Mohee," Carrie repeated.

"Everyone calls him that. His real name is Gray Wolf Running, from a dream he had, a gray wolf, running in snow. Hunters were chasing him. He couldn't see or hear them, but he felt them, coming nearer. The snow was deep. Gray Wolf had trouble in it, hurrying to get away.

"When Mohee woke his heart was pounding. Sweat clung to him. He didn't know if Gray Wolf escaped or if the hunters caught him, but he knew Gray Wolf Running was his name.

"What my name will be, no one knows yet. Until then I am Tiki."

Carrie nodded.

"I was born among the white people too. When I am not very big, my mother and I are captured back. She knew many words from living with them. She taught me some, Mohee a few."

"And how old are you, Tiki?"

Tiki looked at her. "'Hold'?"

"'Old'. How big?"

Tiki stood up, held his hand out at the height of his head. "I am this high now." He lowered his hand. "I was this high when you came to us." He stood on tip toes, moved his hand as high as he could reach. "One day I will be this high, more even than Mohee."

Carrie held her hand out at the same height as Tiki now. "I had a nephew—"

She remembered, from what seemed like ages before, blood pooling in the grass, a boy lying face down beside it. Carrie shut her eyes. Her chest ached. Tears ran down her cheeks.

She thought of the boy there. She took a deep breath, opened her eyes, looked at him. She held her hand out again at his height. "My nephew. I miss him. My daughter too." She was thinking of Hannah. With the memory came pain. In a moment she was crying, soft and gentle. She couldn't stop.

The boy put his arms around her, hugged her. She hugged back.

As her crying subsided, she looked around.

A spider spun down beside them, hung at eye level.

Carrie let go of the boy. "Agh!"

"What?"

She pointed. "There. In the air!"

Tiki laughed. "That's Many Legs."

Carrie drew back until she was against the side of the wigwam. "Do something!"

"She won't hurt you. Remember? She's our friend. Hello, Many Legs. How are you this morning?" Tiki reached his hand out toward the spider.

"Don't. Please. You could die!"

"Die?"

"From her bite."

The boy looked at her.

"Spider bites kill."

He shook his head.

"They do!" There was terror in her voice.

"Not Many Legs."

"Send it away! Kill it!"

"Is well. Let her spin down, she'll go away. Some mornings she comes down and tickles my face to wake me. Whenever we pack, up she goes." Tiki pointed toward it at the top of the wigwam. "And comes with us." He paused. "My name might be Many Legs when I grow up. I like climbing to high places too. Will you be afraid of me?"

"Of you, no."

"Even if I am Many Legs?"

She shook her head.

Tiki smiled. "Is good. Mohee thinks my name will be White Man's Son, the savior of our people." He laughed.

The spider reached the ground, ran off behind the boy. Carrie did not move. She felt paralyzed.

Tiki looked behind himself. "Bye, Many Legs." He turned toward Carrie. "She's gone."

All Carrie's thoughts were jumbled together—Hannah, the spider, the heathens, this boy.

Tiki clapped his hands.

Carrie stared ahead, seeing nothing. "Spider bites don't kill?"

"Not Many Legs. I told you that."

"Oh." She nodded.

"Come. Time to go work. And see how the hunting went." He shook her arm. "Hi, you."

Carrie stood, looking behind her, above, beside, behind, certain another spider was lurking, hidden in the darkness.

Tiki urged her toward the door. "She is gone now. There is nothing to be frightened of. Not with Many Legs. Come."

Still Carrie didn't move.

"We live with Many Legs every day. She doesn't hurt us." He took Carrie's hand, tugged on it. "Come."

Slowly Carrie followed him outside. He led her to the old people and bounded away.

The old woman was making broth for soup. She had Carrie gather dried roots and the first shoots and small leaves, scolded her when she took the wrong ones or left the right ones, wagging her finger in Carrie's face, impatient, as if Carrie had done this many times before, couldn't she remember?

When Carrie gathered enough, the old woman had her squeeze and pound and scrape, the memory returning to her hands and arms. When the soup was ready, she had to feed the old couple. Carrie was hungry; she had not eaten. She started to taste. The old woman grabbed her hand, made her feed them first, wait until they were finished.

The old couple did not speak, to her or to each other.

After she ate, the old woman had Carrie sweep and clean. As she took the broom, simpler and coarser than the one at home, she remembered doing this before, before the snow, a long time before, it seemed. As she started the motion of sweeping, Carrie was back at home, singing to herself as she—

Carrie felt sad, as if sadness lived in her chest, expanded to fill it. The hollows of her cheeks cried. Everything she had was gone. Hannah. Gideon. Her home. Her sharp-bristled straw broom. Her cup. Her pin cushion, needles, thread. She bit her lip.

The old woman snapped her fingers. Carrie was

neglecting her work. She tried to go faster, stroke after stroke, there as at home, knowing the work in her arms and shoulders.

The old woman snapped her fingers again.

What now? Carrie thought. Wasn't she doing it well?

She was finished, the old woman indicated. She took the broom from her, set it to the side, had Carrie sit, removed each moccasin and the cloth under it, rubbed a root over each foot. One spot stung. Carrie jerked her foot away. The woman urged it back, rubbing gently, re-wrapped each foot with a clean cloth, slid the moccasins back on.

Carrie stared at her feet while the woman did this. Where did these moccasins come from? What had happened to her leather shoes and woolen stockings? Did the heathens take them from her? Maybe before the snow?

Carrie was about to leave the wigwam, the last one up, when she saw, standing outside, the man with the jagged scar on his cheek. Lightning, everyone called him, Quick Flashes of Light. They called him that, Tiki told her, because of his scar, and the anger that sometimes shot out from him. He was Tiki's uncle, brother to his mother, son of the old woman.

Carrie stopped to wait until he moved on.

Before he did, Tiki came by.

Quick Flashes grabbed him, held the sharp point of a knife against the skin on Tiki's arm. Quick Flashes pushed. The skin dented in.

Carrie saw Tiki's face. He looked scared.

"Does it hurt?"

Tiki did not answer.

"Does it?" Quick Flashes pushed harder.

Tiki shook his head.

"It does, doesn't it? Me it wouldn't, but you it does. You know why? Your father was a white man. You are no braver than a woman. You will never fight with us or go hunting, but will stay in the camp, pounding and cooking with the other women."

Carrie was about to step outside when Quick Flashes pulled his knife back, stared at the boy, his face inches away. "Next time I will do it harder. So we can see how brave you are." He smiled.

Tiki glanced down at his arm. The skin was still indented.

The old woman walked up to them. Tiki hid his arm behind him.

"What are you doing?" she asked.

"Talking to the stranger."

She took Tiki's arm, pulled it out to look at. "Was he hurting you?"

Tiki shook his head.

"I told you, don't do that to him."

"I told you, send him away. We don't want our enemies here."

"He is no enemy, and no stranger either. He is my daughter's son, as you are mine." She stopped him before he could answer. "As long as I stay, he stays. And you are not to harm him."

Her son turned and walked away, mimicking the walk and voice of an old woman with almost no teeth. "And you are not to harm him."

Chapter Nine

Carrie was wakened by a shot, a shout, another shot, not close, shouts nearby, commotion inside the wigwam. Tiki and the old couple were taking it down. She had to help.

The man Mohee was not there. He had taken his gun and gone.

She heard shouts, more shots, a little farther away.

The wigwam was packed up, the bark piled on the horse, the saplings lashed to drag behind. It had gotten colder. Snow covered the ground. It was still snowing.

Carrie was cold. The old woman gave her a skin to put over her. Shots came from the woods, a few shouts. Do we leave now? Carrie wondered.

They were waiting for something. The old woman stood with a gun, looking in the direction of the noise. There were more shots. Five men came running toward them. The one in front was shouting. The one in the rear was limping. He had been shot in the foot. Two people helped put him on a horse. They had to leave, that minute. As soon as the men rejoined their family groups they set off. It was still snowing, large flakes dropping to the ground, sticking to their hair and clothing.

Mohee had not returned. Carrie kept looking back. They passed through woods. She could no longer see where they had been.

No one said anything. They started climbing. The snow was slippery. They moved slowly. It felt like fall, Carrie thought. Maybe they had skipped spring and summer and were having winter again.

Shots sounded farther behind, fainter. They reached a plateau. The land leveled out. It snowed harder. They walked on, snow piling up on the ground.

Carrie, sweating under the animal skin, settled into a rhythm of walking. She wondered why, when she heard shouts, she didn't shout too, hoping to be rescued? She didn't think of it. Instead she hurried to get away with the others.

She sensed a presence. She had heard nothing. She turned, saw a gun, held by a man walking beside her. It was Mohee!

She grabbed his arm, squeezed it. He was safe! He turned toward her, smiled. His face had blood and scratches all over it. Sweat mingled with the blood, ran down onto his top lip.

Was he hurt?

He shook his head. His hands made a bramble rose. He smelled it, made the prickers scratching his face like a cat's claws.

Carrie laughed, squeezed his arm again. She was glad to see him safe.

Mohee smiled. Snow in his hair melted, dripped down his face. He slid his finger along his chin, looked at the sweat and blood and melted snow that covered the tip of it, and laughed. "Brave man," he said.

Tiki turned around, ran leaping at him. Mohee caught him, held him waist high while Tiki beat on his chest, laughing. Mohee carried him a long way, then put him down, stopped to slip on a heavier covering, walked on with Tiki, hand in hand.

They all trudged along. The snow slowed down, stopped. It was several inches deep, but soft to step in. On the ground it was wet and squishy.

They stopped. People rested, chewed on snow. There was no food.

The next morning they drank water, took down the wigwams, packed the horses, started walking. No one talked about eating. The injured and infirm rode. The rest hobbled along as best they could. Everyone moved slowly.

Everything had gotten harder.

Walking ten feet was difficult. Carrie's moccasins were wet from the day before. They slipped and schlurped with every step.

Her dress was lined at the bottom with mud that had dried overnight. It clanked together, banged against her leg as she walked. The cakes of mud hurt her shins. The extra weight slowed her down.

While they were sloshing through the snow, her time had started. She was surprised. All winter it did not come, as far as she remembered. She did not know why, maybe because of her sickness. Now she tried to ignore it, pretend it was not so, hoping the liquid she felt on the inside of her thighs was melting snow, but there was no mistaking it.

The old woman knew. When they stopped to rest, she took Carrie aside. She dabbed at the red spot on her dress, gave her a cloth to clean herself with. When Carrie finished, she handed her a patch of deer tail and a strap belt, showed her how to hold it in place. When the strange fur pressed against her, Carrie shuddered. All she could think of was bugs, squirming and wriggling and crawling up inside her. She couldn't refuse to wear it or tear it off with the old woman there, fussing over her. She swallowed, tried to think of other things.

She thought she'd take it away later, when the old woman wasn't looking. It did absorb the blood. Her thighs stayed dry. She left it there overnight.

In the morning the old woman had Carrie remove and bury it, handed her another patch of deer tail.

They started walking. On and on they trudged, tired, thirsty, hungry, clanking, discouraged.

Was this the way the heathens always lived? How much longer could they go on?

They walked for hours, each step no different from the last. Carrie kept her eyes down, watching the path and where she put her feet. There was no reason to look up. The day was cloudy, raw, damp.

They came out of the woods into a clearing. The sky seemed darker. Carrie wondered how much worse it could get.

Mohee stopped, let the others pass, held up his hand for Tiki to wait. Carrie, walking behind him, stopped too, stood to the side, feeling dull, tired and achy, with no more sense why she was there than anywhere else, and with no desire to be anywhere.

Mohee stood, alert, as if hearing something. "Do you hear?"

Tiki listened, shook his head. "What?"

Mohee pointed in front of them. "On the trees. Coming toward us. Hear?"

Tiki nodded. "I hear," he said.

Carrie listened. First she heard nothing, only the others walking, a few words between them, a crow cawing. Then, silence. Then, off in the distance, fainter than she would have thought, she did hear a noise, quiet at first, then steadier, louder, like drops, collections and sheets of drops, on a canopy of evergreens.

Tiki smiled, looked at her. "You hear it?"

"What is it?"

Mohee pointed. "Rain." With his hands Mohee indicated drops landing on trees. "You hear?"

Carrie nodded. Yes, she did hear it.

She listened. It was getting louder. It was coming closer. She smiled. It was magical. Even with all this pain and drabness, there was still beauty and enchantment left, just as in the stories of fairies her mother told her growing up. They used to delight and enthrall her, and Isaac too, when they were young. But by the time they were settled in the new country, he was railing against them as if they were the Devil's handmaidens.

They were sad too, these memories. Without expecting to, she was thinking of Hannah.

The way when it rained Hannah clapped her hands, ran, grabbed Carrie by the dress, pulled with both hands. "Mommy, the rain. Come see." Asking Carrie to open the door so they could look out and watch it. Tugging on Carrie's sleeve, wanting to go out into it, run out, head up, mouth open, scooting back and forth, trying to catch the drops and drink, laughing when one fell into her mouth. "Taste it, Mommy. You taste too." Insisting until Carrie tilted her head back, and the two danced back and forth, drinking the rain.

"What heathen practice is this?" Gideon asked from the doorway.

"We are drinking rain. Come, drink it with us." Hannah ran to pull him out, water dripping down her face and arms, her wet hair flat against her head.

Gideon grabbed her arm, yanked her out of the rain. Her mouth opened, as if she would cry out. She made no sound.

"You stay inside, before you catch your death." He held her beside him in the dry safety of the house. "You don't know better. But your mother does." He started to shut the heavy wooden door, leaving Carrie outside.

"Mommy, Mommy," Hannah screeched from behind the closing door.

"She wants to be out in the elements. Let her." Carrie heard his voice through the door. "She thinks it's good for her."

Carrie stood by herself in the rain, drops beating on her head, running down her face, hoping she did catch her death from it.

The shower passed. In minutes the sun returned, drying and warming her and her clothes.

Behind her, the door creaked open. "Mommy, I'm hungry. Look, where did the rain go?"

Carrie, too sad to talk, gestured toward the sky.

"Bye, rain." Hannah waved at the air. "All gone. Come inside, Mommy. Feed me."

Never again would Hannah pull on her dress, drag her toward the door so she could go outside and run in the rain.

The quiet steadiness of the approaching rain was the sadness inside that never left, the tears built up that she wasn't shedding. Just when she thought it was gone, there it was, back again.

Tiki took her hand, held it and squeezed. Carrie looked down to see tears on his cheeks.

"What, Tiki? what is it?" she asked.

He shook his head.

Carrie leaned down and hugged him. He put his arms around her mid-section and hugged her back.

Beside her, Mohee made a noise. Carrie straightened up, her arm still on Tiki's shoulder, turned toward Mohee. He took an object from his pouch, held it out toward her.

Carrie's mouth fell open. There in his hand was, not Hannah, but an exact replica, a clay mask of her face as she had looked, rendered so well it was as if she was there with them. There were her nose, her eyes, her mouth, her lips, parted as if she was about to speak or laugh. It looked so real Carrie could see this mouth asking for food, tipping back to drink the rain.

It reminded her of another time, a time before winter when they buried Hannah—it was coming back to her—and he held out a mask of his own daughter. And here, now, he held one he had made of hers.

Carrie bit her lip, reached out, took the mask from Mohee, pressed it to her chest, holding and loving the daughter she missed so much. She was crying again, not in heaves and sobs, but deeply and steadily, like the rain on the trees that was growing louder, moving closer. She heard it running toward them.

In another moment drops were landing beside them, on them. They were getting wet. They were standing in rain Carrie had heard miles away a few minutes earlier, and they had not moved.

As it started, Tiki broke away from them and ran ahead, his arms out, head back, twirling around and around in the rain.

All of a sudden Carrie found herself thinking of Gideon.

"Better come inside," he admonished in her head, pointing at the sky. "You'll get wet." She saw him shut the door.

This time it did not bother her. She was glad to be left outside. She stood, smiling, feeling the damp softness of the rain on her face, on her clothes, in her hair, dripping down onto her hands and the image of Hannah. Carrie turned the mask face toward the sky, held it high above her, waved it back and forth, trying to catch the drops. Over the sound of them splatting on the mask, she thought she heard her daughter laughing.

They walked for hours in the rain, through woods, up hill, and down, by boulders, over rocks, across streams, through meadows.

Carrie walked with the image of Hannah pressed to her chest; after a while she lifted it up again, moved it back and forth over her head, letting it drink all the rain it wanted. When it had enough, she brought it down and stared at it, still amazed at how much like her daughter it looked. She kissed it on each wet cheek, wiped it off, and slid it into her pocket, where she could caress it whenever she wanted.

Her clothes clung to her, wet and heavy and cold. Her moccasins got soaked through again. They squished whenever she moved. The dried clumps on her dress turned back to mud. Some dropped off. New ones splashed on.

In the afternoon the rain ended. She, Tiki and Mohee stopped and listened. They heard it leaving as they had heard it approaching, as if each drop was a tiny foot, and there it went, step by step, until it was walking off over the tops of trees.

Crossing a meadow they heard a different sound; the whole meadow seemed to be vibrating.

"You know what it is?" Tiki was smiling. "The Small Frog with the Big Voice."

While Tiki spoke, Mohee stepped off the path into the meadow, stood a moment, leaning over, his hand just above the ground. With a swoop he shut it. The noise came from inside his closed fist.

Carrie felt the hair stand on end on the back of her neck. She didn't know whether to run or look more closely.

"Can I see?" Tiki asked.

"Look, Chipmunk." Mohee opened his hand slightly. There in his palm was a miniature frog, smaller than his thumb. While she watched, its throat puffed up until it was the size of the rest of its body, and then that noise came out of it, and was repeated by hundreds of others, all around. Carrie smiled at the sound. If she had not seen it, she would not have believed that such a large sound could come from such a small creature.

Tiki laughed, tried to make the noise himself.

Mohee shook his head. "Listen."

Tiki tried again, better than the first time.

Mohee nodded. "Keep trying." He opened his hand fully. For a moment the little frog stayed on his palm, making its large noise. Then it jumped back into the grass with the hundreds of others and disappeared, while all around they repeated their thrumming.

The dark clouds lifted. The sky cleared. The sun broke through, streaming through a gap in the departing clouds. A rainbow arced across the sky above them, curving down toward where they were going. Above it a second one curved from horizon to horizon, as full and clear as the first. They all stopped and looked, heads back, exclaiming over the colors and the length. It was a good sign, everyone knew. They would eat before sundown.

They laughed and sang as they crossed the meadow.

Carrie saw five deer ahead of them. Mohee lowered his gun. They were too far to shoot. A dozen turkeys crossed their path, clucking and pecking. They disappeared just like that.

Back in the woods, a shaft of sunlight caught a spider web between two trees. Droplets of water hanging from it reflected a hundred tiny suns.

"Many Legs lives here too, blessing our journey. And if we leave it there," Tiki indicated to duck under the web, "the ones following will think we didn't come this way, and will look elsewhere."

Why didn't I walk through it? Carrie wondered, but she was already under it and past.

No, she realized a moment later. That would make no difference. No one is following us. No one is looking for me. She was alone and forgotten. On they walked, left foot, right foot, left foot, right.

Carrie saw the next spider web before Tiki showed her, smiled as she ducked under it, pointed back at it. Mohee whistled. A bird sang from a branch, hopped to one closer. Mohee held his finger out, whistled again. The bird hopped onto it, a small one, no bigger than his hand, with yellow and green and a banded eye, its turned-up tail flitting. It scolded Mohee, flew back off. He whistled to it as it left.

Chapter Ten

In late afternoon they stopped on a bluff, stood looking out. Sunlight embraced them. Below lay a bend of a large river, its water dancing and sparkling in the light.

It was quiet. It was peaceful. Carrie smiled; she put her hand in her pocket, ran her fingers over the image of Hannah. She was happy, and sad.

They started walking again, wound down the path toward the river.

"Soon we will eat," Tiki shouted. He ran ahead.

They reached a clearing by the river. There they stopped, made a camp. Carrie and the old people set up the wigwam.

Some of the men unraveled a net, waded and swam out, laying it in the water. They waited, then hauled it in, heavy with fish, wriggling and squirming; they removed the fish from the net, tossed them onto a pile, carried the net back out.

Others used spears. They stood, looking down into the water. Suddenly, one jabbed his spear down, brought it out with a fish, walked with it onto shore, and laid it, flipping and jiggling, on the growing pile. Another did the same. They would not go hungry now.

So many fish, the river was teeming with them. From the shore, looking out, all Carrie saw was the smooth dark surface, flowing toward the sea, but under the water, the fish must be crowded together.

Carrie helped gather wood for a fire. One of the women shouted at her. Over here, she pointed; not by the river, where it is easier but the wood is wet, but back here, on land. With several others Carrie dragged branches to where another woman was building a fire. Soon it was blazing.

Carrie stopped to watch the old woman, sitting with others, cleaning the fish. Slip, slip, her knife went. Off came the head, tossed into a pile with the other heads. Up the belly she slid the knife; out came the innards. From them, the old woman set aside a reddish sac almost the size of a fist. Eggs, she indicated, holding it up to show Carrie the hundreds of individual dots in the bigger mass. She licked her lips. Very good.

Carrie bent over one fish at the edge of the pile, fascinated by, and afraid of, its eye, staring up past her, seeing everything, and nothing. She reached her hand down, to grab it. Suddenly the tail flipped; the whole body jumped.

"Oh," Carrie exclaimed, jerking her hand away. "It's still alive!"

No wonder they called her Chipmunk—one who is afraid of everything—she thought, smiling, as her fright subsided.

The old woman kept cleaning the fish. This way and that the knife went. Her gnarled hands moved faster than Carrie could imagine, pulling out dozens and dozens of bones, almost as many as there were eggs in the sac. In minutes she held two fillets up, bone free, tossed them to Carrie, took up another fish to bone.

Carrie laid the fillets as the old woman had showed her, on a rack near the fire, watched them sizzle, the fat drip and dry, until the flesh side was done, turned the skin toward the fire for a few moments, took them off, laid them beside the other cooked fish, put other fillets in their place.They ate well that night. The fish was good and filling. Carrie slept contented.

Just before sleep, in her fatigue, she saw Hannah and Gideon. They were sitting at the table at home, spoons in hand, waiting for her to serve them.

The next day they did not travel. Tiki woke her by showing her Many Legs. "See." He pointed up and smiled.

"She's come here too."

For breakfast they ate more fish, all they wanted. The men and boys caught still more, piles of them. Mohee and Tiki offered to teach her how to fish. Carrie shook her head. She did not want to.

"Come." Tiki gestured to her. "Is easy. See."

Mohee stood on a rocky point, a spear poised in air, staring into the water. All of a sudden he stabbed down. Tiki, watching, clapped his hands. Mohee pulled the spear out, a fish impaled on it. He laid it on the ground next to the others, held the spear out toward Carrie. "You try."

Carrie took it, stood as Mohee had, spear in her hand, its tip inches above the water.

"Now," Tiki urged.

She stabbed down, lifted out an empty spear.

Mohee gestured toward her; he brought his hand straight down, stopped it, moved it a few inches to the side, kept it going.

Carrie was puzzled.

"In water," Tiki explained. "You see the fish here." He held his hand out in front of him. "Is here." He moved his hand a few inches to the right. "Try again."

Carrie tried again, and again. She saw the fish, not far below the surface; she didn't aim for it, but a little to the side, the way Tiki and Mohee showed her. She tried three more times, moving it farther to the side each time. Still nothing.

She handed the spear back to Mohee.

"Watch," Tiki said. He took the spear, stood as Mohee did, with it poised above the water. "See the fish?" Carrie nodded. "Now!" Tiki jabbed down. Just like that, he had a fish. Carrie clapped her hands.

Tiki brought it out of the water, smiling, laid it by the others. "Try again." He handed her the spear.

Carrie stood with its tip just above the water.

"Now," Tiki urged.

Carefully but quickly, she jabbed down. She felt the spear hit the fish and hold it, saw it squirming in the water.

Tiki clapped his hands.

"I got it. I got it!" Her whole body moved up and down.

"Pull it out."

She did, held it up toward Mohee. "Look! Did you see?"

"Good, Chipmunk," he said, smiling.

"Nice fish!" said Tiki, removing it from the spear, putting it with the others.

"I caught that!" Carrie kept smiling.

"Again?" Tiki asked.

Twice more Carrie stood with the spear over the water, jabbed it down, brought out a fish. Her smile got bigger. She did that. They showed her how to, but she's the one who did it!

Fishing was finished; all the fish were cleaned and cooked. Work was done.

Tiki and Mohee swam in the river.

Carrie was sitting near them, on a rock, overlooking the water, the sun warm on her face and her clothes. All of a sudden they stood up and, without saying a word, started undressing. One item of clothing came off, another, and another. Surely they were not going to remove them all. But they kept going, as if she was not there, dropping one after another in a pile at their feet.

Carrie stared down to the side, toward the dark water, trying to imagine all the fish swimming in it. She could tell without looking that Tiki and Mohee continued to expose more and more of their flesh.

She felt as if bugs were crawling all over her. She tried to swallow. She couldn't.

Out of the corner of her eye she saw the last of their clothing fall to the ground.

Despite herself, she could not help glancing over. The man and boy stood completely naked, facing away from her, out toward the water. Carrie could not take her eyes off them. She had never seen such a sight in her life.

Mohee touched Tiki on the upper arm, said a few words to him, and away they raced. In a moment they were in the water, laughing, kicking, swimming, splashing. “It’s cold,” Tiki shouted, and splashed some more.

Carrie exhaled, started to smile. A movement to her right made her stop: ankle deep in the water, a naked woman made her way out, it seemed, toward where Tiki and Mohee were swimming.

Carrie held her breath. She did not know how the heathen woman could expose herself like that. She felt shame for her, for this person who, by the slow, upright way she moved, did not seem to feel any for herself.

For her sake, Carrie turned away, looked around on the banks and in the water where everyone went on doing what they were doing—men and boys splashing in the river, old men sitting on the bank, smoking; old women standing a few inches deep in the water, rinsing out clothes or talking. No one seemed to notice the naked woman in the river but her.

Carrie looked back, stared at the woman. She had seen her before, she realized. She was about Carrie’s size, but younger, and prettier, and to Carrie’s surprise she was pleasing to look at, even naked, with her dark straight hair hanging down to her waist, the narrowness of that waist, the flatness of her stomach, the arc of her hips, line of her legs, the round fullness of her breasts.

Carrie had never seen anyone who looked like that. She had never seen herself naked, but she knew that was not what she looked like.

Suddenly she felt ashamed, not for the naked heathen woman, but for herself and her own body, covered from neck to ankle.

She looked back at the river. The naked woman walked in above her knees, to her waist, headed, Carrie was sure, in her slow, steady way toward Mohee.

In a minute, Carrie knew, he would pretend to notice her, stop his games with Tiki, walk to join her in his arms, and the two would embrace, kiss, fondle, and who knew what more, there, in front of her, without any thought to what was decent.

Carrie sat rigid, her jaw tight. She looked up toward the sky. For a woman to behave like that, in the open, in daylight—

A splash made her look back toward the river. All of the woman but her head had disappeared into the water; there she swam in small circles, round and round, by herself.

Straight ahead Mohee laughed and splashed, shouted and guffawed with Tiki, as oblivious of the woman as she was of him.

Up and down the river, others of their group swam and bathed in the water, men and women, young and old, alone or with someone else, even the old couple from her wigwam, all of them naked.

Carrie could not help looking at them, at their bodies. The day she was captured the men wore nothing above the waist. Since then, except when they fought or made raids, they kept themselves covered. She had never seen a man naked head to foot before, or a boy either, other than her nephew Paul when he was still swaddled in diapers. She had never seen a woman naked either. And here there were so many, all of them acting normal and unashamed, as if they wore clothes no one else could see.

At first she had trouble looking at them. She expected to see what Isaac warned about, railing against nakedness and lechery and fornication.

The heathens made so many joyous noises, so many shouts and hooplas, it was hard for her not to turn back toward them. When she did, she saw none of the dangers Isaac spoke of. They were tired people enjoying themselves. Before long she smiled with them in their pleasure.

The longer she watched the easier it became, the less she noticed they were naked.

Some, like Mohee, were pleasing to look at. And Tiki. And the young woman. Some had scars or skin that sagged. But looking at them did not displease her either.

Most amazing, she decided, was that nothing was

amazing. They were people without clothes behaving like people with clothes, only not encumbered.

Tiki and Mohee tried to get her to join them. "Come, Chipmunk." Tiki shouted from the river, standing chest deep in the water. "Cold." He and Mohee pointed at her, laughed, splashed. "Feels good."

She shook her head.

"Why not, Carrie?" a bird seemed to sing to her. Is the Chipmunk afraid?

She needed to. She was dirty. She had not fully cleaned herself since she was captured, had not once removed her clothes. Maybe the old woman cleaned them when she was sick, but they were dirtier than she could remember. In the last two days they had gotten wet, caked dry until they clanked against her when she walked, got wet again, and now were drying in the sun. They smelled more strongly than usual, as if they were part of the slippery ground. And her time was not yet finished.

In the sun, she saw that the old woman was not able to remove all the stain from her dress. It had dried hard, a deep, dark red. She needed to wash her clothes out, as she saw other women doing. And she needed to clean herself.

She stood, took a step toward the water.

No. She knew she shouldn't. Isaac's voice sounded in her head, warning of all the evils that would follow.

Carrie shut her eyes, feeling the sun on her face and hands, imagining what it would be like to stand there without clothes on, its warmth caressing all of her. She wanted to join the others, but she could not. Shame, doubt and guilt assailed her, not to mention the tribe of devilish heathens she imagined lurking behind every rock, waiting until she exposed herself before they swooped down and worked their unspeakable will on her.

Tiki and Mohee climbed out of the water twenty feet away, shook themselves off, stood naked on a rock, shivering.

Tiki pushed Mohee off the rock, back into the water, jumped in himself, ran splashing away. Mohee whooped and hollered, came out laughing. For a moment Carrie laughed too.

Tiki and Mohee stood drying in the sun, talking. They seemed happy. At ease.

No prohibitions, Carrie thought, no "beware of this, watch out for that." She thought of Gideon. Everything he did had rules and "be carefuls." How little he enjoyed himself. Or she, herself.

Mohee caught Tiki, swung him around, pretended to throw him into the water. Tiki squealed. Everyone nearby laughed.

Carrie laughed again too. Laughing felt so good. When did she laugh before. Ever.

She caught herself. She should not be laughing. It was not Christian to laugh. It was a temptation.

All of a sudden a larger laugh welled up. She tried to hold it in. She could not. It came billowing out, grew until her whole frame shook. Chortles and "whees" escaped her.

What was she laughing at? Gideon inside her wanted to know. With all that had happened, what could she possibly find amusing? Did she think such behavior was seemly? Did she forget who she was? or where she was? Suppose someone saw her? What would they think?

In her imagination Carrie heard his stern voice, saw his long face. She wanted to keep laughing, guffaw until her sides ached. Instead she held her laughter in as best she could, as she had, it seemed, all her life, breathing steadily until it subsided.

Carrie felt the mask in her pocket. She had a daughter gone, a husband too. And she laughed? What did she have to laugh at? A naked man and a naked boy, both heathens? She was on the short road to damnation.

Lord, forgive her. She knew she was weak, knew she needed strength. She needed His assistance. It was difficult keeping her faith, so far from those she loved, for such a long time, with so little hope, and so much sadness. Hannah was in her thoughts every day, and Gideon, but sometimes it was good to forget her troubles, even for a moment. She was sorry if that was a sin.

Clouds covered her face. She bit her lip.

She heard the bird song from earlier, looked up. There Mohee stood, in front of her, clothed from the waist down, looking at her and whistling. She did not see any bird, but in his whistle she heard its call. He held his finger out. Nothing flitted to it.

As he whistled, Mohee made his other hand into a bird, fingers flapping like wings, wrist flicking, as if one landed on his finger. Carrie saw the bird, there in front of her. Mohee held it out toward her, the magic of creation in his hands and sounds. She smiled, reached her finger out to take it from him.

"Wren," he said as the bird hopped from his finger to hers, as vivid and alive as any real one.

The whistle changed to a bird flying. The fingers flapped. The hands flew. The bird was gone.

Chapter Eleven

As it grew dark, those from Carrie's wigwam lingered by the fire, telling stories. Each took a turn but the old man. He sat, watching and nodding, but did not speak.

The old woman spoke first. Tiki explained her words in English. She talked about the fish they had eaten, how once it lived on land, its back sharp with the quills of a porcupine. It walked a long way, came to the Long River, decided to swim, not across, but out to the ocean where the river ended. It swam and it swam. It got more and more tired, its wet coat dragging it down. Lower and lower it sank in the water, its mouth bobbing nearer and nearer the surface. Before long it was under the water, but the gods, who were watching as they watch all things, turned it inside out, and it became the fish they had eaten, gliding along, all its quills bones, and, every year, coming in and swimming back out to the ocean and giving them, for that short period, all that good food to eat.

When she finished, everyone oohed and aahed and clapped.

Mohee talked next. He talked some with words in English, some with words in his own language, but mostly with his body. He was the deer he hunted. He stood in the opening, crouched, limbs taut, looking with his head one way and another, so well that Carrie saw the deer she had seen bounding away the day before. Then he was the hunter, bow drawn back, letting the arrow fly. Then he was the deer, watching it miss, leaping away. Then he was the hunter becoming the deer, feeling its danger, alert and aware, knowing how precious and fragile life is. Then he became the hunter again, wearing the deer skin, bending the bow back, shooting the deer, dancing the dance of the deer as it chose to be shot, the arrow entered it and its spirit left, thanking and apologizing to that spirit, dancing the dance of the deer as it died. He finished as the spirit of the deer, alert, aware, watching, and off he bounded, easy and free.

Carrie watched, hardly breathing, as he became the deer, the hunter, the wounded deer, the hunter, the deer again. There was magic in what he did. She didn't want it to end.

Tiki told about Many Legs. He spoke in English, repeated phrases in their own language. It was a story the others seemed to have heard before. How in the beginning there was one spider. She was not Many Legs, only Two Legs, like people. Some said she was a person herself who was changed into a spider. She lived at the top of the dome in the middle of a wigwam.

One morning she wanted to see where she was. She let out her thread and spun herself down. When she wanted to go back up, she couldn't, because she only had two legs, and that was not enough to climb. So she lay on the ground and moaned and complained. She was going to die, she said, if she could not get back up.

The gods got tired of listening to her. They were sleepy, they wanted to rest, she was keeping them awake. "Give her two more legs," one of them said. Tiki spoke in a deep voice for the gods.

All of a sudden she had four legs, but three were on the same side. She was lopsided. She complained some more.

"We want to eat our supper and go to sleep in peace," the gods said.

They gave her two more legs, and, for good measure, two more after that.

"No one needs more than that," they said. "Complain any more and you won't have any."

The spider stopped complaining. She was not lopsided anymore. Look how many legs she had. Look at all she could do with them. She could spin, not only straight lines, but curves and circles and crisscrossed webs. She could swing between bushes and branches, across paths, let herself down, climb back up, fly out, spin back. She could catch flies in her web and eat them. And when she laid eggs and they hatched into babies, they too had eight legs, and could swing off and find their own places to live and spin and climb and build webs.

"Now every path and every wigwam has a Many Legs living there, to protect it from enemies. And that's why we don't kill them, even when they scare us. Because they are our friends."

Carrie clapped her hands. She was delighted with Tiki's story. They all were.

They grew quiet and looked at her. It was her turn. She protested. She did not know any good stories like theirs.

From her religion, she must. Tell one of them.

Carrie thought a long time before deciding what to tell. When she spoke, she paused between phrases, to let Tiki translate. They all listened carefully.

She told about the Garden of Eden, what a paradise that had been. Adam and Eve had all the food they wanted; they never worked, and were happy all day. Only one thing they could not do, and that was eat the apple, the fruit of the tree of knowledge. And that was fine with them, they had more than enough to eat, they did not need an apple.

One day, when Eve was alone, the snake began tempting her. "Wouldn't you like to eat that apple?" he hissed. "All these wonderful things, and only that's forbidden. If everything else is so good, can't you imagine how good the apple must be? Why do you think it's forbidden? Knowledge? What doesn't God want you to know? What harm can it cause, one little bite?"

"He's right," Eve thought. "Why not? One little bite." She picked the apple and took a bite.

Adam came running up. "That's the tree you're not supposed to eat the fruit of."

It was too late. She had already eaten it. She was ashamed. She knew she had done what she was not supposed to. She pretended nothing was wrong. "Mmm. Have a bite. Even a small one. All the food we have, there is nothing as good as this."

Adam took a bite, half the size of Eve's. As soon as he swallowed the first part of it, he knew he had done what he should not have done. He stopped chewing, tried to cough the piece back up. It was too late. It had already gone down. He knew what she knew, that neither of them wanted to know. They had sinned. They both were mortal and would die, and they saw that they were naked, and were ashamed.

Even before God found out and punished them, they knew they had to leave Eden. "And that's why people all over the earth wear clothes, and work hard for their food, and die." She remembered Isaac's admonition in sermon after sermon. "In Eve's fall we sinned all."

Carrie stopped. It was their turn to clap and whistle and stomp, and say what a good story it was, and how well she told it.

They asked many questions about it. About paradise they were very clear, but there were other things they did not understand. What was sin? and what was shame? and why was it bad to be naked?

Carrie explained the best she could. She was not sure she knew either. She did not think she was defending the story very well. She tried to think of what Isaac would say, did not get farther than "Because it was bad. It was wrong. God said so, and that was that. Besides, look what it led to."

When she finished they still did not understand. She was not sure she did anymore either. She had seen, that afternoon, men and women who were naked and were not ashamed and were not lusting after each other either, and this certainly was not Eden.

It had gotten dark. Stars shone brightly above them. The other wigwams were quiet. It seemed late.

The old man was sleeping, breathing evenly. Tiki would have been too, but they kept waking him to ask her questions. Mohee was wide awake, his eyes bright in the dark as he thought about what he had heard.

The old woman touched the old man. He started and

stood up. She touched Tiki. He stood up, eyes still shut. The three headed for the wigwam.

Carrie stood, stared a moment up at the stars. They seemed so sharp, so still.

Mohee pointed up. “No Many Legs up there.” He made a spider with his fingers, spinning down a thread.

She smiled, shook her head.

“No ‘sin’ too.”

She laughed. “No.”

He nodded. “Good sleep.”

She walked toward the wigwam, stopped outside the flap, breathed deeply, looked up again at the stars that were without spiders or sin, listened to the silence all around, then went in, lay down.

A few minutes later she heard Mohee come in, lie down on the other side of the wigwam.

Carrie lay a long time, her eyes open, staring up at the black that did have Many Legs in it, wondering about sin, and nakedness, and shame, and why it was always Eve’s fall, and not Adam’s too.

Carrie slept fitfully. Half the night, it seemed, she was awake, thinking about sin and shame and her own naked body. She was overcome with curiosity about it, what it looked like, compared to the heathen woman’s she thought attractive. She wondered why she had never seen it, remembered the admonition: “Keep yourself covered at all times; it is evil not to.” Having all sorts of inventions to bathe herself, or nurse Hannah, without exposing her sinful body.

She had no sense of herself as a person anyone looked at. She met Gideon young, his father asked her father for her. There was never any question, Did he like her? like what he saw when he looked at her? They were husband and wife, fond of each other. They did their duty.

She wondered what she looked like to others. If someone looking at her would say, as she did with the heathen woman, she is pleasing to look at, or not pleasing to look at, either her body or her face?

Why was she wondering about such things? Wasn't it a sin to think them? She remembered the sermon: "Vanity of vanities. All is vanity. Powdered face, painted lips, gaudy clothing."

But no clothing was bad too. It was sinful.

The sin of what? Lust? Envy? The evil that happens between people who let their base desires rule their beings?

The heathens were evil. She knew that; she had heard it many times. They were naked, proof of their evilness. But they did not lust and cavort. They acted as unashamed as Eve and Adam in the garden. And they were not evil to her either, as Isaac had warned. They left her alone.

How twisted her thinking was. They kidnapped her from her home, took her from her family, killed her daughter, kept her from worshipping the one true God. And she was defending them?

Her temples hurt from so much thinking. She rubbed her fingers against them, stared up toward the dark dome of the wigwam. Many Legs was up there, sleeping. She imagined it spinning down toward her in the dark, its many legs letting out thread, imagined it so close above her she could reach out and touch it, and still not see it. She shrank back against the ground. Her throat was dry. She was sweating.

She must have slept. A giant spider swallowed the light. She saw its shadow against the edge of the wigwam. It was not a spider but Mohee's hands, dancing a spider dance.

Carrie was tired. She wanted to be home. She thought of being there in the evening, cleaning up from supper, while Gideon sat in his chair, studying the Bible, his fingers holding up the next page.

She imagined him walking out to greet her when she returned, saying how glad he was, how much he missed her, how worried he was about her, as close to a smile on his face as she had ever seen.

She tried to picture his face, this man she had been married to all these years. She saw his beard, his ears with their large lobes, his bushy eyebrows, his crooked teeth, his scowl. Was it a pleasing face to look at? She did not know. It was her husband's face, not a face you looked at to see if it was pleasing.

Mohee was pleasing to look at, both his face and his body. She was surprised she had noticed.

No, no. She was thinking about her husband. She felt good in her chest about him. She missed Gideon, missed his hands, tearing bread at the table; his fingers, turning a page in the Bible. She missed his boot steps ringing on the wooden floor as he walked in to eat, or the soiled, sweaty smell of his shirt, with the missing half button he insisted she did not need to replace.

She wondered what he looked like under that soiled shirt, why she never saw him naked. She would suggest it when she got back, that they should bathe together naked. She giggled inside at the thought.

Bad thinking.

What was wrong with her? The heathens with their insidious ways were making her thoughts evil. She was no better than a modern day Eve. Shame on her.

"Shame."

She, fully clothed her entire life, felt shame. And men and women, naked in front of her and themselves, hiding nothing, felt none.

Her temples throbbed. She pressed her fingers to them, shut her eyes. She wished she could sleep.

Chapter Twelve

The next day they moved on.

Day after day they got up, ate if they had food, took down the wigwams, walked all day, stopped, ate, slept, got up the next day and did the same. Sometimes they stopped a day or two to hunt or fish or rest. Less and less often, they saw white people, off at a distance. Once in a while they fought.

They walked through the cherry trees blossoming, flowers blooming. They walked through the songbirds singing, the turkeys gobbling, the whippoorwills whooping, the leaves filling out, the woods darker and cooler, but often still, warm and humid in the increasing heat.

When the wild strawberries were ripe, Mohee led Carrie and Tiki to a bed of them. He picked a few, handed several to Tiki, others to her. She did not think of rejecting them, or waiting until they ate first. She popped them into her mouth.

She was amazed that berries so small could taste so sweet. She, Tiki and Mohee feasted on them until their hands were red and sticky from the juice, stopped for other clusters scattered along the path.

The old man grew too weak to walk. For several days a horse carried him. He got even weaker.

One morning when Carrie woke, his eyes and mouth were open, his skin cold.

"Many Legs touched his face," Tiki told her, "and he didn't brush her away. Many Legs wrapped her thread around him and took him away."

Carrie bit her lip. He was a sweet old man. The way

in the winter he had fed and cared for her, and, now that she was better, let her feed him, not fussing, patient, taking her hand and squeezing it to thank her. Smiling when he was happy, but never saying a cross word to anyone. Because, Tiki explained, he could not hear, an accident with a musket exploding took his hearing away.

It made her think of her father, who had lived and died in England, never made it to the "New" England, "where men are free to worship as they believe." He urged Isaac and Rebecca, and Gideon and her, to go, died before they left, made them promise they would go without him. It had been so long since she thought of him. She remembered helping him eat when he was too sick to feed himself, just as she had fed the old heathen. How much the same the two of them were, more similar than different.

They stopped two days for the old man's funeral.

Mohee made a mask of his face, gave it to the old woman. He hummed the song of funerals, played sad songs on his flute; Quick Flashes beat the drum in a slow, mournful way.

Together they dug a grave, put the old man's body in a sitting position, wrapped him in birch bark, laid him in it on his side; with the others they chanted, played their instruments, told stories of his long life, said their sad good-byes.

As at Hannah's grave, the old woman made a mournful sound that seemed to come from deep within the earth. She wailed and wailed, cut her hair, blackened her face, slept with his image pressed against her, whimpering and moaning. They had been together since they were not much bigger than Tiki. She could not remember how it was before him. How could she go on? She was not herself without him. What was the point of living?

Carrie sat with her night and day, bringing her broth and dippers of water, soothing her brow, holding her hand, happy to do for her as she had done for Carrie. The old woman looked so sad and so old. Still, from time to time, she squeezed Carrie's hand, or leaned her head against her.

They waited two more days before moving, walked more slowly in sadness, yet one more of the old ones gone, and with him a sense of how the days before used to be.

In time, night after night, Carrie heard many of their stories—about gods and heroes; the characteristics and uses of different plants and creatures, how they got their names. Over and over she asked about their customs. If Mohee would not tell her, she asked the old woman, had Tiki translate.

She wanted to know about their cercmony of marriage. She had seen one couple go off and stand together near a stream, with two or three others around them. When they returned, not much later, Tiki said, "Now they are husband and wife." The man, she noticed, slept every night in the wife's wigwam, with her family.

"Tell me about yours," she asked Mohee, "you and your wife getting married."

"Pah." He waved his hand. He did not remember. It was nothing.

She persisted.

It was not the ceremony that mattered. It was the feeling inside here—he touched his chest—being two yet one, sharing Special Places together, making every place they shared Special.

Carrie thought of her own wedding, how important the event was for her, and for all the young girls, even those who lived simply and shunned excess. It meant becoming a woman, leaving behind childhood and her parents' home where she had lived all her life.

And the ceremony itself. All the girls whispered among themselves about other people's, how wonderful they were. Even if they had little, and were admonished to avoid ostentation, each girl tried to make her own dress as pretty and striking as possible, so everyone would remember her and how she looked. Carrie herself, like so many others, sewed in small adornments that would be subtly visible during the ceremony.

She asked the old woman about her marriage to the old man.

The old woman was quiet a minute, then smiled. It was so long ago, it was hard to remember. This was back before there were white people. Everything was different then. Everything was simpler; they did not travel so much, but stayed in one place, with fields and woods all around and the long river nearby, hunting and fishing; then, with the turn of the seasons, they moved to another place where they did the same.

"Is that what you wanted to know?"

What about the ceremony?

The old woman closed her eyes, remembering. "Everyone was there. His father was a Medicine Man; he talked about our spirits joining. Those were good times, with lots of food. As his gift, my new husband gave me a basketful of corn. I gave him another in return. We passed a long pipe and everyone smoked it.

"After that, he came to live with me and my family. And we were together from then until—" She grew quiet.

Carrie nodded. "I'm sorry."

"Is well," Tiki said.

After a minute the old woman smiled and went on. "We had three sons and two daughters. The only ones left are Quick Flashes," she paused thinking, "and Mohee, and he's another woman's child. And you, Chipmunk." She took Carrie's hands. "Like one of the daughters, come back." She thought a moment. "One of the sons, the oldest. He went off when he was young, and we never heard from him again. He might still return. He appears in my dreams from time to time."

She stopped for a moment. "There have been so many changes since then. If you had told us then all that would happen, we wouldn't have believed it, or we would have said, 'Better to die now than to see so much gone and taken away'."

The old woman shrugged, her jaw moving, chewing on a root. "Like the marriage ceremony. It is not how it used to be, all hurry up and get it over with before another attack happens or we have to move again. It should take time, the ceremony; slowly. Like marriage. But, so often, it seems, we don't have time anymore. Where did it go? I want to know. Is someone stealing it?" She was quiet a moment. "This now." She spread her arms and hands out. "It is not what we expected, or the way we would have wanted it to be. But it could be worse." She smiled, showing gaps in her teeth. "Me and the old man. So many years together, so many close escapes. And never an argument or cross word, the last thirty years. Because he couldn't hear." She laughed.

"Isn't it hard?" Carrie asked, thinking of the long marches, so many days without food.

"It has always been hard, and always been good," the old woman answered. "Isn't that how it is everywhere?"

Chapter Thirteen

Mohee told many stories, especially when his friend Quick Flashes was not around, and he was around less and less.

He seemed to delight in telling them, and Carrie, and the others, in hearing them. Some Tiki had to translate, but more and more he told them with simple words and gestures, so Carrie could understand.

He told how, after she was captured, the snow surprised them. Neither he nor the others knew it would come so early or be so much, except the old man. For three days he pointed at the sky, but because he said nothing, no one paid attention to him. In the old days they would have stopped and looked until they understood. But now they were in such a hurry, going this way and that, they did not think they had time.

Even the first, wet flakes of snow they ignored.

Overnight it turned colder. The wind picked up. The air smelled and the silence sounded like snow, but Mohee and the others still did not realize what the old man was trying to say. It took waking to snow inches deep in the night before Mohee knew. He roused the others; they left in the dark, hurrying toward the nearest Long House. Before they left, the snow was already above their ankles. It fell harder and faster, as if it would never stop.

It was a two day walk in clear, dry weather. It took them four, the snow reaching half-way to their knees by the time they arrived, everyone slipping, wet, tired, hungry, wishing they had listened to the old man and had gotten there before the snow started.

Several of their party floundered in the snow, slowing them down. The captive woman was the worst. Part way there she fell on the ground and couldn't get up, had to be carried the rest of the way on the back of a horse. Quick Flashes wanted to leave her behind. Mohee wanted her to stay with them, did not want to fight again with his friend when it seemed they fought more and more. He was glad when the old woman put her on the horse and brought her with them.

As it got dark on the fourth day, they reached the Long House. Mohee, Quick Flashes, and a few others fished while the rest unpacked. It was as if the fish were waiting for them. They ate well that evening, slept soundly, and in the morning woke to winter at the Long House.

Life seemed easy then. No raids or attacks. Every few days it snowed. Between snows the air was cold. The sun dazzled, stars sparkled. They fished from the shore or at the stream until the lake was frozen. When the ice was thick, they drilled holes in their favorite spots, brought back an abundance of fish. No one went hungry. Everyone slept contented.

The owl lived in a tree by the lake, calling at night, deep and haunting. Mohee called back, hoo, hoo, hoo.

Mohee took out his flute, made the same deep note with it. He whittled one for Tiki, taught him to blow and finger it, to follow with his tunes. Quick Flashes beat a rhythm on a drum. They played quietly to pass the time, more loudly while others danced.

By himself, Mohee played his flute in a corner of the house, or outside in the sun, under the overhang where the ground was bare, or in the shed, between two sleeping horses, warmed by the heat of their bodies.

While he played, he thought about the year gone by, the year ahead, how he liked this life of winter, wondering why it couldn't always be like this. As soon as he thought that he knew: it was because of the white people, more of them there, all the time, taking what belonged to his people, making it so they could never be still, always had to be moving, this way and that.

For him, so much of what he did was a reaction, a lashing back.

When he was young, already it was not the same as

it was when the old ones were young. They stayed, they told him, in one place as long as they wanted. But even for him, it felt as if the world was his, it was his tribe's. They could still go to all the places that were theirs. They traveled only when they needed to, following food. Sometimes there was much, often there was little. Sometimes they fought other tribes or among themselves, but every moment felt as whole as any other. Much of their life was difficult, but their universe was still entire.

His constant companion in this was Quick Flashes. They were inseparable. Games, adventures, fishing, hunting, fighting, if one was there, the other was nearby.

In all the stages of their journeys, as they ranged up and down the Long River, Mohee had "Special Places" that were his favorites, ones he had gone to with his father, played at with Quick Flashes, returned to by himself when he was grown, went back to with his wife Mouse—White Deer Mouse, Quick Flashes' sister.

One of those Special Places was a high meadow, with a stream falling at one end and woods below. There his heart was content. He sat in the middle, hearing the water tumble, looked out to the west at hills leading to hills leading to hills, watched birds fly, deer graze, turkeys scratch, and smiled at how happy he was. Many times he and Mouse made love there. Afterwards they lay, body close to body, skin touching skin, and dozed, or talked, about each other, their past together, what their life would be like in the future.

And then one spring, he and Quick Flashes went back there, sat in the sun by the stream, the last of the snow melting around them. The silence was shattered by a gunshot, a musket ball screaming into a tree above them. Mohee looked around, startled. They were not dressed as a deer or dancing like one. They had come to be quiet. He did not know who was shooting at them, or why.

At the top of the field stood a man with a beard. He yelled words at them that sounded angry, waved his arms. Mohee stared at him, trying to understand. The man knelt, reloaded, took aim again with his musket.

Quick as his friend's name, Mohee and his

companion were gone, rolling down out of sight, wading across the stream, running off on a path through the woods.

They told the others what happened. Several said the same had happened, there or elsewhere, to them.

Quick Flashes was angry. “And what did you do about it?”

The old wise men shook their heads. “We did nothing.”

“You think this is how it should be?”

“This is how it is. Settlers come and our home is no longer our home.”

“These people came from somewhere. They can be made to go back there. I am ready to go in the dark before dawn with torches, burn their houses, kill as many of them as I can. I will do it tonight. Who will go with me?”

No one answered. A few of the old men shrugged.

“No one?” He turned to Mohee. “Not even you?”

“What is the reason for burning? What does that do?”

“It drives them away.”

“It doesn’t shake them up like a hornet’s nest?”

“It makes them afraid, and then they take the bee’s path back where they came from. You will see. Go with me tonight, carrying fire and guns.”

Mohee shook his head. His friend turned away as if he had been slapped.

“Reconsider,” said one of the old men. “There may be a better time for what you say.”

Long into the night Mohee sat by himself, watching, thinking. He saw Quick Flashes ready his horse, load it with guns and torches, lead it to the edge of the clearing and ride off. Mohee was still sitting there when he returned.

Mohee nodded, as if to say, “How was it?”

His friend smiled. “Four houses are gone that were there before, the sky bright with their flames.”

“And the people?”

“Three or four I shot and saw fall.”

“No more?”

“There is only so much one person can do alone. Work with me and it will go faster.” He smiled again. “It was a good night. I saw their fear. I do not think the others will remain.”

Only it did not happen the way he thought. Not much later Mohee was lying in his wigwam, sleep had not yet closed his eyes, when he heard hooves thundering toward them. By the time he was outside, two of the wigwams were burning and three of their own were wounded.

“Attack!” he shouted. “Everyone defend.”

In moments, men emerged from every wigwam, shooting at the horses and riders, drove them off into the night while the women took the wigwams down and made ready to leave.

They walked for two days before it felt safe to stop.

The night after they stopped, Quick Flashes burned houses at the nearest village. Before the sun rose, white settlers attacked them, killed one of theirs, burned two more wigwams.

As they began walking, the sun showing red on the horizon, everyone exhausted from the previous two days without food, Mohee stood in front of his friend’s horse, took the reins, held them.

“Do not do attack again, the next place we stop.”

“It is the only way to get our places back.”

“How is this getting our places back? It drives us farther away.”

“I will do what needs doing.”

Others stood listening. One old man spoke. “No, you will not. You will do what we decide, what helps us all.”

“I will decide what I will do.”

“Not if it endangers us. Or you will not live with us.”

They went north, they went west, they went south. Quick Flashes stayed by himself, speaking to no one, not even Mohee or Mouse.

Many nights he went out, did not return until dawn. They were often attacked, forced to take the wigwams down and move on as they fought off the settlers.

They returned to the Special Place where the settler shot at Mohee and Quick Flashes. The settlement had grown.

Mohee snuck back there, but the peace was gone. The gunshot from the other time had shattered it, all the gun shots. A cabin stood in the meadow, at the top of it. Mohee could not sit in the field in silence and contentment. The special spirit of the place was gone, driven away by the man with his gun, the cabin, the trees hacked and cut to build it. The whole time he was there, Mohee stood behind a tree, loaded gun in hand, watching the door of the cabin, sure that at any moment it would open and an armed man burst out, shouting and shooting.

He went back there with Mouse. They walked around the edge of the meadow, kept their eyes on the cabin. They could not relax or make love, not knowing who was watching.

On his next visit, there was a fence between him and his meadow. Inside it stood not one but several buildings, each bigger and more imposing than the other. The biggest had two large crossed sticks in front of it.

Mohee could not go there, except at night or early in the morning, and then only by being so careful and alert he felt like the deer. From outside the fence he smelled people, heard their voices, the strange sounds of their language, their cows mooing, their chickens clucking.

The next time they came near there on their journey his heart leapt up, thinking about going, stopped in mid-jump when he remembered how it had changed. He decided not to return. It would be too painful. The meadow was no longer his Place.

The same happened to many other Places, each one a deeper hurt, a greater sadness, and, taken together, an even greater one. He did not know which one would be taken from him next. He expected soon none would be left. If he returned and a Special Place was still there, untouched, he could not enjoy it. He kept looking around and listening, expecting the arrival of settlers. Before long, he knew, this Place too would be gone.

Wherever Mohee went he felt that sadness. At every step it cried inside. He was no longer taking a journey from happy place to happy place, but from sad one to sad one, hurt to hurt, from what was gone to what would be. Many times, as he put one foot in front of the other, he wondered, Why? Why not sit in one Special Place they had not taken yet, and wait until they came, and fight for that one until they were gone or he was dead?

Each step filled him with dread. There was sadness in everything he did.

"You have to fight," Quick Flashes said. "If you go to a Special Place and a cabin is there, you have to come whooping and yelling, shooting with guns, burn it, chase the people away, kill them if you can."

Why? Mohee asked. Did that take the spirit of the cabin away, or make the Place Special again?

"If you don't, the people will think what they have done is right, and, before you know it, everything will be gone."

After they were attacked twice in one day, once from the east, once from the south, when they didn't have time to stop and bury their dead but had to lash them to horses like animals and keep moving, Mohee said to his friend, "Lead where you want. I am ready."

Chapter Fourteen

Mohee dressed for war, armed himself, went looking for battles. He came shooting with arrows and guns, hooting and yelling, swinging his war club, lighting fires. He did it well. Sadness became anger at the people who made him sad. Over and over he led raids, killed settlers. He did it bravely. He was not afraid. He did not care if he was caught or hurt. Sometimes what he and Quick Flashes did scared the people away.

But it did not make the cabins go away. And even if they won, and all the people died or left, and they burned the cabins, so nothing remained but corpses and ashes, the sadness did not go away. He could not make the Place be as it had been. It had changed. Its spirit was gone. It was no longer Special.

And the people were not going away. They built cabins, cut down trees, made clearings, put up fences, plowed the land at more and more Special Places. And they fought back, defending what they thought was theirs.

Mohee and his people could not travel as they used to, on their paths along the Long River, fishing and hunting. Cabins, fences, settlements blocked their way; they had to go farther and farther around.

It is our place too, Mohee wanted to say, land I and my people have gone on for as long as the story tellers can remember. Before we came there was only the earth and the sky. Then we were here, and those were the paths we walked on.

Mohee could not walk, hunt or eat without being on the alert. There was always the tension of not knowing when or where the next fight would be, or which Special Place would be gone; even fighting for a Special Place, he realized, took its spirit away. All that was left was the pain of losing it, or being hurt, or having those he loved hurt or killed or captured, each time a bigger hole inside where before there was only wholeness.

More settlers came. They blocked more paths, made more raids, burned more wigwams, took more captives, killed more of those they found.

In one of those raids, Mouse herself was taken. Mohee shot at and followed the man who captured her, but they got away.

Mohee was sadder. Even when another Special Place was gone, Mouse was still there, a Special Place in herself.

And he was angry. They had taken, it seemed, everything from him but his life. What reason was there for living?

He made more daring raids. He did not find her.

With those who were left of his tribe, Mohee continued his travels. They journeyed up the Long River. They returned. He did not find or hear word of his beloved Mouse. She was gone too. Most likely she was dead, but he still hoped not.

The few Special Places that were left he sat at alone, but he took her spirit there with him. It comforted his heart, talking to her inside, telling her how it made him feel that she, like so many of the other Special Places, was no longer there.

Spring, summer, fall, winter, spring, summer, fall, winter he traveled without her, living in the wigwam with her parents as they both had done before, until hope was gone. It was more likely for a Special Place with a cabin in it to go back to being as it had been than it was for her to return.

Mohee walked into a clearing in mid-afternoon, hoping one of their musket balls would find him. Instead, nowhere near where she was taken, he found Mouse. She was working with a boy child, in sight of a cabin. Without a word he grabbed her, started to run.

The boy too, she indicated.

Mohee turned around, scooped the boy child up in his arms, and off they went, so quickly and quietly no one saw them leave.

They did not stay near there that night, but moved three days without stopping. And then they celebrated. He with her and she with him, loving each other, loving who they remembered and who they were. He found a mouse in her pocket, held it up and laughed. She they called Mouse still had mice come to her. She told how she found one in a drawer in the settler's house, left crumbs there for it every day. In a few days a dozen mice were there, looking for her crumbs. They crawled on her when she lay down, slept on her when she slept, waited in the mattress for her when she went off, climbed into her pockets and sleeves when she returned. In a week there were dozens of them living in the room she slept in. They came from the rest of the house, the barn, from all over the woods, looking for her and her crumbs.

One day the owner's wife lifted the cover to her bed. Dozens of mice ran out. "Oh, my!" she called out, and fell to the ground in a faint. Mouse had to lead them all outside, to sleep outside herself. She was forbidden to feed them, forbidden to play with them. This was not the wilderness. They were not heathens. She had to learn to be civilized.

Mouse brought three of them back to their wigwam with her, tokens of her love for him. "Oh, my!" she exclaimed as they peeked out and scurried up her arm.

Mouse and Mohee laughed. They were happy.

Mohee was happy with the boy too, that she called Tiki. The white man's child, Mohee called him, tossing him into the air, taking him in his arms, clasping him to his chest, loving him as if he was the one who brought his mother back.

They traveled together as they used to. Maybe there still was hope. Even if the Special Places were disappearing, wherever they were made a new Special Place.

Mohee fought less. He was not so angry. Not so sad either. He looked at Mouse, or at Tiki, and he smiled.

Quick Flashes seemed angrier. He took Mohee aside, pointed at Mouse. "What did you take her back for?"

Mohee stared at him.

"She has been with them so long she has become like them. She uses their expressions. 'Oh, my!' 'Oh, my!' Our words aren't good enough?"

"Oh, my!" he said, mimicking her. He said it so often, everyone started calling him Oh My.

That made him angrier. "Do not call me that," he snarled. "I have a name."

He did not let up. "And the boy she brought with her, he is one of them. He brings their poison with him. He cannot stay here, polluting us. The only way we can go back to what we were is to rid ourselves of all contamination, to be the way we were before we heard of them. We need to get rid of him. And if you won't do it, I will."

"You will do no such thing."

"You will let go of my arm."

Mohee held on.

"I have never raised it against you, but if you don't let go, I will."

Mohee removed his hand, but stayed face to face with his friend. "He is her son, as much one of us as you or I. You will not hurt or harm him in any way. If you do, whatever you do to him, I will do to you."

Before long Mouse's belly was growing. She had a child, a girl for both of them. Mohee danced when she was born. "Wren," they called her. He made bird shapes with his hands and whistled, whole flocks coming to show their pleasure. They laughed and giggled together. He was happy.

But the settlers did not go away. There were more of them. They didn't take only Special Places. They took ordinary ones too—woods, trees, streams, even paths. Every day more of what was theirs was gone.

Mohee was not so happy. He fought more, not because he was angry or he wanted to. He had to, before everything that was theirs was taken away.

Everyone fought now. Mouse had a gun. The old

people too. Even Tiki was learning.

One day Mohee came back from hunting, quiet and happy in the woods, to find signs of a raid—the wigwam knocked down, fire scattered, torn clothes on the ground, patches of blood. No one was visible. He called and called.

One by one people came out from where they were hiding—Tiki, Mouse's parents. On a path off to one side he found what made him sadder than he ever thought he could be, Mouse and Wren, face down on the trail, bloody wounds in each of them.

Mohee cried inside and on his face. He wailed. He howled. Bears bellowed. Wolves howled too. The woods were filled with the sounds of birds mourning—song birds, hawks, owls, doves, wrens. The whole universe was sad.

He hummed the song of funerals, beat his chest. Why were Mouse and Wren taken, and not him?

He hugged and hugged Tiki. They sat all night, the two wrapped together, quiet. From time to time one or the other sighed. In the trees nearby owls hooted. He hooted with them.

Mohee blackened his face, cut his hair short, played his sorrow on his flute and in his bird songs, with the others told stories of Wren and Mouse.

He made a mask of Wren, his first one ever. So he could still have something of her; so she wasn't gone completely.

He thought he would make one of Mouse too, but when he set out to do it, his hands could not form the shapes. It hurt too much.

The tribe buried both bodies, side by side. He would see them soon, he knew, would join them on the long journey to the place that had no such heartache.

They moved on. Mohee walked with such sadness it was as if it was raining inside. He did not care if anyone caught or killed him. He hoped they would. But no one did; their shots missed. He survived for days. He survived for weeks. He started to feel. He was angry. Angry at the settlers, as angry as his friend. Everything he loved they were destroying.

He could not get it back. And there were too many of them, he could not drive them away. But he could burn their cabins, shoot their animals, make them sad.

He started fighting again. It did not make him happy. It made him sadder and angrier. But it showed he was still living. They had not destroyed him yet.

He burned many cabins, shot at the men with guns, made many settlers unhappy. The one thing he would no longer do is shoot at children or women, no matter how much Quick Flashes or Limping Bear urged him to. He touched his chest. He would not do as was done to him.

Still, the settlers were afraid of him. They called him Rabid Wolf, hunted for him, put out a bounty on his life. The wilderness was not safe with him alive.

In one raid—Mohee did not look at Carrie as he told this part—they went back to the Special Place where he and Quick Flashes had been shot at by the man with the beard. A church, house and fence destroyed the meadow they loved. Only children and women were there. Limping Bear shot at one, raised his gun toward another.

"No!" Mohee yelled. "No children or women!"

Before Limping Bear could shoot again, Mohee rushed to the closest woman, holding a child in her arms, pushed her ahead of him, down the hill, out of the meadow, into the woods, meaning only to keep her and the child safe, as he would have wished with Mouse and Wren. All he wanted was them back, and that he could never have, any more, he slowly realized, than this woman could her child.

Chapter Fifteen

They walked the rest of the day, Mohee, the others of their group, and the captive woman, clutching the limp child to her. She wanted to stop. She was tired. She was unhappy. He could see that. She had to keep walking, long after she had strength or desire, whether she wanted to or not.

Now what? he wondered. He didn't mean to take a captive, but here he had one. What did he do? He had never taken one before, but he knew the rules for captives. She was the servant for his family and the tribe. She was to sleep in their wigwam, eat with them, take care of the old people, do the hard work. That was how it was.

Whether they should try to get ransom for her or keep her, or what beyond the end of that day they should do with her, never occurred to him, just as by now, for their smaller group and for the tribe as a whole, what they did was no longer part of a larger plan.

When they stopped, Quick Flashes stood in front of him, pointed at the captive woman. "Why is she with us?"

Mohee shrugged. He did not know. He was only trying to save her and the child, and look how that turned out.

"She is not staying here. She is not."

Mohee shrugged again.

"We are not having one of them living with us. Look over there. When you turn around, she will be gone."

Mohee nodded, turned to look at others of their group.

Quick Flashes started to go up to the woman, to push her by the shoulder, lead her out of the clearing.

Before he reached her, his mother stood in his way.

"Move aside, old woman."

She stayed put. "Where are you going?"

"I am doing a favor for Mohee."

"It is too late for that now."

Quick Flashes stared at her, raised his arm, pointed for her to move.

She stared back. "She is staying here. Unharmed. Now you go back where you were."

They both stared at each other. Quick Flashes took half a step back. "You will regret this."

The old woman watched the captive woman carrying her dead child. It made her think of Wren dead, she went on, taking up the story, how sad that made her and Mohee, and how angry. Did this make sense, she wanted to ask. The woman may be a settler, but she did not kill Wren. But because his daughter was dead, hers was too. Two people were unhappy. That made it better for Mohee? for any of them? That brought his daughter back? or hers?

The old woman was sad for the captive woman too, that she was feeling what *she* still felt. "I am sorry," she wanted to say. "They thought it would help."

Taking her away maybe made the man who was her husband sad. It did not bring Mouse back. Killing her child did not bring Wren back or make anyone feel better.

Even if it had no Special Places left, the world was not like that. Life was hard enough without making it harder.

When they stopped, the old woman indicated the child, offered to help bury her. The mother was not ready yet. She understood. She would have wanted to carry Wren until her arms gave out, hoping to breathe life back into her.

The next morning it was time. The woman could not

keep carrying the dead child. The gods would not like it. Bad things would happen, more than already had. The child needed to be buried.

The old woman helped the captive woman, knowing her grief. She led her away from the wigwam, down a path that led to another Special Place. They stepped out into a long field, stopped. The old woman looked down it and smiled. It was still the same.

The field sparkled in the early morning light. Five crows cawed and gossiped, flying across it. Two hawks whistled, gliding above it. Half-way down, three turkeys scratched and strutted and gobbled. All around, blackbirds trilled.

She prepared to help the woman as best she could. She expected Mohee to, but he would not. How could he? he asked, touching his chest. All the killing made him too sad.

She scolded him and he ignored her.

But as she was scraping at the dirt with her fingers, Mohee came with a shovel and did as Mouse had told him they did. He dug a hole in the ground, buried the child, placed a '+' of sticks on top of the burial mound. When he did, the old woman felt the same sadness she felt when Wren died.

He watched the captive woman, Mohee said as he started talking again, and saw, yes, she was unhappy. She was suffering because of her child dead and her husband gone. But her suffering did not make his less. Her child dead did not bring his back. It did, though, make him think of Wren. His hand went to the mask of her he carried in his pouch. His fingers ran over the face he loved.

The old woman saw this. She urged him to bring it out. When he did, she took the mask from him, held it toward the woman, to show her she knew, it happened to them too.

The captive woman contorted and turned away.

Why did she do that? That was his love for his

daughter the old woman held there. His child was gone but her spirit, and his love, and his sadness, were always present in the mask.

He wanted to put the mask of Wren back in his pouch, but the old woman kept holding it out.

His heart was heavy. His Wren was gone. And the old woman was telling her about it. He shut his eyes.

When he opened them, the captive woman was staring at the mask.

His, the old woman indicated. Ours. Won't you take it?

The captive woman took it. She touched it, kissed it, handed it back. And she started moaning, as sad for her daughter as he was for his. All the birds started speaking with her. The air was full of them: crows cawing, owls hooting, hawks whistling, warblers warbling.

Mohee bit his lips together, held the mask to his chest, kept the same sound tight inside. The birds were speaking for him too.

One by one the birds stopped twittering. The air was empty. The woman was still. It was time to move on.

Life with a captive went on as it did without one.

They walked, they hunted, they ate what they caught. Settlers attacked, they fought, they walked. Sometimes they looked for Special Places, hoping a few were still there, trying not to think that not long before Special Places were everywhere.

The woman was still afraid, Mohee saw as they walked, afraid of things that were not harmful. A fly landed on her arm. Not a mosquito or a deer fly, a common fly. "Ahh," she called. And she jumped. Even after all this time.

The next fly he saw, he swooped his arm over, caught it in the cup of his hand, slid his fingers in, held it up toward her by the wings. "Bzzz," his lips went. She watched, looking wary. He moved it toward her hand. She drew back. He pointed at its head, its delicate legs, the fuzz on its body, showing her how small and harmless it was.

He grabbed her arm by the wrist. She tried to pull away. He held it firm, coaxed it forward, tipped her hand over, opened her palm. He laid the fly in it. See. Nothing to be afraid of.

Her hand jerked as if tickled. She watched. The fly did not move. Then it rolled over onto its feet, flapped its wings and flew off. She watched it rise into the air.

As they walked on, three crows flew low over them on the path. She cringed at their shadows. Caw, their raucous greeting called, caw. They perched on a branch over the path, cawing, ca-ca-cawing, ca-ca-ca-ca-ca-ca-ca. She stopped. Mohee indicated to go on. The rest of their group kept walking. The captive woman did not move, watching the crows above her.

"Caw" sounded near her. She jumped. "Ca-ca-ca." Mohee stood beside her, his voice repeating their sound, even the scratchy catch in their call. "Caw." As she watched, his two hands made their wings, thumbs joined, fingers flaring out, closing up, flaring out, ca-ca-ca. Slowly she followed his hands, flying forward, walked under the tree, not looking up. When she was past it, his hands circled back and up, calling their leaving call, caw, caw, caw. From the tree the three crows glided off the branch, raucous and flapping, flew off into the woods.

A small green snake sunned itself on a rock in their path. The others went around it. The captive woman almost stepped on it before she saw it. "Ahh!" She called out her fear. "Ahhh."

It is only Little Snake, Mohee wanted to tell her. He's our friend. More than that. A relative. His own father was Little Snake. Many others before him.

She would not move. "Kill him!" She pointed. "Smash his head."

Smash the head of his father? No, no.

Mohee walked up to it, making low, soothing noises, leaned over, quickly reached his hands out, caught it just behind the head with one, down on the tail with the other. He held it up. It curved and slithered in the air, its tongue darting in and out. Mohee stepped to the side with it, made room for her to pass. As she stepped forward he held it out at eye height. See? he said. Nothing to be afraid of.

She walked by, watching the whole time. After she had passed, he set it back in the sun, watched it slide off over brown leaves.

Trees. The shade. A snake on the path. Birds. Owls. A wind stirring the leaves high above. Insects. Spiders. Mohee saw the woman's fear of everything. She was like the Chipmunk, always frightened.

How could a person who is afraid of what is be happy?

What kind of life was that? How could people live without knowing that all life is one. It must make them very unhappy. No wonder they came and destroyed the Special Places. They did not recognize what they were. They did not know any better.

Why couldn't they stay where they were, or go somewhere else and be unhappy? Why did they have to come there and make his people unhappy too?

When the Many Legs of their wigwam spun down to wish her good morning, the captive woman huddled against the edge, clutching her clothes to her.

What was wrong with her? One Many Legs petrified her. "You don't know by now that Many Legs is our friend. You are worse than the Chipmunk. You are afraid of everything."

The words came into his mouth, formed on his tongue, but he did not say them. He saw how weak and small her fears made her. He felt bad for her, and the life she must have been leading, a world full of fears and unhappiness.

He saw that maybe taking her away from that life and bringing her to his was not a bad thing, but a good one, even if she did not know it yet. And the only way to make it bad was to beat and maim her. He did not know any reason why he should do that except that he was angry, and he was not so angry anymore. Even if he was angry, she was not the one who had done bad things to him.

From the beginning, the old woman was kind to her, sharing their water and their food, even putting Mouse's shoes on her. That made him angry, but he also saw it made her walk more easily. She did not slow them down so much.

He saw too the way Tiki treated her, how good he was to her. She was not his mother, but she was still a person. She smiled when she talked to the boy, and he smiled too. It made things better, not worse. If they all were living together in the same small space you wanted friendly, happy people, not angry, sad ones.

Bit by bit, Mohee started being nice to her too. Not when Quick Flashes was around, urging him to torment her, asking if he wanted her gone, just say the word and it was done.

Then Mohee growled or looked sullen, or pushed her hard on the shoulder to speed up.

But when Quick Flashes was with his own family, or in another part of the clearing, then Mohee could be kind. To show her how they lived. That before she went back, one settler would know how good it was, and would stop hating them and wanting them dead.

Mohee missed the peacefulness of winter, but the warmth of the sun on his skin in the spring made him feel alive again; so did the call of every new bird, the sight of every green bud or shoot. Each one he pointed out to Tiki, sharing his joy of it. It was hard not to include the captive woman too.

Little by little, day by day, he shared the wonder of every new thing. He shared it too because he was sad, because of Mouse and Wren and the Special Places, and he was lonely, and doing this made him less so.

It took him a long time to realize this, even longer to know the captive woman was sad and lonely too, and his sharing was as important to her as it was to him.

He shared all that was good, and the miseries too. Many times, he brought them to life with his hands, and taught Tiki to too—each of them making a wren with his fingers, a large one and a small one, side by side, whistling with their lips. As they finished, Tiki burst into laughter, ran and threw himself into the woman's arms.

All of life was alive at every moment in anyone who was alive, and Mohee was alive as long as he had people to share that with. Like birds flying north or south, his anger had gone far away. He looked forward to each day, to see what new he could show her and Tiki, or what old they would see and delight in again.

He stopped being sad. Only when Quick Flashes was there did he not feel happy.

Without warning, Quick Flashes would be beside him on the path. "What are you smiling at? Are you glad we are moving again, farther from the places where you and I used to play, where the spirits of all our departed still dwell. Does that make you happy?"

"You can't be angry all the time."

"I see you." Quick Flashes held up his finger. "I am watching you." And as quickly as he appeared, he was gone, and Mohee might not see him again for days.

More and more, Mohee stayed with the others of his wigwam—the old woman and the old man, Tiki, the captive woman. Together they walked, they went hungry, they walked, they feasted, they walked, they fought with raiders, they ate, they slept, they walked. And in the evenings, and when they rested, they told stories, sharing their lives, as he was doing now. If they saw anything Special that day—a butterfly, a tree, a stream, a place—it made him and Tiki and the Chipmunk feel good. And they felt good again when his hands became the butterfly, flitting here and there, or his throat gurgled like the stream beside them.

Chapter Sixteen

Carrie loved their stories about themselves, and their past, and about her too, even if they were also painful. She told stories of her own about what she had heard and observed and about herself, how much she had changed since she was with them. How frightened she had been of everything, of the Small Frog with the Big Voice, or of Many Legs. No wonder, she said smiling, they called her Chipmunk.

Now, when they walked, she slowed down to admire Many Legs' web, hanging across the path, glistening in the sunlight. And when they stopped, and set up the wigwam, the first thing she did was look to see if it had come too.

She did not tell any more of the stories she had brought with her, and she never told stories about her past, and the people she had left behind. She tried not to think of them when the others were around.

When they were not, she thought sometimes of Gideon and Isaac and her other home. More and more, it was a place she had lived at some time in the past, like England. When she was there it was good. Now she was somewhere else.

A few times she thought of telling Mohee and the old woman about them. Some day she would. It never seemed right. It would bring a different mood to where they were, that had nothing of her past life about it. She was not ready for that.

Tiki slipped and hit his head against a tree. Carrie put cold leaves on it until it stopped throbbing.

The old woman coughed all night. Carrie sat up with

her, made a tea from pounded leaves as she had taught her, helped the old woman sip it to soothe her throat.

In her time with the heathens, Carrie had learned to gather leaves, roots, and later, when they came, berries. Now she made the soup, cleaned the fish, the deer, shot the gun, while the old woman rested.

One day, by herself, a few steps from the camp, Carrie looked up and stopped. It was on a day like this, with the sky the same clear blue, the sun at the same high angle, the woods the same deep green of leaves newly filled out, that she and Gideon were married. Gideon did not like ostentation, and open expression of feeling he frowned at, so she used, in a quiet way, to say to herself, "Today is another anniversary of our nuptial day," and be amazed that she had lived with this man, who had been a stranger, so long. But try as she might, she could no longer remember what he looked like, except for his large ears. And there were many times, even from the beginning, when she felt she hardly knew him, and he knew her even less, the girl she had been who had gone to him in marriage, the person inside she had to hide whenever he was around.

She had no idea what month or date it was, or how long she had been gone, so much time spent in nothing more than surviving.

She looked back at the sky. It had been such a long time. And today, wherever she was, Gideon seemed as far away as England where they were married.

Carrie stopped trying to remember Scripture or think about the Sabbath. It came and went and came and went, and she never knew when.

Sometimes she thought about how the Lord God had made all the creatures about her, and how, if she was a good Christian, she should instruct these heathens in His ways, but she was not Isaac, or even Gideon, she did not have the zeal. She knew full well, as she had heard so often, that the heathens, if they did not believe, were on the path to everlasting damnation, and she, if she did not remember her beliefs and return to their practice, was traveling there with them.

In time, though, she began to think that perhaps this vision of her brother's was too extreme, that it was also possible to be good, to be kind and loving and gentle, and respectful of all living creatures, the way so many of the heathens were, and not be Christian.

Do what she could, Carrie could not make this thought go away. The longer she lived with the heathens, and saw, every day, how they were, the clearer it became.

"What heresy is this?" Isaac's voice boomed inside her. "Only believers can truly be good; only believers will be saved. All others are to be damned to Hell for all eternity."

"I do not believe the Lord God would treat so harshly those born outside the faith who are also good."

"That is how it is. You know it full well. Why do you question it?"

Carrie tried not to listen as his voice in her head grew louder, condemning her thinking, and reminding her where such thoughts would lead—she saw him raise his right index finger in emphasis—"If you do not change your ways."

She knew, despite all he said, that what she had observed was true: that these heathens, who couldn't read and knew no Scripture and certainly were not "saved", were still better people than some of the most "devout" Christians she had known. And, she felt, they deserved a place at the table of the Lord as much as anyone.

Carrie woke sweating from a dream. The hot white light of hell blazed before her. She was shaking. She thought of the Lord and tried to pray. Before she could frame her thoughts into words, everyone was up, the wigwam was coming down, and life went back to walking, eating, sleeping, walking, all the daily details that left her too tired to think, and made Gideon, Isaac, and the Church of her Redemption seem too far away to be real.

Instead, first thing next morning after they moved, she looked again to make sure Many Legs was still there with them, pointed it out to Tiki, both of them smiling. And while they walked, or after they stopped for the day, she listened for the booming sound of the Small Frog with the Big Voice.

She learned many more of the heathen's words, still used some of them wrong, making everyone who heard her laugh, taught more of hers to Tiki and Mohee. The old woman never learned any. She had trouble enough, she said through Tiki, remembering the ones she already knew.

One night, Mohee pretended with his hands to be a bird perched on a limb above the wigwam, broke the night silence with a "whip-poor-will, whip-poor-will." Tiki answered with a "whip-poor-will" of his own.

Tiki spread his fingers in the fan of a tail and gobbled like a turkey. Mohee responded, his fingers spread wide, with a gobble of his own, the way one on a nearby hill answered one in the valley. Carrie giggled and clapped her hands.

Many nights when she lay down, Carrie smiled before she slept.

At the sound of the galloping of a single horse, Carrie opened her eyes, sat up, heard Quick Flashes' yell as he rode past.

"Settlers!" Tiki translated. "We're being attacked."

She heard a whoosh, followed by the clumping of many hooves, saw the red of flame begin at the base of their wigwam, scrambled outside with the old woman.

Mohee was already there, smothering the fire before it spread.

"Stay behind the wigwam," he said to her and the old woman, as he and Tiki turned their muskets toward the attackers, fired at the closest ones. Muskets flashed from other wigwams. One attacker slumped, slid off his horse. Another circled around, picked him up, galloped away. The rest of the marauders followed. None of them had torches.

By the time the sound of the retreating hooves faded away, all the wigwams were down and they were moving again, Mohee, Tiki and Carrie walking in single file behind the others.

"What's that you have there?" Carrie asked Tiki.

In his hand he carried a half-charred torch. "It's the torch that was burning the wigwam." He kept looking at it, turning it around and around.

"Is it interesting?" Mohee asked.

Tiki nodded, pointed at the jagged mark on its shaft. "It is not the kind the settlers use."

"Where did it come from, if not the settlers?" Carrie asked, taking it from Tiki, and holding it out toward Mohee.

He took it from her, glanced at it quickly and, without looking at either of them, threw it off into the woods.

They walked on, waiting for his answer.

"Ask Quick Flashes," he finally said, still not looking at them. "He is the one who makes them that way."

Late in the afternoon they stopped. They had three wounded themselves, and two injured horses. From where they made camp, near the top of a steep open hill that dropped off in three directions, they could see anyone approaching half a mile away.

After the wigwams were set up, people went off by themselves.

Carrie and Tiki walked together to the side of the hill where it dropped away to the east. Carrie sat, staring out at the view, miles of green trees below her. How calm and peaceful it looked, like a painting of tranquility and harmony, yet how violent and unsettled it was. Below this canopy of trees, she knew, were angry people, loaded muskets, pain and death waiting to happen. Thinking about it made her feel tired, and sad. Wouldn't it ever end?

Nearby, Tiki followed swarms of butterflies, white with black spots or orange with black edges. He chased one over a ridge, he told her later, down a slight ravine, trying to flutter and fly as it did.

He was startled by a voice in front of him. “Having fun?”

He looked up. Quick Flashes stood in his path.

Tiki stopped, backed up, turned around, started to run. On his third step he tripped on a loose rock, sprawled onto the ground. He heard the rock rolling down toward the edge.

Before he could scramble back up, Quick Flashes’ foot pinned his leg to the ground. “Don’t leave so quickly,” he said. “I have something to show you.”

“I don’t want to see.” Tiki struggled, but could not get away.

“You don’t know what it is.”

“I don’t want to know. Let me go.”

“Don’t fight me. You’ll get hurt.”

Quick Flashes lifted him to his feet, his strong hand gripping Tiki’s arm. Tiki tried to jerk free. The grip tightened, dragging Tiki toward the edge. Tiki’s feet dug into the loose rocks; his legs resisted as best he could, but he kept being pulled closer.

When they were almost to the edge, Quick Flashes grabbed each of Tiki’s wrists with his hands, lifted Tiki up and began spinning him around. Tiki swung out over the drop off, back over the land, out again and back.

“You know what happens if I let go? You fly like a butterfly. Isn’t that what you wanted?”

Tiki spun around faster and faster. Everything was a blur.

“Stop scaring him.” A woman’s voice, badly accented, spoke from higher up the side.

Tiki was swung back over land and let go. He flew a few feet, landed on rocks, rolled over and over, stopped with a thud against a larger rock. The sky spun. Everything hurt.

“Look who is here, the cause of our problems.” Quick Flashes started toward her. “I should have done this long ago.”

Carrie backed away as fast as she could, tripped, sat

down on the ground.

Quick Flashes reached for her foot.

She kicked.

He grabbed her leg at the ankle, started pulling her over the rocks toward the edge.

Tiki jumped up, ran toward him, hurtled through space, knocked Quick Flashes down. Carrie's ankle slipped out of his grasp.

She scrambled to get to her feet. Before she could, Quick Flashes had gotten back up, grabbed her foot, started pulling again.

"Let go." She tried to hold the loose rocks. He pulled her over them. She picked one up, threw it at him.

Tiki picked some up too, threw one after another at him. They all missed. "Let go of her." Tiki ran at him, started beating on him with his fists.

"What is going on here?"

At the sound of the familiar voice, Quick Flashes let go of Carrie's foot, took two steps back and stopped. They all looked up at Mohee, standing at the top of the ridge.

"He was trying to throw us over the edge," Tiki answered.

Before anyone could say more, Quick Flashes held up his hand. "That is not how it was. I was showing them how Quick Flashes of Light are. Like this."

While they were watching, before any of them realized what he was doing, Quick Flashes backed up three steps, and sprinted as fast as he could toward the drop off. When he reached it, he jumped straight out over the precipice and, his right hand making zigzags in the air above his head, disappeared without a sound.

He was still alive when they reached him, near the bottom of the cliff. He had come to rest half sitting against a tree.

"Are you still with us, friend?" Mohee asked.

Quick Flashes opened his eyes, saw Mohee staring down at him, looked at Tiki and Carrie beside him, shook his head, and smiled. "Now you know the power of lightning." And his mouth fell open, and his head lolled back.

Mohee bent over, hugged him, kissed him on the forehead, laid him down.

Tiki and Carrie clung to each other, their hearts still pounding.

"He was the bravest of us all."

"He swung me around over the edge." Tiki pointed up. "He would have—"

Mohee nodded. "Bravest, not wisest."

The ceremonies for his death lasted several days.

They left his body out for viewing in the center of a clearing, placed his belongings around him. His wife, Running Deer—the one Carrie watched walk naked into the water—threw herself on him, imploring him to come back, not to leave her there alone, begged the others to let her follow.

She cut her hair short, painted her face black, wailed as all the birds did when Carrie lost Hannah and Mohee lost Wren. A heathen child, no bigger than Hannah, wailed beside her. Carrie's heart tugged. She felt so sad for them.

The old woman wailed too. So many times he had opposed her, but he was still her son, the last one living.

Carrie went to the woman, meaning to hug her. As she reached toward her, Running Deer flung herself to the ground, writhing and thrashing. Carrie knelt beside her, wishing to find some way to console her, took from her pocket the mask of Hannah, kissed its cheek, hugged it to her, held it out. Running Deer glanced up, reached out, took the mask, kissed its cheek, hugged it to her chest and wailed, handed it back to Carrie, gathered her daughter in her arms. The two sat, rocking and wailing.

Carrie put the image of Hannah back in her pocket, was about to move away, when she noticed Mohee, standing nearby. He was—Tiki had told her, and she saw now in how he behaved—Running Deer's brother. It made her understand even more how close he and Quick Flashes were, best friends marrying each other's sister.

Mohee leaned over his sister, an object held out toward her. It was Quick Flashes himself, in a mask so real it looked as if he had come back to life. Mohee touched her arm, spoke to her. She looked up, let out a gasp. He kissed its cheek, handed it to her. She took it, held it clasped to her chest. She and her daughter wailed even louder.

Different members of the tribe hummed the song of funerals, remembered Quick Flashes in different ways: they danced, they sang, they chanted, telling his brave deeds, the stories of his life. Mohee danced him as a hunter, bringing in the deer, danced him as a warrior, slaying many enemies. Tiki played the flute; Mohee beat Quick Flashes' drum, slow and mournful, put it with his belongings beside him. When the ceremonies were done, every warrior together lifted him, placed him in a seated position, on his side, wrapped in birch bark, in the grave they had dug for him.

For three days after, they did not move. They hunted and fished, they sat, they ate, they rested, the air around them thick with the sad sweet scent of grapes in flower.

Some grew restless. "Shouldn't we go now," they asked. "Isn't it time?"

His sister could not, Mohee said, and neither could he. His heart was heavy with the death of his friend. He could not make his feet go farther from where he was born. He would die of sadness before he reached the place where the wild geese landed.

The small group divided again. A few kept on for the north. The others stayed with Mohee and Running Deer, drifted back toward where they had come from.

Chapter Seventeen

For several days as they traveled, Tiki and the old woman talked about a pool in rocks in a stream, off to the side, high above the Long River, a Special Place they would be at soon. There was excitement in their talk, and worry too. The last time they were there, the previous summer, it was untouched. Would it be still?

Tiki told Carrie about it, kept mentioning it to Mohee. "Remember last time, swimming, and splashing, and sliding in the water on the rocks?"

Mohee was quiet, tight. "It might not be like that."

"It was last time. I remember. You do too."

Mohee nodded. "Things change."

When Mohee said, "We'll find out soon," and "Let's not talk of it anymore," Tiki talked to Carrie about it, telling her about the stream high above the river, higher than you would think to look, so high it was hidden among overhanging branches. It came out of the greenery, tumbled down into deep pools full of fish, a straight-down waterfall hitting the rocks and water so loud you had to shout to be heard.

He talked about bathing under it, swimming in another, higher pool, so clean and clear he thought when no one else was around the gods must swim in it; the large flat rocks around it, and, off in the distance, way below, that you almost could not see, the Long River, so far away it looked like a stream.

Carrie was excited herself, hearing about it. She looked forward to seeing it, hoped it was still the same. She could see Mohee's worry too, as if afraid it would be different, as if preparing himself not to be disappointed.

The half day before they reached it the walk was

quiet, full of anticipation. When they heard a roaring they stopped.

"What is it?" Tiki asked, smiling. "Is it?"

Mohee nodded. "It is."

Tiki turned to Carrie. "It's the waterfall!"

"It might still be changed," Mohee shouted.

They came around a boulder. In front of them a swollen stream dropped a hundred feet down the hillside, the water black and white as it fell, foaming into a lather in a pool at the bottom.

Carrie's heart stopped, jumped into her throat. This was a Special Place.

Mohee whooped. He smiled. His body relaxed.

"We're back!" Tiki raced ahead, clambering up the path toward the higher pools. He turned back toward Mohee. "Beat you."

"No, you won't." Mohee ran after him.

Carrie smiled. This was a very Special Place, a Special Place of Special Places. This was the way things used to be, that Mohee and the old people talked about.

She breathed in. The air felt fresh, from the water, and the pine smell of the woods.

Tiki and Mohee and the others were already splashing and laughing, bathing in one of the pools. She could hardly hear them over the roar of the water.

Carrie climbed up after them, smiled watching them. "Thank you," she mouthed toward them, for bringing her there, for sharing it with her.

She looked down at the ribbon of water that was the Long River far below, up at the hills, climbed up to another, smaller pool, surrounded by tall pines, reaching from the banks above it toward the sky. This was another Special Place, quiet, peaceful, gentle and still.

She walked out onto one of the flat rocks, worn smooth by the stream, sat down by the pool. For a long time she looked down into it, deep and dark beside her.

She lowered her left hand into it. It felt cool and sharp. She pushed her hand back and forth, watching the surface ripple away. She held her hand still. The ripples subsided. She pushed her hand through it again.

She pulled her hand out of the water; drops fell onto the stone.

She drew her knees up, wrapped her arms around them, sat with her eyes shut. The voices of Tiki and Mohee rose from below. She opened her eyes, sat up on her knees, pulled her sleeves above her elbows, dipped her arms into the water. She cupped both hands together, splashed water over her face.

Carrie wanted to wash herself, to feel that clean coolness over the rest of her body. She reached her fingers toward the top button of her dress, stopped, afraid she was about to do something forbidden. She looked around, let her fingers slip the first button from its hole, and the second. She pushed aside the cloth until her neck and the top of her chest were exposed.

She dipped her right hand in the water, ran it over the patch of naked skin.

She stopped, looked around, listened. Except for the voices from below, she was alone. Everything was silent, still.

She brought her fingers to the third button. She unbuttoned it, and the fourth, and the fifth, and the sixth. There were so many buttons, set so close together and sewed so tightly, tilting them through their holes was not easy.

Down her fingers moved, from hole to hole, button to button, until they were all undone, and her dress hung open, revealing her shift to the light, the air, the sun.

She held her breath. The sky did not turn black. Lightning did not flash. The trees above did not bend and thrash. The water did not swirl and boil away from her in horror. Nothing changed.

She pulled her arms from the sleeves, slipped the dress off her shoulders, let it fall to the ground, surprised at the weight she was carrying.

Goose bumps rose all over her arms and legs.

Carrie stopped, listened. At a soft breeze she grabbed

the collar of her dress, ready to pull it back up and hold it before her. The breeze died. She let go of the dress.

She knelt, removed her moccasins and what remained of the cloth around her feet, worn through at the heel and caked with dried mud, pulled her stiff shift, stained from her time, off over her head. She undid her hair from its bun, shook her head until it fell loose over her shoulders and back, and, with her milky white skin, stood in the sun, naked for the first time since the day she was born.

The whoops and splashes from below did not change. No one noticed her. No one cared. She heard Mohee and Tiki hollering and laughing.

At the first sound, she crouched down, crossed her arms over her breasts. As the sounds continued, distant and unchanging, she stood, let her arms fall back to her sides.

She felt the sun warming her body, caressing her skin. She breathed out, tightness and tension disappearing in the heat of the sun. She smiled. She did not remember ever feeling like this before.

She sat on the flat rock, put her foot into the water, drew it out, surprised at the cold.

Below, Tiki yelled and Mohee whooped.

Carrie braced herself, slid forward, careful not to look down at the parts of her body exposed before her, and stepped in to the water up to her thighs, slid down until all of her was submerged, her hair floating behind her. She stood up on the rocky bottom, ran her palm over the dark surface around her. She rubbed her hands over her body, washing herself, cleaning the accumulated dirt off, reluctant at first to let her hands touch her 'there', gradually combing the mats and snarls out of her pubic hair with her fingers.

Her pale skin was covered with goose bumps. Her wet hair clung to her head and shoulders.

All of a sudden a laugh welled up inside her. It came burbling out, as surprising and unexpected as a belch. In a moment, giggles, guffaws, chortles and "whees" echoed from the rocks. Her whole frame shook. She could not have stopped if she wanted. And why should she? She felt free, alive, herself. The leaves fluttered with the happy sounds, as if they were laughing with her.

After a few minutes the echoes subsided. She was left with a smiling feeling inside.

When she was sure she was finished laughing, and would not choke or take in water by mistake, Carrie put her head under the surface. She did it again and again. She lifted her feet, pushed her arms through the water, turned over, laid her head back on it, took a deep breath. Her knees, toes and breasts floated up. She drifted in the pool, bumped into a rock, paddled back, the water swirling around her hands, rippling to the edge.

She stood up, ducked her head under the surface one final time, held it there as long as she could, climbed out of the pool, stood dripping on the flat rock.

Inside she could not stop laughing. All of her tingled—her arms, legs, knees, thighs, stomach, shoulders, breasts—as if every inch of her body was awake for the first time in her life. She stood on the rock, head held back, hair dangling behind her, letting the sun and breeze dry her.

Carrie heard feet on the path, climbing toward her. She reached for her dress, tried to call out, "Who is it? I'm—?" She could not think what word to use: naked—not decent—happy—clean.

Before she could say anything or get her filthy dress back on, the old woman's head came into view. Carrie sighed, waved to her with one hand, let the dress fall with the other.

The old woman climbed up to the rock, sat on it, indicated for Carrie to sit in front of her, with her fingers combed the snarls out of her hair, began braiding it.

It made Carrie think of when she was little and had pigtails, how her mother would comb and twist them into two tight strands. When she finished, Carrie would lean her head back against her mother's knee and stay that way as long as she could. She never wanted that moment to end. But, no matter how long it lasted, it always did. Someone called, something happened, there were more chores to do.

Carrie shut her eyes, leaned back, rested her head against the old woman's knee. The old woman's hand stroked her head, settled on her shoulder. Carrie reached up, took hold of the old woman's hand, and held it, smiling. She felt peaceful, calm, still, as if she was home again.

They sat that way a long time. The noises from below ceased, the breeze shifted, the light changed, pockets of cooler air drifted by.

With a sigh the old woman leaned forward, kissed Carrie on the cheek, gently urged her up, stood, handed her a deerskin skirt and top, removed the mask of Hannah from the pocket of the dress, slid it into a pouch she lay beside Carrie, and picked her way back down the hillside, taking Carrie's dirty dress and shift with her.

Carrie looked down, surprised. She had forgotten she was naked. She put the new clothes on, feeling the softness against her skin, slipped her moccasins back on.

All evening she sat by herself on the rock, her body glowing from the water.

Before he went into the wigwam for the night, Mohee climbed up, stood beside her. His hands made a small bird pumped up at the throat. His mouth opened. His voice sang, "Whip-poor-will, whip-poor-will."

A real one responded from a tree across the pool. He called and the other answered. Another, farther up the hill, responded as well. "Whip-poor-will, whip-poor-will."

Carrie and Mohee laughed together. The sound of the bird was so joyous, so infectious. He squatted in front of her. As if by one instinct, their hands joined, palms to palms, fingers intertwined with fingers, meeting in the space between them.

Mohee leaned over, kissed Carrie on the lips, mouth open, his tongue finding hers.

When he stopped Carrie pulled back, asked, "Why did you do that?"

Mohee's hand closed to a fist, touched his chest over his heart twice, pointed toward hers, formed, again, the bird he had just made. When it was half-way toward her, Carrie reached out with hers, caught it in mid-flight.

"Do it again," she said, and, taking his face in her other hand, ran her fingers over Mohee's jaw, his cheekbone, his nose, his eyebrow.

After the second kiss Carrie smiled, let go of his hand.

Freed, the bird in it called "whip-poor-will, whip-poor-will", turned, and flew away.

She watched Mohee descending until he disappeared down toward the wigwam.

Carrie sat a long time after everyone went to bed. The whippoorwill was quiet. The only noise was owls, booming and calling out over the hills, and the stream, falling over the edge, tumbling down onto the rocks, and, from below, the muted roar as it splashed into the lower pool. The air was cool, the night crisp and clear and sharp. Stars sparkled all over the sky.

Carrie loved the feeling of her clean body, still tingling under her new clothes.

She did not go to bed until the moon rose through the trees. She walked down in its white light, stepped into the wigwam, heard the different rhythms of Tiki, the old woman, and Mohee sleeping, and, above in the night, the constant din of the stream hitting rocks.

She removed her moccasins, her pouch, skirt, and top, laid them by her place, stepped past Tiki to where Mohee slept, lay down beside him, pulled his cover over her, touched his naked shoulder, ran her hand over his cheek and forehead, seeing them with her fingers in the dark, turned his head toward her.

"Mohee," she whispered in his ear, "love me."

Chapter Eighteen

Carrie opened her eyes. Beside her, Mohee slept. They had loved and slept, loved and slept all night. She lay against him, started laughing, had to cover her mouth with her hand. She could not believe how she felt, alive from the tips of her toes to the top of her head. As if waterfalls tumbled inside her, deep pools swirled, winds blew, whippoorwills whooped, turkeys gobbled. She laughed again.

She drew closer to Mohee until their skin was touching along the length of their bodies, shut her eyes, breathed in, settled smiling back into sleep.

"Chipmunk?" Tiki's voice woke her.

Carrie opened her eyes. It was light. "Over here."

Tiki looked at her.

"Now," she thought, suddenly aware of her naked body, and of Mohee's, beside her. "Now comes shame and guilt and sin."

"Morning." He smiled.

Carrie smiled back. She felt none.

Without warning, Tiki whooped and jumped into the middle of them. They tussled for a minute. Then he lay on his back between them, their hands joined on his chest.

"See." Tiki pointed up.

Carrie looked up. "She seems farther from over here."

Many Legs spun part-way down toward her clothes.

"And not so scary."

"She likes you over here," Tiki said. "More room for her."

Carrie leaned over, kissed Tiki, then Mohee. "Time to get up," she said. "Many Legs says so."

Neither Tiki nor Mohee moved. Tiki was looking up, watching Many Legs. Mohee was staring into space.

Carrie waited. Tiki and Mohee stayed as they were.

Her throat was dry. Now what?

She took a deep breath, pushed aside the cover, and, not believing she was doing this, stood up and stepped naked over to her clothes, acting as if this was what she did every morning; as she started putting them on, she couldn't help glancing back. Tiki was still watching Many Legs. Mohee was watching her. He smiled, made a fist, touched it twice to his chest. Carrie smiled and almost burst into tears. She turned away, finished dressing in her new clothes; when she was done, she turned back, smiled again at Mohee, touched her chest with her fist and then, like Tiki, stopped to watch Many Legs spinner her way down.

That morning, as they pounded berries with venison meat into a meal for later, the old woman stopped, reached over, took Carrie's hand, squeezed, looked at her, half smiled and nodded, held her hand a moment longer, let go, and went back to pounding, all without a word.

Carrie turned the old woman toward her, and hugged her hard, both arms wrapped around her short, solid body.

"Thank you," she said to her in her thoughts. "Thank you, thank you, thank you." She felt so happy she could hardly keep it in.

Alone, later, Carrie thought of what her brother would say about her conduct.

"I have done nothing wrong," she thought.

"Have you fallen so far? Have you forgotten you are married? Is not adultery a sin?"

"Can't widows and widowers remarry? Am I not dead to one life, alive in another?"

"Are you married to this heathen? Is one night of sin

equivalent to a state of holy matrimony? Are you damned already beyond redemption and don't even know it?"

"Didn't Gideon and I, even you and Rebecca, join bodies before the ceremonies were held?"

"We were betrothed in the sight of God and family, not lewdly come together in the heat of lust." Isaac droned on in her head. "And we were Christians, not a fallen Christian consorting with a heathen in the appetites of the body."

Carrie stopped listening. She turned to watch Tiki playing in a pool, smiled as Mohee walked to join him.

Carrie bathed in many streams, pools, and rivers, at dawn, at dusk, in the brightness of mid-day, in the darkness of night. She learned to swim and hold her breath under water, to lie back, naked, give herself up to its gentle caress, no part of her in the air but her nose.

She slept under Mohee's blanket skin every night. Some nights they were tired, and lay entwined together and slept. Many nights they made love.

Carrie loved to know Mohee's face with her hands. She loved to explore his whole body, its muscles, skin, and bone, even his stub finger that he had lost the end of to an ax, and learn how it worked. She loved the way he touched and loved and kissed her and her body, amazed he could give her pleasure she did not know existed.

Her whole being delighted in being alive. She smiled when he kissed her, giggled when he winked at her, laughed when his hands made a bird, flapping in the air. And she loved to love him, her soul shaking and convulsing from their lovemaking.

One still night they were making love in the wigwam, she had come once, was coming again, she felt his closeness, his skin against hers, breast to chest, stomach to stomach, groin to groin, legs to legs, lips to lips, when she heard the quiet patter of rain on its walls, and in the middle of her ecstasy she was crying, sobs heaving up from deep within, all the emotion of the last year contained in that one moment—Hannah dead and buried, her head back laughing in the rain; Gideon gone; finding Mohee; loving him. Carrie clutched him to her. She was coming and crying at the same time. She could not stop.

She was happier and sadder than she knew a person could be.

Carrie thought about Gideon. Mohee held his fingers up, the tips of hers touched his, and currents ran between them. She could not do that with Gideon. If he even brushed against her, he apologized, as if it was an accident. He shuffled around, changed the subject.

When she kissed Mohee, their souls mingled, lingered, made love. When she kissed Gideon, she liked it, but she could not call it by the same word.

And when their bodies coupled, she and Gideon? There was not a word that described it. Made love? had intercourse? he mounted her and thrust? did his duty and procreated? Did he feel anything but obligation? He did not act as if he did. She never had. She liked the closeness, but none of the rest ever happened; too often it hurt, and she could only hope it would be over soon. Before Mohee, that's how she thought it was supposed to be.

And the other things she and Mohee did that were part of loving, kissing and touching and stroking, and lingering, not acting as if it should have been over before it started. Not to mention being close and happy together all day, and sharing everything that happened, good and bad. None of that seemed to occur to Gideon, or to her. She did not know they could.

Sometimes, when Gideon held her, she felt it start. Then he moved away.

She did not know she could feel the way Mohee made her feel. The first time she came she thought she was dying. She had no idea a woman could come at all, much less so many times, and each time be as varied as a rainbow, as surprising as a shooting star, as deep and sparkling as the Milky Way on a clear, still night, or that a man could wait for her pleasure before he took his own.

She had not known about such pleasure at all. She wondered why no one told her about it. Didn't they want her to know? Didn't they know themselves?

Carrie felt sad for Gideon. She wondered if they could have been happy together like this. She did not know. But if nakedness was shame, and laughing and pleasure were sins—

She smiled. She would go to damnation happy.

Carrie woke in the night. She and Mohee lay together on the ground outside the wigwam, near the edge of a clearing. So the stars could kiss them while they slept.

She was too happy to sleep. She lay, eyes open, staring up at the stars and, below them, at the fireflies, silently blinking and flitting. Her toes giggled, her feet laughed, her thighs and stomach guffawed, her heart and chest and mouth and soul gurgled. She could hardly keep it in. It wanted to burst out, surround the camp of sleeping heathens, drown them in the sound.

Beside her Mohee slept. She heard his rhythmic breathing, felt his leg intertwined with hers. She smiled, sighed. "Oh, God," she thought. If she died now, she would die happy.

She turned her head to watch him sleeping. She could not believe what she saw. She shut her eyes, opened them again, propped herself onto her elbow for a better view.

His arms, from his wrists to his shoulders, his neck, even his hair, were covered with fireflies, spaced every few inches, rhythmically blinking: on, off, on, off.

She laughed in surprise.

"Carrie," she told herself. "What are you thinking? Imagining he glows!"

She looked back at him. It was true. She was not dreaming. He did glow.

Carrie wanted to kiss him, did not want to disturb the fireflies. They pulsed on and off, on and off, lighting his hair, his face, making a halo around his head, like the angels in Gideon's big Book at home.

She saw Gideon sitting there, poring over his Bible, the candle flickering beside him, licking the tips of his fingers to pick up the corner of a page. Without wanting to, Carrie was thinking of him, and her life before.

She did not feel guilty, she realized. It surprised her that she didn't. She wondered why not, if she should feel guilty for not feeling guilty?

She turned away from Mohee, lay back down, stared at the fireflies lighting the darkness above her the way he lit her, and tried not to think about Gideon.

It was no use. He was in her head now. She could not get him out.

How had it been? she wondered. She was not unhappy with him. The life they made together had many contentments—their union, their children, being blessed in all they did by the righteous way they lived; all this united their beings as vessels of the Lord. It felt good. There was peace, harmony.

But pleasure? happiness? ecstasy? Were these not meant to be as well?

Carrie had moments of pleasure, times she was happy with him, giving him—duty? children? obligation? Kissing him could be not unpleasant. Why no more? Why never more than that? Was it not allowed? Was it a sin? Were these desires of her body always bad?

Didn't she remember Isaac saying so, over and over? In Eve's fall sinned we all.

Being with Mohee did not make her feel unnatural or unclean. When he touched her body, her whole body, the skin of her legs, arms, stomach, neck, gently, tenderly, as if he loved all of her and every part of her, he looked at her with his eyes wide open and told her how beautiful she was.

She did feel beautiful when she was with him, whatever she looked like.

Was that bad if it felt so good?

Isaac in her head talked to her as if she was three. "Do you honestly not know? This man you are with is a heathen. Do you not see what he is, a Devil who tempted you, and you have fallen, and are so abject and depraved you don't know it and don't seem to care?"

Carrie looked over at Mohee, glowing in the dark beside her. The sight of him made her glow inside, in every corner of her being.

He is not a Devil, she thought. He is a saint, a saint of love. She clasped her hand over her mouth. Such blasphemy.

If Isaac knew she had such thoughts. Or Gideon. If Gideon knew what she was doing, and how it made her feel.

Surely she was a woman fallen beyond redemption. She would fry in hell for it.

And with a heathen, wallowing in her wickedness.

Fine lot of faith she had. She had a husband who waited sorrowfully, longingly, faithfully for her at home, and she caroused with the enemy, willingly entered a contract with the Devil, not forced, not coerced, but willingly. Was there no hope for her? Was she already damned forever? Would Gideon, poor betrayed soul, be better never to set eyes on her again? Had she fallen so low, become so unworthy, she could never touch or love or see him again?

Was there even an inkling of hope? Could she, if she proved her self-control, from that moment forth abjured the sight, kiss, touch of that man—bad because she enjoyed them so much, more than was seemly for any woman—never thought of him and what she did with him again, but whenever she felt lust stealing over her, purified her thoughts, thought only of her lawful wedded husband, family, church, quoted Scripture, prayed, might she possibly redeem herself enough that she would be worthy of re-capture, worthy to set the table of and serve that humble, devoted man, her husband? Couldn't she at least try, Lord?

With this pledge of abstinence in mind Carrie started to rise, to steal away in the convictions of her faith. One last time, before she left, she glanced over at Mohee, to appreciate once more how close her soul had come to everlasting damnation.

In his sleep Mohee sighed and smiled at the same

moment as the fireflies encasing him pulsed on. Carrie looked at him glowing and all her resolve melted. She couldn't leave him. She couldn't move.

She couldn't believe how she felt about him, didn't know how it had happened. But there he was, beside her. Words could not describe how full she was of him, of this, of love. That was what the word meant. For the first time in her life, she knew it. She loved him. She loved Mohee. With all of her being. Maybe she shouldn't, but she did.

It reminded her of a place she once was, where a spring of fresh, clear water bubbled to the surface. There was a river underground, someone told her, and this was where it came out. Mohee was that spring for her, that river. And this was where she belonged.

She leaned over, lay back down beside him, put her fingers on his skin, slid them along his arm so that any fireflies they encountered would not fly away but would glide onto her, until they were one unbroken being, intertwined. When they were totally united, Carrie woke him by kissing his illuminated lips.

Mohee opened his eyes to see Carrie glowing beside him, both of them wrapped in a robe of fireflies.

She whispered to him as he pulled her closer and his body responded to hers, "Love me," as if his loving her as only he did would make everything else not matter.

A few nights later, Carrie and Mohee lay, nestled together in the dark of the wigwam, talking, touching.

"Shh." He held his finger to his lips. "Listen."

Far off they heard thunder coming toward them. As it rushed closer, they stopped talking, listened and watched.

The earth rumbled. Lightning lit the wigwam.

"Quick Flashes," Mohee said.

Carrie started to reach her hand toward him. A second flash showed Many Legs, up in its home at the top. She leaned her head on Mohee's arm, moved it onto his chest, smiled; between the rumbles and the flashes, she could hear his heart.

In the days before Mohee, she would have huddled in the corner with Hannah, her beloved Hannah, as terrified as her child was. Of what? Thunder, and the Lord, and other things she could not name. But now—?

It took courage not to be afraid, but she wasn't, not then. Lying there with Mohee, she felt safe, secure.

She jumped from the suddenness of a flash, the loudness of a thunderclap. She was startled, she reassured herself, not afraid. Even standing outside at the height of the storm, as rain lashed at her and thunder boomed all around her, she would not have been.

"Look, Chipmunk." Mohee squirmed beneath her, raised his hand above her. His index finger, held up in the air, wiggled, stopped, wiggled again.

Carrie sat up to see better.

It moved with the flash, stopped in the dark.

"What? Mohee. What is it?"

A tremendous clap shook the wigwam.

"Watch." His finger moved again.

She did not understand. "Does it make a noise? Make the noise for it." She had to shout to be heard over the thunder.

"No. No noise. Only." It moved again with the lightning, stopped with the darkness.

"What? Tell me."

Lightning flashed, the ground rumbled, rain pelted the side of the wigwam.

"Didn't you tell me, the other name for our friend who lights us at night is Lightning Bug?"

"That's what you're making?!" Carrie clapped her hands. "Do it again."

His finger fluttered in the light, was still in the darkness, fluttered again in the light.

"Yes. I see! It's wonderful!"

She loved his fingers making magic of everything.

She grabbed his other hand, brought it to her lips,

kissed it just as lightning lit them up, like an old painting, revealing both of them smiling, while the thunder cracked around them.

Carrie let his hand go, held her finger up, wiggled it back and forth the best she could.

The two of them kept fluttering their fingers in the air, making lightning bugs going on and off, on and off, as lightning flashed and the storm raged around them.

Chapter Nineteen

Carrie sat by Mohee in a clearing. Tiki was playing a few feet away. The old woman and the rest of their dwindling band were nearby. They were eating, their weapons set to the side.

Mohee seemed so weary the last few days, quiet and sad, sitting beside her for long periods, holding her hand.

"We have fought too long," he said. "There are so many of them, so few of us. Their guns and their diseases are killing us. Soon none of us will be left and none of our way of life."

Mohee talked, again, about how life had been before the settlers came. It was a kind of Eden, the way he described it, simpler and yet more difficult than the Christian one, a way of life that was unified and one. And it was gone.

He said this not in anger, not in blaming anyone, accepting it as how it was.

As if, Carrie thought, it was all twisted around. The world Mohee described was the real Eden, and it was not because of a serpent that it was lost, but because of Isaac, trampling through the underbrush, righteous and afraid, spoiling Special Places, killing or driving away all the creatures that lived there, building fences, converting or condemning or controlling, making divisions where none had been.

Carrie had seen Mohee's vision of how it was. She had lived it. She could never go back to living as she had.

She might have to, he said.

She started to protest.

He held up his hand for her to let him continue. "We have so little food, there are so few places left where we can fish or hunt."

The serpent, she thought, has slithered everywhere.

The day before Mohee had taken her to a different clearing. In the middle of it he stopped, turned toward her, held his arm out as if to indicate, "Here."

Carrie looked around. Was he showing her another Special Place?

The clearing was like so many other pretty places she had seen, a field surrounded by woods, green hills visible in the distance.

Mohee took her hand, kissed her fingers, held them to his chest. With his other hand he pointed toward a small mound at the high end of the field, near where the woods began. Slowly they walked toward it. Carrie's eyes darted left and right as she tried to figure out why he had brought her there. At the same time, without her noticing, her hand went to the mask in her pouch, her fingers caressing it over and over.

They were almost to the mound when Carrie realized. It was Hannah's grave. She stopped, hand over her mouth. Hannah's grave!

In another moment she was on her knees beside the grave. She was crying, quietly. She leaned forward over the mound, put her right arm around it, hugged it, brought her lips down, kissed it.

Mohee knelt beside her, laid his right hand on her arm. She raised herself onto her knees, put her hand over his, squeezed it, moved her hand back to the mound, felt all over it. More tears came out in a burst. She scraped a little dirt off the top, clasped it in her fist, moved her hand back and forth, the dirt, as from an hour glass, making a pattern on the grave.

While she did, Mohee started humming. It was the song they hummed at funerals when sending the spirit of a loved one on its way, and he was doing it for Hannah. She cried even more.

He started talking. It reminded Carrie that telling stories was part of their letting go of the dead. "There was a woman who lived in the time of Special Places," he began, talking about her and Hannah. “She came here from other people. She had a child she loved as much as any mother loved a child. She carried her in life and she carried her in death, she buried her in a Special Place at a time when she was sad, and now she has come back.”

Carrie was crying, not as she had before, but in the way the old woman did when the old man died, with a mournful sound that felt as if it came from the earth itself. The sound went on and on, spilling out of her. She looked at Mohee, meaning to apologize. He shook his head, moved his hand in a circle, as if saying, “This is the time for crying and for telling stories.”

While he hummed the song of funerals, the sadness continued to pour out of her, coming into her body from the ground, passing through her heart, out her mouth. “Uunhh. Uunhh.” She was expressing in sounds what she couldn’t before and couldn’t stop now. Her whole being vibrated.

“I did love her,” Carrie began when she stopped crying, talking in a way she never had before, “and she loved me. The way she giggled and squealed.” She smiled as she remembered. “She had a dimple here.” Carrie touched her cheek. “And when she laughed... We played Peek A Boo. She’d hide under a blanket. ‘Where is Hannah?’ I’d say, and out she popped: ‘There she is!’ And she squealed. And a moment later said, ‘Play Peek Boo, Mommy. Play it again.’ We’d play it over and over until she collapsed giggling against me. We played ‘Patty Cake’ too, ‘Patty Cake, Patty Cake, Baker’s Man,’ patting our hands together, against each other’s.” Carrie patted the air as she talked. “Going faster and faster until one of us made a mistake or she started laughing and couldn’t stop.” She smiled again. “Her father did not approve of these games,” she said, making a stern face, “but whenever we could we played them, and laughed and were happy. It was the only time I could ever laugh, with her. And then this wonderful happy child.” Carrie stopped. She was crying. Mohee laid his hand on her back, all the time still humming. After a while her crying subsided. “She was shot in your raid. She died in my arms. Everything went black. I was sad, so sad for such a long time. I felt alone. Abandoned. No one came for me. I was forgotten. And I was afraid, afraid of you and the others, afraid of what you would do to me, if you were going to kill me too. Sometimes I wished you would and all my pain would be over. But you didn't. The Old Woman brought me and Hannah here and you helped bury her. Then I was sick for a long time, and you and the others took care of me. And kept being kind to me after I was better, sharing your lives, your sorrows, and your joy too. Even walking two or three days without food you noticed beauty in the rain and in flowers and in birds, even in Many Legs. And little by little I did too. I started getting back the joy I lost with Hannah."

Carrie stopped. While Mohee continued humming, she clapped her hands together, kissed her right hand, patted it on the mound to her left, let it linger there, kissed her left hand, patted it on the mound to her right, let it linger there, brought both of them back up and clapped them together. Mohee beside her turned toward her, put his hands over hers, patted all four together, then leaned forward and kissed her finger tips.

She smiled at him, reached with her right hand into her pouch, pulled out the mask of her daughter. There she still was, her face as real as when she was alive. Carrie stroked her cheek, then, as she did so often when Hannah was sleeping, kissed her lightly on the forehead, held the mask against her heart. "I know her body is in the earth and her spirit is in Heaven. It is here inside me too. And in the rain, laughing in the drops splatting on the ground, and in the sunshine sparkling on Many Leg's web. And other places too, the way Wren is in your song, and in your whistle.

"She would have loved you," Carrie went on. "And you would have loved her too. As I would have loved Wren, and already do," she added, as his hand went to his pouch, and brought the mask of his daughter out. Carrie kissed it on the forehead, lifted Hannah's mask toward it. The two masks rubbed cheeks, almost as if they were laughing.

"Sisters," Mohee said, touching his chest with his fist.

Through all this he kept humming the song of

funerals more and more quietly until he stopped, and all that was left was vibrations in the air, like memory. Then that was gone, and all that remained was feeling. Before long that too was gone, and it was just Carrie and Mohee, breathing as one. She felt empty and full, exhausted and at peace. "Thank you," she said quietly. They stayed that way a long time, until she turned toward him, took his hand, and said, as simply as she could, "Mohee, marry me."

"Here?" He asked as they both stood up. "Now?"

Carrie nodded. Maybe what she was about to do had no bearing in the eyes of God and man, as she had lived before, but she was no longer there, and did not know if she ever would be.

This is where she was, and this is what she wanted to do, to join their beings and their hearts, not in the fashion of her ancestors, but in the simple manner she had seen others married in. They had no medicine man or respected elder to offer them a blessing. They would have to do it themselves.

Was he willing to do this?

Mohee nodded. Yes, he was.

He stepped toward her, paused a moment, took both her hands in his.

When he touched her, Carrie almost burst into tears. She tightened her jaw, managed a slight smile.

Mohee cleared his throat.

From the woods nearby, Carrie heard voices. "Wait." She saw two shapes past the end of the field, heard a whistle so like a wren she could not tell if it was real or not.

"Who is it?" she called out.

From the path in the woods Tiki's voice answered. "It's us." He and the old woman stepped into the field.

"Come," Carrie urged.

When they were standing beside them, Mohee started. He began by speaking in his own tongue. He gestured while he talked, pointing at the sky, the earth, her, and touching himself on the chest, then spoke again in her language, saying, "Before earth and sky, I am joining here with you."

Carrie smiled, squeezed his hands.

What he had said was so simple, she wanted hers to be simple too.

"And in this Special Place," she began, made even more Special, almost holy, by what they were doing in it. "Before earth and sky." And before God too, she thought but did not say, who sees and knows all, and who approves, she was sure of it, despite what Isaac or Gideon might say, "I am joining myself to you, freely, because I want to, more than anything else I have ever done."

Now came the moment when they exchanged one gift that was meaningful and important to them. They each had only one such item with them, the clay masks of their daughters. Nothing could be more fitting, Carrie felt, especially here, where she had parted with Hannah a first time.

Again she took from her pouch the mask of Hannah, hugged and kissed it, while Mohee did the same with the mask of Wren. They held the two masks in the space between them, had them touch cheeks, first one, then the other. "Ours," Mohee said. He took the mask of Hannah from her, gave her the mask of Wren. She kissed Wren on both cheeks, hugged her against her chest, and, after a minute, put her in her pouch, while he did the same with Hannah.

Mohee spoke again in his own language, commending them both to the spirits of earth and sky, to watch over and protect them. And to the Lord God too, she thought again, if He is not as harsh and forbidding as Isaac would make Him, but is also the God of Forgiveness and of Love, and does not begrudge anyone a few moments of happiness in this vale of tears.

They rubbed cheeks, first one, then the other, hugged, and kissed each other with a kiss that joined their souls. As they did, the old woman clapped her hands, Tiki whistled the pretty song of the wren, and they were married.

They did not know any of the things about each other that everyone thought so important—heritage and lineage, where they were born, even last names or birth dates. They simply knew each other to the depths of their souls, in a way Carrie could never before have guessed possible, and that for her had become the true meaning of marriage.

That night, when they made love, Mohee touched her face, her cheek, her neck, stroked her belly, her leg, her thigh.

"Sweet Little Chipmunk, if we never make love again," he said afterwards, sounding tired, "know that I loved you, and remember me."

Why did he talk like that? she wondered. He had given her so much—love of him, love of herself, love of the whole world. He let the love she had in her already come out, showed her it was not bad or sinful to love, but natural and wonderful. Why did he speak of it ending now?

They could still go away together, she told him the next day, find new paths where they were not known, where there were no settlers. She felt there was so much more life ahead for them.

He shook his head. "When I found you, here we were, and here they were." He drew two marks in the dirt, one for the heathens, one for the new settlers, with a space between them. "Now they are there, and all around us too." He filled the space with marks, crowding against them, leaving them no room.

"We can go to Canada."

"Too far." He touched his chest. "I do not have the heart. A person cannot live all his life fighting. He becomes small and hard, his own worst enemy. For however much time is left, I want to be who I am, nothing more."

As they ate, Mohee told how so much of his life was determined by the settlers. His daughter, shot and killed in a raid, and his wife, whom he loved as deeply as he loved Carrie, maybe more, because it was longer, and in so many ways of thinking they were the same, they did not have to say it to know it. But no, maybe that was not so, maybe his love for Carrie was more: they were two people who seemed to be so different, in their love they were joining the differences, discovering how much they were the same. And he loved her when his heart was darkest, when he thought there could be no more love in the world, nothing but sadness.

He remembered other encounters with settlers. His father, killed one place. His uncle and aunt there too. A cousin, of one of their diseases. Another cousin another place, betrayed by one he had befriended. His good friend and brother, Quick Flashes, made mean and killed by them in so many ways, though they were nowhere near when he died. His mother of a broken heart, that so many were gone, but most especially his father, that she loved so deeply—and with them all a way of life that could never be recaptured.

"I felt that too, when Mouse died." But when he met and knew Carrie, there was again a reason. She gave him back hope. Even that was not enough anymore. There were a handful left in this group, a few more in another. Soon it would be his turn too. Before long, maybe even by the next spring melt, it would all be gone. They had fought well, but what could they do? "Do not become like your enemy in fighting," one of their sayings went, "or you lose even if you win."

They were almost finished eating. Carrie held a turkey wing bone in her hand. As she lifted it to eat the meat off, a man on horseback burst into the clearing, shooting and shouting.

"Settlers," Carrie said, jumping up. "We'd better hide."

Mohee stood, shook his head. There was a shot, he grabbed his arm, started to sit.

She took a step toward him. "Mohee?"

Two arms reached down, scooped her up onto a horse. Before she could begin to struggle and fight, a voice in her ear said, "Carrie, you're safe. It's Isaac."

Carrie looked back, watching Mohee as the horse galloped away. She saw his fingers flap up and down, his hands make a small bird pumped up at the throat. His mouth opened. She imagined she heard his voice singing, “Whip-poor-will, whip-poor-will,” the sound so joyous and infectious she could not help smiling.

III

Chapter Twenty

After Carrie was recaptured, before she was reunited with her husband, Rebecca—who, Carrie learned later, had only been rescued a few weeks earlier herself—unbraided and cut Carrie's hair, and dressed her in more appropriate clothing than the heathen garb she came home in. Isaac knelt in the next room, praying, the door between the two rooms open.

The entire time she brushed and pulled and twisted, working her hair out, Rebecca talked to Carrie in a voice too low for Isaac to hear. "Sinning with the heathens," she hissed. "Won't that go over well? You couldn't resist temptation—the naked loincloth, the muscles on his arm? No. You had to lie with the Devil. You couldn't be strong and virtuous and prove yourself a worthy Christian wife? Where is your faith? Don't protest." Pull. "Don't say you were forced to it." Twist. "No one forces you to braid your hair or wear moccasins. I know," she said, her voice rising so Isaac could hear. "I was there. No one forced me to anything. I came home in the dress I was taken in, my Bible still in my pocket. That is what is meant by virtue. That is what we call fidelity.

"You know," she said, lowering her voice again. "I don't have to remind you. They are vermin. They are snakes and Devils, all of them. And anyone who consorts with them"—yank, pull, twist —"knows what to expect as her reward."

Through it all, Carrie said nothing. She sat, staring straight ahead. Rebecca didn't finish until Carrie's hair was cut, shorter than necessary, and she was dressed again as was fitting for a Christian woman of her status, the wife of a Deacon and the sister of a Minister, in case she had forgotten what that might be.

"Do you know what happened to him, the man standing next to me?" It was the first time Carrie spoke since her recapture.

Rebecca pulled the strand she was holding tighter. Carrie's head tipped back, her mouth opened, but she remained silent.

"Forget him, you fool," Rebecca hissed. "Whoever he was. You are back in the land of prayers." She indicated Isaac, kneeling, through the door.

"Or the old woman, or the boy Tiki, who was playing nearby?"

"They are all dead."

Carrie started. "They are not."

"Oh, yes, they are. Didn't you hear? Your brother killed them, every last one."

Was that true? Did Rebecca know or was she being spiteful, jealous because for a short time in her life Carrie had found happiness?

Rebecca must have known about her and Mohee, without knowing who it was. Wasn't it obvious in the way Carrie stood and moved and carried herself? Even with the shock of being recaptured, the uncertainty of not knowing what happened to Mohee, she still must have looked different.

She wanted to ask Rebecca, Can you find out from Isaac: What did happen to him, to Mohee, the man I love, my one true husband, that I was eating with when I was captured? Was he shot? Wounded? Killed? If so, tell me. Let me know, so I will not long for things that cannot be, and can truly mourn him. And the boy Tiki, that I love as much as a son, what about him? Or the old woman, his grandmother, a second mother to me?

She stayed silent, the thoughts going round and round in her head.

In the other room Isaac knelt, hands together, lips moving.

As she watched, Mohee appeared in the air beside him, lit up by fireflies.

Carrie's heart stopped. Her mouth fell open. "Mohee," she started to say. No sound came out.

Mohee nodded, put his finger to his lips. He stepped toward Isaac, moved his arm in a circle around him, and all the fireflies blinked on and off, as if lighting up her brother, while he kept silently praying, completely unaware.

Carrie laughed at the sight. Laughter bubbled up inside her. She clamped her mouth shut, tried to keep it inside. And then Mohee was gone. Isaac was as he had been. Carrie was still laughing, her whole body shaking, though she made no sound, and Mohee had disappeared.

Rebecca jabbed her in the back. "Shh."

It had no effect. Carrie's body still shook.

"You find this humorous?" With her head she indicated Isaac. "Shhhh." Rebecca jabbed her again, harder. "Shush."

Slowly the laughter inside subsided, and Carrie was still again, except, behind the mask of her face, she was smiling.

She wanted to ask Rebecca, Did she see him, just now, that man, lighting up the room the way he lit her up inside? He was her one true love. Wasn't he handsome? Did she think Carrie could walk out and look, to see if she could find him, see if she could see blood where they had been while it was still fresh. It was not far.

Well? she thought, watching Isaac's stern figure, praying.

She knew that would never do.

Chapter Twenty One

Isaac looked the re-made Carrie over. Gone were the clothes of the Devil, the offending skirt, top and moccasins burned, replaced by more fitting attire—long stockings, a new shift, and a dark woolen dress that reached from her neck to her ankles, with buttons every inch and a half.

He had known her when he rescued her, he told her later, despite her hair braided in the heathen style, despite her moccasins, deerskin clothing and sun-darkened skin, because of her red hair, but most especially because of a look of her top lip he had never seen in anyone other than their mother.

He nodded his approval, led her into the other room. A man wearing the same black clothes Isaac wore came toward her, stopped six feet away, stared at her.

Carrie studied him. Who, she wondered, was this man, a little large and ungainly, with nothing distinguishing about him? Was she supposed to know him? He looked like no one she had ever seen before, except his ears did seem familiar.

"Carrie?" he said.

Before she could speak, Isaac answered. "I brought her back, brother. On one of my 'senseless' raids."

"Thank you." The man smiled. "Praise the Lord God. It is a miracle."

It was Gideon.

He moved toward her. "You are here. It is everything I have hoped for. Oh, my sweet wife."

Gideon started to put his arms out to hug her, this man she had not recognized except for his large ears.

As he did, she stepped back. He took her hands,

studied her. "You look so good, so healthy. It couldn't have been as awful as they say. Tell me about it. Tell me about the ordeal you've been through. Was it as bad as what I've endured here, without you, missing you every hour of every day? All I went through, alone. Cooking my own meals. Until cousin Hetty could do it for me. But she is such a poor cook compared to you, it's a wonder I haven't wasted away." He laughed and patted his belly, which seemed to have grown in her absence. "But tell me, I'll listen."

Before she could figure where to begin he went on.

"What about Hannah? Where is she? Is she here too?"

Carrie shook her head.

"Where did you leave her? Is she safe? Did Isaac rescue her too?"

Carrie stared at the ground.

"What? Tell me. I cannot bear the suspense."

Carrie pursed her lips, shut her eyes. "She is dead."

"Oh, no."

Carrie opened her eyes, nodded. "Yes."

"How did it happen? When? Where did it occur? Tell me, please. Why do you torture me? What happened to my child? Why are you not answering me?"

Couldn't he slow down? This was hard enough as it was.

"Well?"

Carrie tried to remember, to put herself back in the situation.

"I am waiting."

"It was here," she finally got out. "When they attacked. We were standing on the hill, not far from the door—"

"And what were you doing outside? That is something I have not been able to understand. Why were you not inside as I instructed? And the child with you? Why did you let her go outside when I specifically told you not to? She might well still be alive if you had done as I said." He grew tight around the eyes.

There it is, she thought. Home ten minutes, and it was as if she never left.

Did he know, she wanted to ask, that at the time of the attack Rebecca bolted the door from the inside and locked them out?

And did he have any concept what an attack was like? How sudden it was, how little time one had to do anything but grab the child, look around for a place to hide, and that was it?

"Well?" he asked. "How did it happen? Can't you at least explain that?"

Carrie did not say how she had carried Hannah all day, able to do nothing more than clutch her dead child to her and walk. She did not want to start thinking about how lost and scared she felt when she was taken captive, the same as she felt now that she was home.

"She was killed during the raid," she answered. "Shot. She died in my arms. A moment later I was prisoner with her. I buried her the next morning as best I could, without a Bible or a Minister."

It is not far from here, she thought. We could go there together and— She did not say it. She could not go there with him.

Carrie felt on the verge of tears. She bit her lip, held it in.

"I am sorry," Gideon said, laying his hand on her arm in a jarring way meant, she knew, to be tender. "I didn't know. It must have been hard."

Carrie nodded. Very hard, she thought, trying to figure out what to say next and how to say it.

Before she could speak Gideon went on. "Well, enough about that. You know the Lord giveth and the Lord taketh away." He looked at her. "But you are here." He started to pull her toward him.

Carrie tensed, her body closing away from him.

"It looks so changed," she said, stepping to the side.

"It is all as it was the day you left." He smiled.

Carrie shut her eyes. This is going to be difficult, she

thought. She opened them. Gideon was smiling at her.

"I am so glad you are back," he said. "Everything will be as it was." He squeezed her hands.

"Oh, I am forgetting. Stay right here. I have a present." Gideon walked a few feet, bent down, picked something up, walked back toward her, one hand behind his back. "For you." He smiled a wide grin, his teeth showing long and crooked. "For your Homecoming." He brought his hand around.

In front of him he held a pair of women's black shoes, well oiled and polished.

Carrie stared at them. "What is this?"

"It is your shoes." His smile got bigger. "Aren't you going to take them?"

"What shoes?" She never had a second pair. Did he have these made for her, in hopes she might return?

"You don't know them? Here. Here!" Gideon laid them at her feet and knelt, trying to pick her right foot up and force it into the dark leather.

As his hand reached out, Carrie took a step backwards.

"They are the shoes you left in."

"These?"

Gideon nodded, his head going up and down. He was almost laughing. "I found them in the stream where you left them, where you were forced to leave them, before you were made to wear their heathenish garb, to cast off these signs of civilization. Here."

Without getting up, Gideon slid a stool over behind her, beckoned for her to sit. "Look at them. You wouldn't know they had been left in water, would you?" He picked the right shoe up, held it in front of her face.

"When I came back, and you and Hannah were gone, I didn't know if you were dead or alive, or, if you were alive, where you might be, or if I would ever see you again. But when I found these, months later, can you believe it, in a stream, way off the path, I knew you would be coming home again. I knew. For that long time, when I didn't have you, I hoped and prayed, and said to myself, these hopes and prayers are foolish, but if the Lord wills it . . . And then I had these, and they sustained me!"

Gideon brought the shoe to his lips and kissed it. "But now you are back! I have you again, and you have these, and your Homecoming is complete!"

"Thank you," Carrie tried to say. Her voice broke in the middle. She tried to smile. Her face couldn't.

Gideon put the shoe down in front of her, pushed it toward her.

Carrie was crying. She didn't know why.

"Do you want me to help?"

Carrie shook her head. "I can."

Please don't make me, she thought. She could not say it.

"Well?"

Gideon looked so expectant, as if he was happier about the shoes being used again than her coming home.

Thrift, she thought. Thrift.

That was not fair. Gideon seemed so pleased, like a little boy. Not merely because of the shoes. About her too.

He kept looking at her, waiting.

Was she really going to have to wear these?

He leaned forward, elbows above his knees.

Couldn't she take her own time about it?

He nudged one shoe toward her. "They still fit, don't they? Your feet haven't grown?"

She shook her head.

"Well?"

It was like the heathen marching behind her the first day, his hand shoving her forward whenever she moved too slowly.

Carrie slid the shoe under her, pushed the tongue up, lifted her right foot, pointed her toes, brought her foot down, wiggling and sliding against the hard leather that pinched and scraped as her foot went in.

Inside her heart was breaking.

She knew these shoes.

She remembered the blisters on her heel and sole, her knob rubbed raw, her toes cramped together. She flexed her foot. She forgot how stiff and painful they were, how hard to walk in, how heavy and unyielding.

These are not my shoes, she wanted to say. Not anymore. I did not come back with the same feet.

She wanted her moccasins, soft and supple and gentle, that Isaac took from her and burned, calling them "the fiendish work of the Devil".

Gideon was already holding the other shoe out for her, like Prince Charming in the old story, the tongue bent out of the way. As Carrie lowered her foot he jerked and pushed the shoe to make it fit.

When it was on and she stood, in pain, afraid to move, Gideon grabbed her arm and said, almost with a shout, "You are home!"

Chapter Twenty Two

Carrie stared at the floor, spoke in fits and starts, looked off into the woods. Gideon touched her. She pulled away.

Of course she was grateful for all he and Isaac went through to recapture her, to bring her back to civilization. Of course she understood what agony it was for him, without his wife or child, not knowing where she was, if she was dead or alive, if she was safe, what atrocities she might be forced to undergo or witness. She certainly was not the only one who suffered. She appreciated that. But couldn't he see—

Of course he could, he said, interrupting her. He certainly understood how difficult it was, the contrast between that life of barbarity, surrounded by coarse, heathenish Devils, and the one of civilized sanctity they led here. He would not dwell on that, but didn't he do well, even in her absence? The garden was thriving, though a little behind in the weeding, she was always better at that than him. He had bought another cow. There was always more than enough to eat, morning, noon, and night; he patted his stomach. He did not suffer in that regard. And that reminded him, pancakes would be just right for supper, no one did them like her, and for breakfast, Johnny cakes would be perfect, he had not had them the whole time she was gone.

Already, that afternoon, she tried to fall back into the rhythm of working, being home again among the objects she had missed so much. They were all still there: her pin cushion, needles, and thread; her smock; her apron; her comforter; the one wall ornament, that she had embroidered, The Lord Bless and Keep Our Home.

Even her broom. She half laughed, half cried when Gideon handed it to her. She missed it too, didn't she, in the beginning, especially, when it meant home to her.

Now none of these things seemed important. A person could have a happy home, she had learned, and have what looked like nothing.

Gideon hovered near her, expecting her, she gathered, to use the broom as if she had never been away, as if nothing had changed.

Carrie began sweeping, not with a vigorous stroke, stroke, stroke, as she used to, but gently, tentatively, making a few strokes, stopping, thinking how hard this was.

"Are you not well?" Gideon was still there, overseeing. "Have you forgotten how to do it? Do you want me to show you? I did a fair job, if I may say so, when I had to. You did not come home to a dirty house."

Carrie shook her head. She would not let him take the broom from her. I can't go faster, she thought but didn't say, can't you see: my feet hurt, my heart is sore, I do not want to be back here, doing this, with you here, smothering me, acting as if nothing has changed.

In a corner she stopped to watch a Many Legs spinner down, left a ball of dust where it landed.

"You missed a spot."

"A spider is there." She smiled for one of the first times since her return. "Did you see? Many Legs the—they call them. Every house has one."

"Not if we can help it."

"Gideon!" she cried out.

Before she could stop him, he brought his foot down on the clump of dust, ground it back and forth, grabbed the broom from her and swept it out of the corner toward the open door.

"A house which is civilized does not have spiders in it. Surely, you have not forgotten that?"

After that first supper, while Gideon sat in his chair and talked about how good it was, how happy he was to have her back, wasn't life wonderful again, thank the Good Lord, Carrie cleaned up, and stared out at the woods, dark in the moonlight.

As she watched, Mohee appeared in a swarm of fireflies. They rose together into the sky, blinking on and off, illuminating his face. "Mohee." She whispered his name. He looked at her, blew her a kiss.

Before her eyes the picture transformed. The fireflies became him, forming his face, one blinking in the center for his nose, two above that for his eyes, as bright and sparkling as they were when he shared something Special with her—a place, a bird, a rainbow, a storm, the sound of rain on the trees.

Carrie thought she would burst. Like a bubble, pleasure rose up inside her. She could hardly keep it in.

And there, in the middle, were his two index fingers, making lightning bugs, blinking on, blinking off, blinking on, blinking off.

It was all she could do to keep from opening the door and rushing out to join him.

Instead, she stood there, happy and sad, watching as one by one the lights of the fireflies went out, and he was gone.

"Come here, my sweet wife," Gideon said, trying, she knew, to be gentle. He smiled. "I am so happy you are home." He touched her on the shoulder, pushed his face against her, gave her a peck on the cheek, meaning to be warm, she knew.

She turned her face to him, to kiss him. He turned his cheek toward her.

In the bedroom he blew out the candle, climbed into bed. The moon gave more than enough light to see by.

Carrie sat, pulled her right shoe off. One toe throbbed, a second was rubbed raw, a spot of blood on it. She stared at it.

"Why do you delay?" Gideon's voice startled her back into the room.

"I am sorry, I—"

She unlaced the second shoe, as gently as she could slid it off. It seemed to pull her skin off with it. She bit her lip to keep from calling out.

"I am waiting."

She started to remove her dress, her fingers undoing all the many buttons, dreading what was to follow, that she knew was a sin, she had heard Isaac intone it she did not know how many times, a sin against her one true husband that she had chosen of her own free will. But she could not tell this to Gideon, could not tell anyone.

"You'll want your night robe."

Carrie took it from its hook, untouched since she had left, slipped out of her dress and, what she had never done there before, out of her shift as well; she stood a moment naked, enjoying the feeling of her body unencumbered by clothes.

Gideon cleared his throat.

Carrie hurried to put the coarse wool on. All her skin itched from it, as if it was crawling with strange creatures that needed scratching.

"Is it new?" she wanted to ask. She knew it was the same one she had worn every night. This too would take getting used to.

Carrie got into bed beside him, thinking he was a good man, she had been fond of him before, she could be fond of him again. What happened was not his fault. Why should he suffer for it? Now, if she was tender, and talked, and told him all she went through, so he might understand, and he talked, and told her all he felt, they could begin to be a couple again, and might in time be intimate.

As soon as she was in bed she reached to touch his face.

He was already rolling over on top of her, bunching up her robe, pulling his erect member out of his night clothes, pushing it against her.

No, she thought.

Before she could speak he was inside her, thrusting back and forth.

With his left hand he grabbed her shoulder, held her still, thrust twice. "Ahhh, ahhhh!" he cried, jerked around a little more, kissed her on the cheek, whispered "I'm so glad you're home," rolled off her. In moments he was breathing deeply.

Carrie lay there, her night robe in a clump over her belly, trying to pull it down, smooth it out, stop the pain between her legs. Even when it was down as far as it could go, she still kept trying to pull it farther and smooth it, pull it and smooth it.

It didn't help; it didn't stop the pain.

It was all she could do to keep from crying.

Nothing had changed. How could she have forgotten how much it hurt.

She stopped trying to smooth the robe, clenched her fingers by her side. Never again, she thought to herself. If that was what passed for tenderness and love, she would rather do without.

All she heard was Gideon's breathing; all she felt was throbbing. It didn't matter how she lay, which way she moved, it didn't go away.

She rolled over away from Gideon, stared at the patch of moonlight on the floor, feeling as bad as she had ever felt in her life.

She tried to relax, to sleep. Gideon's breathing seemed to get louder, until, she thought, if she heard it once more, she would scream.

She slid out of bed, followed the moonlight out of the house. Outside, at least, she could breathe.

She sat on the ground, her knees pulled tight against her, staring at the dark woods. A few scattered fireflies flew back and forth, blinking on and off. One by one their lights stayed out.

"Mohee," she thought. "I love you. I want to be with you. That's all I ask."

She thought of their souls mingling when they made love, or when they talked, or with his hands and whistles he made a wren.

One last firefly blinked and went out.

She felt so sad. She did not know how she could stand it,

Hours later Gideon found her there, asleep. “There you are. Thank the Lord you are safe. You don’t know how worried I was. I didn’t know what happened to you, if you’d been kidnapped again or what. Come back to bed, you’ll catch your death of cold out here. Come back, come back.” He leaned down, helped her up, threw a blanket over her, put his arm around her, started to lead her in. “You don’t want people to see you out here, dressed like that. There’s no telling what they would think.”

Chapter Twenty Three

Carrie heard Gideon's stories over and over, filling in the days from when she was captured until Isaac brought her back.

When she wanted to speak, to tell what happened to her while he was suffering without her, it was never the right time.

Sometimes her throat felt so full of what she wanted to say, she thought she would choke if she did not let it out. If there was a lull, and she started to speak, he rushed on with endless details of the same old story, or hurried off to do whatever daily tasks he deemed more important than listening to her.

Still she did not give up. She tried to forget Mohee. She did not stand yearning at the window, looking for fireflies. She focused on trying to make it work, sat by Gideon as he studied his Bible.

The silence as she waited felt empty, hollow.

"Gideon," she began.

He cleared his throat, turned the page, his glance never straying from the Book.

There might be a way. There had to be.

If there had been no raid, no forced march and capture, she would still be content.

What would she be doing in the evening while he read his Bible? she wondered. Playing with Hannah? Putting her to bed?

Was that what was missing from this house? Put a child back in it for her to tend and love...

No, that was not all that was missing.

Gideon started another chapter, oblivious to her

presence.

Why did he ignore her? Why would he not let her speak? He never asked about what happened to her while she was gone, or mentioned one word about it. Did he assume it was uneventful? Did it not matter? Did she?

She knew what to say. She had rehearsed it: we cannot go on as if everything is the way it was before I left.

The problem was not in what to say. It was in being able to say it. How could she tell him if he would not let her?

Maybe the one who was at fault was not him. She had never talked or expected to before. She was the one who had changed. Shouldn't she be the one who changed back to the way she had been?

Maybe she should. Maybe that is the only way it could be.

But she could not. And she was not sure she wanted to. She liked the person who came back, better than the one who left. Gideon was the one who needed to change. But if he didn't know that, or saw no reason to, or wouldn't even listen to her...

It was like the shoes. Maybe they had gotten smaller and stiffer from the water of the stream. Maybe her feet had grown. Maybe nothing was different except inside her, and she could no longer tolerate what she had never questioned before.

Whatever it was, her feet did not accept the stiff black leather. They stayed raw, blistered, bloody. Whenever she could, she removed the shoes, slipped them under the bed, hoped her feet remained hidden under the hem of her long dress.

Once, as she sat, she lifted her dress slightly and Gideon noticed.

"What is this?" he asked.

Carrie pulled her feet farther under her. "It is nothing."

"Oh, but it is. Let me see."

Carrie did not respond.

"Let me see," Gideon commanded. He held his hand down.

Carrie brought her bare right foot forward. He grabbed it. She winced.

"What is this about? Have you lost all sense of civilization? Did you come back a beast? Have you no appreciation for all I have done? finding these shoes, cleaning them, oiling them, working them, in the hopes of having you return, when I didn't know if you were dead and had only my faith to sustain me?" His eyes were moist. "And you don't wear them?"

"My feet—" Carrie started to protest.

"You need to put them back on."

She did not move.

"This is not a matter for discussion. Do you not know where they are?

"I know."

"Well."

Carrie stood, went into the bedroom, returned with them in her hand, sat back down.

Gideon waited.

"They hurt."

"Of course they hurt. You cannot go from the wild abandon of the heathen life back to ours and not expect discomfort. That marks the difference between us and them. Any monster can go without shoes. Only a civilized being, one at ease in the sight of the Lord, can wear them. That is still you, is it not?"

Carrie nodded.

Gideon smiled. "That is how it should be. A little discomfort is to be expected. It means your feet are getting used to them. But you must not do this again, however much it hurts. Suppose Isaac came by during the day, or another of our compound, and found you without them. Do you know how that would reflect on me?"

Carrie nodded.

"And you will do what is right?"

"I will."

Carrie leaned forward, started to push her foot into her shoe.

"Would you like me to help?"

"I can do it myself. Thank you."

She put both shoes back on, trying not to show the pain she felt, tightened the laces as loosely as she could.

As she tied the second knot, she felt Gideon pat her on the head, saw him move away.

Carrie wore her shoes as long as she could. When the throbbing and the pain became too intense, she kept them on a few more minutes, and a few more after that. When she could not stand it any longer, she took them off. She was more careful to keep them, and her feet, hidden.

In the first few days after finding her without them, Gideon checked her at random. "And how are your shoes today?" he asked, putting his hand down toward the hem of her dress.

The first time, he touched her shoes before Carrie realized what he was doing. After that, when she saw his hand move toward her, she reached down and grabbed it. "Gideon. Have some decency. Suppose Isaac walked in at this moment, or another of the compound. What would he think? How would that reflect on you?" He never tried to touch them again.

"They are doing better," Carrie said, pulling her feet farther under hcr.

"You see," he said. "I told you they would. Was I not right?"

She moved where she kept them, went without them as often as she could, tucked her feet up behind her whenever she sat.

Carrie was restless. She flopped back in her chair. She stared at the ceiling.

In the shadows in the corner she saw movement.

She sat up, watching. Shh, Many Legs, she wanted to say. Stay busy and quiet in the shadows.

She glanced at Gideon, absorbed in the Good Book.

It's our secret, she whispered in her head.

She watched the delicate legs spin down. It made her smile inside. Many Legs was still there!

Stay hidden until morning, she thought. I will see you then.

She had adopted a strategy to help Many Legs stay. When she found one while cleaning, she took it on her arm, let it rest there, its feet tickling her skin, while she swept out the cobwebs, put it back in a hidden spot on top of the cross beam. She apologized about breaking up its home. It was the only way to keep it there. She hoped it understood.

When Gideon complained about how quickly the cobwebs returned, how many there were, and she had just finished sweeping, she took Many Legs outside the next time she cleaned, balanced on her hand, shook it off by the door.

"Can you live here, Many Legs?" she asked, "Bless our house from here?"

Was the one she saw now, she wondered, the same one she put outside that morning, come back inside before bed time, bestowing its blessing on them? She didn't know, but she hoped so.

Carrie watched until it disappeared into the darkness of the corner. Good night, she thought. I will see you in the morning.

Gideon had not moved or looked up, his finger, every few minutes, lifting the page and turning it.

Carrie sat back, sighed. Gideon made no response.

She stood, walked to the window, looked out. There was no point in pretending. She was looking for Mohee, and the fireflies that brought him. She saw none, only the reflection in the thick pane of glass of the yellow light of Gideon's candle.

She moved toward the door. "I am going out to look

at the stars," she said.

Gideon did not answer.

Carrie stepped out, pulled the door shut behind her, looked up. There were no stars; no fireflies either. The sky was cloudy, the air heavy.

It smelled like rain.

She sat on one of the steps, stared at the darkness of the night above and the woods below. Mohee was in those woods. She lifted her right hand by her side, bent her fingers back and forth in a silent wave, brought the two front fingers of her left hand to her lips, blew him a kiss. Rest well, she thought. Wherever you are.

Twice Carrie had gone back into the woods, when Gideon and Isaac were off about their business. She walked down and stepped in, started on the path. Her resurrected shoes pinched and rubbed with every step.

She stopped, sat on a rock, took them off. She held the left one up, looked at it, well oiled and shining.

It was going to take more than oil and rubbing to work her back in.

She took off her long stockings, stood, picked up the shoes and the stockings, carried them under her arm.

She walked alert, aware of the birds, the wren hopping, crows cawing. She saw the sun sparkle on a spider web, hung from tree to tree. She ducked under it, stopped to watch Many Legs, silently working.

She found where they had been when she was recaptured. She was sure it was the place, so close to Isaac's compound. There was the clearing in the middle, there the stream, there the large oak, the clump of four white birch trees, one leaning inward that they had put their wigwam under.

Carrie stood silent. She felt close to Mohee and Tiki, felt their presence. She found the circle where the fire ring was, the ashes covered with dirt. People might have been there a week ago, a month, a year. There was nothing to tell her more.

She searched along the path for the face mask of Wren. She did not find it. She had it in her pouch when she was recaptured, remembered it when she was seated on the horse. Having it there when she got back would not do.

She pried and worked until it was at the edge of the pouch, then looked up, twisted around and glanced behind to her left while with her right hand she slid it free and with a slight shove let it fall to the ground. She hoped she pushed it far enough off the path so leaves would hide it.

Chapter Twenty Four

The latch lifted behind Carrie. The ground lit up beside her. Gideon's thick boots and heavy tread clumped outside.

"Carrie!" he called.

"Right here."

"Oh. You surprised me. I didn't see you. What are you doing?"

"Watching the night. I miss it. I lived outside while I was gone."

"That also distinguishes the civilized from the heathen, that we have a home, blessed in the sight of the Lord, and we live in it." He held his hand out toward her. "Besides, it is bed time."

"Can't we stay out here another minute? There's no harm in it." No one can see us, she thought, but did not add.

"I suppose."

"Won't you sit?"

He sat on the step above her, a foot to her right.

She slid over, leaned her head against his knee. He pulled it away.

She sat back up, stared out at the dark. "It is a pleasant night," she said after a minute.

"Warm," he agreed. "No stars."

"It is going to rain."

"Do you know this for a fact?"

She turned toward him, smiling slightly. "Yes."

"How? Did the heathens turn you into a sorceress?"

"No." She laughed, knowing a sorceress was a dangerous thing to be, one step removed from a witch.

She did not know what was bad about knowing it was going to rain. No demonic power had told her, only her own observation.

"It smells like it."

She heard Gideon sniff the air.

"And the tree frogs have gotten louder," the Small Frog with the Big Voice. They were, all of a sudden, almost deafening, their one-note orchestra emanating from the small marsh down in the woods. But they were not infallible. They drummed louder whenever it turned more humid.

"We should go in then. We don't want to get wet."

"It isn't raining yet. I don't think it's going to flood."

There was a silence.

Carrie wanted to lean back against Gideon's leg, enjoy the night together. Again she moved her head toward him. Before it got there he pulled his leg away, sat straight and still on the wooden step.

"Do you have any other predictions?"

"Predictions?"

"Pronouncements for the future?"

"Such as?"

"Saying it was going to rain?"

"No."

"Don't you think that is presumptuous of you? Only the Lord knows what will be before it happens. No matter how much something seems like it might be, He always has the power to make it not happen. You know how often it has felt like it might rain or storm, and it hasn't."

"Yes."

"I think what you meant to say was not 'It is going to rain', but 'It feels like it to me'. Am I not right?"

No, she thought angrily, you are not. It is going to rain. She stopped herself. Was she being willful again, countering his authority, the way she did the day of the attack, when she used her senses, and made a judgment to stay outside?

Wasn't that why she was captured?

No, it was not. Staying inside did not spare Rebecca. The only ones not captured were Sarah and her children. They fled the safe place she was told to wait. If they had stayed, she would have been taken too. There was nothing wrong with Carrie using her own mind and powers of observation then. And that is what she was doing now too.

They sat silent. Carrie's anger seemed to seep out, to slip away into the quiet of the night, but the silence still felt tense.

Why was it so hard since her return to talk to each other? and why did every conversation seem to end in an argument? She did not remember it being this way before. Had it been? Was it because they never talked about anything that mattered?

While she was gone, there were so many things she thought about asking if she ever saw him again. Why couldn't she remember them now?

She remembered one. She smiled at the thought.

Have you seen yourself naked? Why not, do you think?

Did you ever want to see me naked? Weren't you the least little bit curious what I look like under these clothes?

Mohee was; he loved what he saw. We bathed together naked many times, exploring and knowing each other's bodies with our hands and eyes.

Laughter chortled up inside her. She had to clamp her jaw shut to hold it in.

She knew these questions would never do. No one but a sorceress would think of them.

There must be something more proper she could ask.

"Am I not right?"

She looked at him. She had no idea what he was talking about.

She could say yes. That would please him. That was her Gideon, always needing to be right, like her brother, the Good Minister Isaac. Even if you did not think he was, you were supposed to say so.

It got quieter. The tree frogs were silent. A breeze ran up the hill. And then Carrie heard it, on the tops of the trees out over the woods, like the patter of a hundred tiny feet. She sat up straight and listened.

Gideon's hand settled on her shoulder, heavy and cold, like a trap.

"Do you hear it?" she asked.

"You haven't answered me."

She pulled her shoulder free, stood up to listen better.

"On the trees. Do you?"

"I do not hear anything."

"Listen. Running like little feet across the tops. There." She smiled. "The rain!"

"I hear nothing."

"Listen," she urged him. "Coming this way." She heard it clattering and scurrying toward them. "Don't you hear it?"

Gideon was looking not at the night, or out toward the dark where the sound of the rain was coming from, but at Carrie. He looked alarmed.

"That is another thing sorceresses do. They claim to hear things that are not. You don't need to be examined for sorcery, do you?"

Carrie shook her head. What was he talking about? Did he really believe hearing rain on the treetops was sorcery?

"Are you sure? My little Carrie has changed. She has not been herself since she returned." Gideon adjusted how he sat. "It is true. The simple things that used to please you you have no interest in. You find it difficult even to have a conversation with me. Don't think I haven't noticed. And it pains me that after all this time I still don't have my Carrie back. Perhaps that would explain it."

Carrie heard the rain run over the leaves to the edge of the woods at the bottom of the hill, stopped hearing it as it splatted across the field, up the hill, and then there it was, the drops hitting the grass in front of them, the roof behind them, the steps, her arms, her head.

Rain! Her lovely rain. Here it was!

"Come inside." Gideon reached to grab her arm.

Carrie had already bounded down the last two steps and stood, turning around, her head tilted back, mouth open, trying to catch the drops she had heard minutes before, as she did with Tiki and Mohee, as she had done there with her beloved Hannah.

Gideon stood, watching from the safety of the doorway. For several minutes he did not speak.

Carrie held her palms up, catching raindrops. She turned her hand toward him, arm outstretched, as if to say, Won't you come dance with me?

Gideon shook his head. "When you are ready," he said, after watching several moments longer, "I invite you to come inside." And he stepped into the house.

Carrie nodded, smiled, spun around, catching drops in her mouth, her nose, her eyes.

She laughed.

Maybe she could still be happy.

The empty doorway stayed open, the warmth of yellow light beckoning her in to where, she knew, Gideon resumed his seat and reopened his Bible.

Carrie kept dancing until the shower passed, the feet ran off on the leaves to the east, the drops stopped falling, and her clothes clung to her in a most unseemly manner, knowing that in the house, Gideon stared at the Bible, open in front of him, not seeing the words, wondering what had happened to his little Carrie, as she spun and twirled in the rain, a heathenish practice if ever there was one.

A few minutes later, when he looked up from his Bible, Carrie stood in the open doorway, her garments hanging wet about her, her hair dripping around her head, looking at him, and smiling.

Her smile faded. The two of them kept staring at each other, as unfamiliar one to the other as the day her father summoned her into the parlor, and there stood the stranger who was to be her husband.

Chapter Twenty Five

Isaac came to Carrie, his face ashen. “Can you help?” he asked.

It must be about Rebecca, Carrie thought, as without another word he led her back to the compound and into his house.

Isaac stopped before the barred door of the birthing room. “Hopefully, she will respond to you,” he said, handing her a dish of food.

“I have brought Carrie,” he said to the shut door, “the way you’ve been asking.” He removed the bar, opened the door enough for Carrie to slip through, shut it and, she could hear, re-barred it behind her.

In the small room, Carrie’s eyes took a moment to make out Rebecca, huddled on the floor.

Carrie leaned over, holding the dish in front of her.

Rebecca turned away.

Carrie set the dish down, sat on the floor beside her. “Rebecca,” she began. “It’s Carrie. Can you hear me?”

Rebecca’s head moved up and down.

“Are you sick?”

Rebecca shook her head.

“Well?”

Rebecca nodded.

Carrie took her hand. “I am here.”

Rebecca kept nodding. There were tears in her eyes.

“What? What is it?”

Rebecca started crying, softly at first, then harder, until sobs and convulsions shook her. Carrie wrapped her arms around her, hugged, it seemed, a long time before

Rebecca's crying subsided.

"What? You can tell me."

Rebecca nodded, wiped her eyes. She seemed more composed. As she was about to speak, she started crying again. Carrie reached to hug her some more. All of a sudden, Rebecca jerked away, stopped crying, and huddled back into herself, knees pulled up, arms around them, staring at the floor, as she had been when Carrie came into the room.

After a while she started talking.

She was with child.

Carrie started to smile, stopped. Before, this would have been happy news, after losing one child in a raid, having a second be still born. It did not seem so now.

"Are you glad?"

Rebecca nodded. "A child, with the blessings of the Lord. To make us a family again."

"Is it Isaac's?" Carrie started to ask, stopped. She thought it unlikely. She was there when Rebecca's second child was born dead. She remembered Isaac, his eyes wild, shouting "Sex is Death!" over the still-born deformity. And Rebecca telling how he avoided her after that.

Carrie thought back to when they were both taken captive, went off in different directions. Now, here they were, back again. And Rebecca was pregnant.

They both were quiet.

Carrie broke the silence. "Is it one of them?" she asked.

Rebecca jerked her arm away. What kind of woman did Carrie think she was? She was captured virtuous, came home as she had left. She was not one of those women who did despicable acts with the heathens when no one was looking, and then pretended to virtue when she was recaptured. She went on and on, defending her virtue, expressing her indignation, that Carrie could dare to suggest—

"One of them?" Carrie asked again.

Rebecca slid her hand into her apron pocket, pulled

out her Bible, held it up in front of Carrie. "I had this with me when I was captured. My hand on it let me watch and see and know, suffused with the strength of the Lord. It kept me safe. It kept me free from sin." She raised the Bible again. "And it is with its aid that I am home, the same as when I left."

Rebecca sat quietly, breathing so evenly Carrie thought she was sleeping, until she reached over and took Carrie's hand.

There was a tap on the door. Isaac's muffled voice said, "Carrie, you need to go now."

"Shortly," she answered. She picked the dish up, held it toward Rebecca. "If you are with child, you need to eat."

"I have no appetite."

"For the child."

Rebecca nibbled at the food.

Carrie started to rise.

Rebecca's hand reached over, held her. "You will come tomorrow?"

Carrie squeezed her hand, nodded.

Rebecca shut her eyes. "Thank you," she mouthed.

The door opened. Carrie stepped out. Isaac shut and re-barred the door.

"Did she eat?"

"A little."

"Did she rave?"

Carrie shook her head.

"Why is she like this?"

"I don't know," Carrie answered.

"Has she lost her wits?"

Carrie shook her head. "She knows where she is, knows who she is talking to."

"She is not as she used to be."

"No. Perhaps not."

Neither am I, she thought but did not say. Nor would

you be, if you'd been taken captive and held as long as she was.

"What more should I do?" he asked.

You could treat her like your wife, and share your bed and house with her, instead of keeping her locked up like a prisoner, Carrie thought. All she said was, "I don't know."

"You will come tomorrow?"

Carrie nodded, let herself out the main door, pushed it shut behind her.

The next day Isaac handed her a dish of food and a pitcher of water, let her in, shut and barred the door behind her.

Rebecca, huddled in the same spot on the floor, smiled when she saw Carrie, took her by the hand, stared at her. "What I am about to say, I would not tell anyone other. And if you repeat it, I will deny it."

"I will not tell."

Rebecca nodded, smiled. "I do trust you, sister. I do not know what I would do without you." And without waiting for a response, she went on. "Yes." She paused. "You asked me. Yes; it was one of them."

Carrie nodded. It was as she thought.

"No one forced me. But, in the evening, when my Bible was not in my pocket, and the men danced—" She stopped a moment, half smiled. "This is where I am kept now, because of my sin. Do you think I deserve it?"

Before Carrie could answer, Rebecca went on. "Beware. I hope you did not sin too. I know the temptation, you don't have to tell me: alone; far from here, from everyone, thinking you will never see home again; and the men dancing, and one of them, playing the drum—

"Maybe I shouldn't have told you."

"Does Isaac know?"

Rebecca nodded.

Of course he does, Carrie realized.

"Since my return, I cannot sleep. One night, he found me outside, naked, loving myself. His voice startled me. 'Cover yourself,' he said, flinging the robe I had discarded at me and railing at my nakedness, my evil ways.

"He saw my growing belly, and said, 'You are with child!?'

"'Yes, I am,' I said, 'but it is yours.'"

"'That cannot be, harlot. You have consorted with the Devil. Pray to the Lord for deliverance,' he said. And brought me here to this jail, keeps me locked in here, while he sits outside the door, praying, 'Rid her of these demons.' So I will not tempt him, as the Demons tempted me." She stared off in the distance. "He is my husband, Carrie. Husband and wife is no sin. Isn't it so?"

Carrie nodded.

"He says it is. That I am evil. He will not touch me, has not touched me, will not let me touch him. Aren't I his wife?" She was quiet a moment before going on. "But it is no sin. Didn't you say so, husband and wife. Is it?"

Carrie shook her head, took Rebecca's hands. "Oh, sister. Sister." She pulled her closer, hugged her. They stayed together that way a long time.

Chapter Twenty Six

Carrie missed her time.

She already thought she might be pregnant from her swelling breasts, the queasy way she felt in the morning, a heaviness in everything she did; and a tingling all over her body, as if her skin was alive.

It made her smile. She couldn't, until now, admit how much she wanted another child.

"Mohee," she thought, "we are going to have a baby, a child of our love. Wherever you are, make your hands flap for our child, the way you did your Wren. Can you do that for me?" And she smiled at the thought of his hands making beauty from nothing. Just like a baby, she thought, in her mind hugging him and their child-to-be against her.

She told Rebecca.

"Is it one of them?" Rebecca asked.

In the middle of nodding, Carrie realized: she did not know. It might be Gideon's.

No. It couldn't be. Copulation was not love, even with her "lawful wedded husband."

She tried to remember when she first felt the signs. It was only a few days earlier. Her heart sank. It could be Gideon's. Or Mohee's. She had no way of knowing.

"Do not tell them. Whatever you do, do not let them know."

Carrie nodded. She wanted it to be Mohee's, with all of her being. So she could have this piece of him with her, could still love him in the child.

She was sure it was his. It had to be.

"What if it's born heathen?" Rebecca asked.

Carrie smiled, started to nod. All of a sudden, she

was crying, tears streaming down her face.

"Oh, Carrie." Rebecca hugged her; Carrie hugged her back. Look at what had happened to them. Because of that one afternoon.

Rebecca sat with her ear to the wall.

"What is it?" Carrie asked.

"The drum," Rebecca answered. "Don't you hear it?"

Carrie shook her head.

"There." She pointed toward the wall. "There. You don't hear? It does not stop, day or night. And when you are away. Shh. Look. Look!" She pointed toward the one small window. "They are out there now; if you stand on your toes and look out you can see them, men from the settlement, saying unseemly things, calling me temptress, adulteress, asking me to undo the door, let them do to me as I let the heathens do, that I am damned to hell for doing, saying, they are going burn me here if I do not.

"They are there now. Don't you hear them? Don't you see them? Look. Look!"

"I don't hear anyone."

"There they are, taunting me!"

Carrie stood on her toes, looked out the window. All she saw was the open space at the top of the compound. She heard nothing.

Rebecca sat, hands over her ears, huddled behind the bed. "Go away. Rebecca is gone," she called out. "No more Rebecca."

"No one is there."

"No?" Rebecca smiled. "All gone?"

Carrie nodded, "All gone. It is quiet. See?"

Rebecca peered out, looked around, nodded.

"Is there anything I can do?" Carrie asked.

Rebecca started to laugh. She did not stop.

"Rebecca. Rebecca. it's Carrie. This is not the time."

Rebecca shut her mouth. Her body shook. Laughter

burbled out.

"Please."

Rebecca smiled, nodded, holding it in. It felt so good to let it out, even for a little, the first time she had laughed since her rescue. Carrie must know how hard it was to live and not be able to let your feelings out, to keep them clamped up tight inside. She would not begrudge her a few moments of laughter.

"Laugh then, if you need to. But we are short of time."

Rebecca laughed a moment or two longer and stopped. "It is no matter. Laughing time is past." She fell silent.

Carrie asked about her health.

She was given enough to eat. Carrie knew that. She could not complain there.

What about the child?

Rebecca said she could feel him kicking.

"Already?" Carrie answered.

Rebecca nodded, smiled. "A child is alive in there, Carrie. A child to save our marriage. For Isaac to love again, as he loved our Paul, doted on him." Her smile changed to a frown. "Only one thing. What if it's a heathen child. What is going to happen to him?"

Carrie didn't know.

"And if it's a girl?"

Carrie didn't answer.

Rebecca asked if there were any heathens around.

"None that I know of," Carrie answered, thinking of Tiki and Mohee and the old woman.

"No more raids?"

"Not in a while. Everyone says we have triumphed."

Rebecca sat with her eyes shut. "I hear the drum." She smiled.

"Again?"

Rebecca nodded. "So loud and clear. You don't hear it?"

"No."

"There." Rebecca pointed through the wall. "It is back. It is even louder."

"I hear nothing."

"Listen. Listen!"

Carrie listened. All she heard was silence.

Rebecca listened a moment. "Now it is gone. It comes and goes, comes and goes. It feels nicer when he is here, the drummer. He is my friend. He talks to me; he listens to me. He doesn't think what we did was bad." She sat with her eyes still shut. "Are you still there?"

"I am."

"Can you get me out of here?"

"I don't think so."

"Try."

"I will."

"Can you get Isaac to take me back?"

"I don't think so."

"Can you get them to?"

"I don't know."

"If you can—" Rebecca spoke in fits and starts. "I don't know anymore if I am bad or not. Am I, Carrie, the way he says?"

Before Carrie could answer, she went on.

"Maybe if I get away I won't be bad. Don't you think. Otherwise—" She stopped, opened her eyes. "I don't know if I am going to make it."

She said it so quietly, Carrie barely heard.

Carrie took her hands, squeezed them.

"I see the baby," Rebecca said, smiling, imagining, Carrie knew, the child already born.

"I can't see if it's a boy or girl, dark or fair. It doesn't matter. It is mine.

"My breasts hurt; they are swollen. Come, baby, come to the nipple." Rebecca held her arms together as if a baby, wrapped in swaddling clothes, was in them, nursing;

after a minute she moved it away from her breast, rocked it back and forth, talking and singing to it.

"Do you like her nursery?" She smiled, looking around at the room. "A room for a child of God. Yes?

"And you know what will happen," she went on. "Isaac will love me again. I know he will. The child is his. He is my husband, sworn to in eternal vows taken before God. I have never known any other man. I swear it on my Bible." She held up the pocket of her apron.

"The child will make everything right, Carrie. All will be well again.

"I never was captured. Don't let anyone say otherwise. That was a dream that never happened, a bad one, over and done with. I am awake now. The child is his."

Carrie watched her, swaying back and forth, the imaginary child in her arms.

Rebecca leaned over, as if nuzzling its nose.

Rock a bye, baby, in a tree top...

Suddenly she stopped swaying. "Isaac," she said, talking to her husband through the door. "The child is yours. Born of our union, here, at the edge, the way you say, where the savage and the civilized meet.

"After all these years, our marriage will have a child again. Our home will be a happy one, with the sound of a baby, a child of hope, a child of promise. Nothing will take it away from us." She smiled, started swaying with the baby again. "Our union will be blessed, as it was before."

Chapter Twenty Seven

Carrie was in the kitchen, kneading bread for dinner, pushing it back and forth, her hands covered with yeasty dough, staring out at the woods. She remembered playing patty-cake with Hannah, slapping doughy hands together. It seemed like years before.

She pushed down onto the counter. She had been back not even a month. It seemed longer, seemed forever that Gideon treated her like dough, beat and pounded and shoved, trying to reshape her until she fit into the pans, like the wearing of her old shoes that still left her feet bloody and raw.

Carrie stopped a moment, dough thick on her fingers, wiped her cheek with her sleeve. She realized what she felt most every morning when she opened her eyes, every day as it went along, was dread, a weight as heavy as unleavened bread sitting in the bottom of her heart.

She started working and shaping the dough with a kind of frantic desperation, thinking of his reaction when she told him, in response to hints of fulfilling their conjugal duty, that she had missed her time.

"There is going to be another little one?" Gideon beamed, awkwardly hugged her to him, pecked her on the cheek. "A son? A daughter? To start again in the wilderness. To make us a family again." There were tears in his eyes. "Virtue triumphs! Thank you, Lord. We have conquered." He turned to her, smiling. "We can name him Isaac!"

"No!" Carrie started to say, but he had already gone on.

"Or, if it's a girl, Sarah or Mary, if Isaac thinks it proper to use the name again."

He still did not know how that felt, how the mention, even now, of Mary's death stabbed at her heart.

In that one moment, the canyon between them grew so wide she could see his mouth moving but could barely hear what he was saying.

From across the abyss she made out, "Isaac will want to know."

No, he will not, Carrie thought, No, Do not tell him, please, as if not telling him would keep him from knowing.

She wanted the child for her and Mohee, a part of him still with her, to birth and raise, nurture and love. If it was a boy, to be like Tiki, to run in the woods, listen to rain, stop to watch Many Legs. In one breath, that was gone. The child is mine, Gideon was saying, to raise like Paul, toyless and joyless.

She looked at Gideon almost laughing in his happiness, and somewhere inside she died.

Even then, she might have kept trying, hoping to make what seemed the only way tolerable, except, the next day, as a light rain fell, interspersed with rumbles of thunder, she walked toward the compound, on her daily visit to Rebecca, later than usual, between supper and dark, going the back way, stopping to look out at the woods, wondering if Mohee was still there, or Tiki, or the old woman, or any of their group, until she recalled her errand and hurried on. Above, thunder rolled, low and steady.

She started to push open the wooden door that led into the compound. From inside she heard a man's voice. She stopped.

"Why do you tempt me thus, Lord? Why?" It was Isaac, speaking loudly. "What do You want of me?"

It rained harder.

"She is the serpent, but I shall triumph. This new Eden will not be lost because of her." The voice was quiet.

Slowly Carrie pushed the door open, peered in. Thirty feet away, not far from the house, stood a man and a woman. The one facing her was Isaac. Who the woman was Carrie could not tell, but her hands were tied behind her.

"Rebecca?" Carrie started to say, stopped, as her

supper rose into her throat. She swallowed.

Isaac began removing his clothes.

Carrie watched, mouth open, as more and more of his clothes fell away.

Was this her brother, who railed so against nakedness, kept locked in a room his unfaithful wife, and here, button by button—

Yes. It was. Of that there could be no doubt.

Carrie continued to watch, fascinated and horrified. She should not, she knew, but could not make herself leave.

Isaac took off his shirt, boots, pants, dropped them in a pile on the ground. "Now yours," he shouted, his words disappearing in the rumble of thunder. He jerked a rope Carrie had not noticed, that ran around the woman's waist, was tied to a post beside him. He pulled her toward him, grabbed her top by the collar, ripped part of it off.

The woman turned around, started to run. The rope jerked her back.

"Now!" Isaac shouted, ripping off more clothes.

What was going on? Carrie wondered. What was her brother doing?

It rained even harder, sheets of large drops splatting all around them.

Who was this woman? Carrie wondered. It was not Rebecca. But who? And why?

In moments, Isaac and the woman stood facing each other, fully unclothed, as the rain changed to hail, a storm of it, bouncing off their heads and arms, clacking and clattering on the ground. More kept falling, harder, faster.

Carrie put her arms above her, trying to protect her head from the falling pellets of ice, but otherwise she stood, not moving. She could not stop watching.

The woman moved back and forth like an angry cat, hissing, Carrie heard in a lull.

More thunder rolled, closer, longer. The wind blew, stronger and steadier.

Isaac scooped up a handful of ice from the ground,

held it against his chest, rubbed it over his arms, his stomach. "Submit," she heard him call out over the wind. "Submit to the will of the Lord!" He scooped up more ice, rubbed it over his legs, his thighs.

"No." He bellowed, beating his chest.

He reached toward the woman. Her mouth closed on his hand. "Aggh!" he howled, "Vixen!" He grabbed her hair with the other hand, yanked back. Her mouth opened; he pulled his hand free.

Then he and the woman were falling onto the ground.

Carrie turned away. She knew she should leave. She could not make herself do it.

There she remained, half sick, not watching, but listening despite herself to the wind and the thunder and the sounds of the man and the woman, huffing and grunting like animals.

What fault was it of hers that kept her there, she wondered, spying on others?

And what was happening? Was Isaac indeed committing the crime too horrible to mention, there in front of her?

The huffing and grunting increased. Thunder rolled; the wind roared. A noise from the compound startled her. She heard a loud thwack, followed by a moan. She could not help looking. Even in the almost dark, she could make out Isaac, naked and lying face down, thrashing about, and the woman beneath him. As he thrashed, his hand brought her head down on the ground, thwack. A loud moan followed; another thwack, another moan.

Carrie stood as if frozen. Before she could move or think what to do, Isaac yelled "Yes!", there was a final "Thwack!", a louder moan, and Isaac, and the woman, lay still.

It hailed harder. Small pieces of ice accumulated inches deep on the ground all around her.

Isaac pushed himself away from the woman, shouted words Carrie could not make out up at the sky, and sat back on his haunches, on the ice; beside him the woman lay, as if sleeping.

The wind blew louder. It whistled through the tops of the wooden boards of the compound's fence. Thunder rolled. The ground shook.

As it reached its worst, Isaac lifted his head and began speaking.

Carrie heard only a word here, another word there, the wind and thunder drowning him out. "Lord," she heard, several times. He pointed at the woman, pointed toward the sky, the dark lit by sudden flashes of lightning.

Isaac went on and on, gesturing to the elements. Then he stood, brushed the ice off his bottom, speaking the whole time. He seemed to be preaching, pointing down at the woman one moment, up at the heavens the next.

A moment later the hail turned back to rain, pouring down. A flash of lightning lit the air. A crash of thunder clapped so fast and so close the whole compound shook.

Carrie stood petrified, the ground rumbling beneath her feet. Was this her punishment for not leaving?

No. The target appeared to be Isaac.

The next flash spiked down toward him, seemed to end a few feet above his head. In the same instant, thunder cracked and rolled and boomed.

The flash lit up Isaac's face. He looked so pale and contorted, for a moment she thought, It is the Devil, with the fires of hell raging around him. A moment later she corrected herself: No, it is Isaac.

Isaac raised his arms into the night, spoke to the dark. She heard nothing, only the wind and thunder.

There was another flash, and another, first on one side of him, then the other, as if the Lord were the whip master, making him dance, but Isaac's feet did not move. They remained anchored in the firmament. He turned around, looking at the sky, preaching to the night.

Rain pelted him, matting his hair down, streaming down his naked body. Lightning flashed on one side and another, silhouetting him against the night. The earth rumbled so loudly Carrie expected a chasm to open at her feet.

Through it all Isaac remained standing, strong and resolute.

"My Lord!" he shouted at the night as the thunder subsided, raising his arms toward the sky, "I am Yours."

By the time Carrie reached home, walking slowly, stopping from time to time, trying to make sense of what she had seen, her teeth were chattering. The wind, rain, thunder and lightning had vanished as quickly as they came. In the west, along the horizon, there was already a thin line of light where the sky was clearing.

Gideon stood in the door way. "You are wet, even for you."

"I was caught in the storm."

"No sorceress gave you warning?"

She shook her head. "No. It surprised me."

Gideon surveyed her. "Your attire is hardly seemly. Cover yourself." He reached behind him, handed her her cape. "You have no time to change."

"Change for what?" she asked. Did she not know? She shook her head. Know what? They had been summoned to the church. "Now?" she asked.

"Now," he nodded. Isaac had repulsed an attack. The attendance of all was required.

Chapter Twenty Eight

"Tonight, the Lord has given me a sign," Isaac began when their small congregation was seated, with nothing more by way of an introduction.

He was wearing, Carrie noticed, clean dry clothes, as if what she saw didn't happen. But it did. She had seen him not that long before, wet and naked in the rain and hail and thunder. Was she deceived by the shadows and the flashes of lightning? She stared at him; he looked the same as he always did, except that his hair seemed wet.

"You know me, my brethren." Isaac's voice rose. "I never rest. I never cease my vigilance on your behalf. You know it is because of me that you are all sitting here safely, and will sleep secure in your beds tonight, no matter how much the lightning flashes and the thunder rumbles. Are there any among you who doubt this?"

There was no sound as Isaac looked around at the congregation, no movement save a few heads shaking from side to side.

"You are right to trust in me. Tonight, you felt the ferocious storm we had, and as God-fearing believers, you were afraid, were you not? You had no need to be. You know why? It was the Lord testing me and sending me a sign. I stood, alone and unprotected, while the storm lashed around me, and here I stand, now, triumphant.

"What you do not know is that earlier, while you were in your homes, digesting your suppers, reading Scripture, preparing your little ones for bed, I repulsed yet another heathen attack, another outrage that might have killed all of you, and that none of you were aware of.

"Even though two sisters of ours, by my diligence, are returned to the fold, our enemy does not rest. No. The godless heathens have not given up. You may think so, but I know better. I am zealous in defense. I am zealous in attack, and today, while none of you thought of the danger near at hand, I made a raid. Close to here, too close for comfort, I came upon a rapacious party of heathens, planning to attack when we were not suspecting. But I surprised them. I attacked first. Two of them I wounded. A third, a young woman, I took prisoner. Why? Because the Lord God told me to.

"I was wise to listen to the words of the Lord, wise to learn in what pleasing shapes the Devil might appear.

"As soon as we were within the walls of our compound, while the storm raged, this licentious heathen began removing her clothing and, crazed by the lusts that destroy, she attacked me. But virtue triumphed! Though she was most pleasing to look at, I knew she was the Devil in disguise, and I repulsed her. I did battle with the Universal Enemy of Mankind, and, once again, I have emerged triumphant! I did this for you. Which of you would have done the same?"

His speech done, Isaac reached to his left, took hold of a cloth that Carrie had not noticed and pulled it toward him, revealing a naked heathen woman, lying on her belly.

A gasp rose from the congregation.

Carrie felt her stomach turn over. It was true. There no longer was any doubt. The woman was dead, her head turned at a grotesque angle, her eyes still open.

Looking more closely, Carrie had to clasp her hands over her mouth to keep from crying out. The woman was Running Deer, Mohee's sister.

"Now go," Isaac's voice boomed out, "and when you return to the safety of your homes, and bolt your doors for the night, do not forget who did this for you."

He stepped down from the pulpit, stood by it, silently watching while the couples filed out, the men staring at the lifeless shape, or looking a moment, turning away, turning back to look longer, the women hurrying by, their eyes on the ground.

Carrie felt dizzy. Everything spun. There she was,

Running Deer, Quick Flashes' wife. Isaac did this to her. Carrie had seen it.

Carrie and Gideon were the last to leave. She couldn't stand. She couldn't move. She sat, mouth half open, staring at the dead woman.

"Carrie," Gideon whispered to her as he stood up. "Everyone else is gone. Isaac is waiting. Let us go." Carrie made no response. She kept staring at Running Deer's face. It seemed to be both in pain and at peace. "Carrie. Carrie!"

"What?"

"We need to leave." She nodded. She couldn't take her eyes off Running Deer. "Come."

Slowly she turned toward Gideon. "It is time for us to go." She nodded again.

With Gideon lifting her under one arm, Carrie was able to stand. Once she was up, he held her steady and led her out, one small step after another, Isaac watching the entire time.

Outside, she hadn't gone five feet before her knees buckled. She would have fallen if Gideon hadn't grabbed her and held her up. "Is it the sickness, my little Carrie?" She nodded.

"You must take care. You must not upset yourself; try not to think about it if it bothers you. You have to protect the little one."

With Gideon's support, Carrie took a step, stopped, took another step.

"Would you have believed it?" Gideon said. "That things which seem so fair can be so evil? I would not have known, I confess it. But thanks be to heaven Isaac did."

On they walked in the same slow way, Carrie leaning on him. Gideon patted her hand, smiled. "We are beginning to be a family again, are we not? Is it not the way Isaac says: virtue triumphs over evil!"

Carrie turned her head toward him, her eyes wide, and as quickly turned away. No, she thought, staring at the dark ground in front of her. It was not as Isaac said. He took his own clothes off, ripped Running Deer's off her. She was tied up, a prisoner. He threw her on the ground, and he— Carrie took a breath. He committed the crime too horrible to mention. He did that. To her. Carrie saw it all, in the storm. And he lied about it. Running Deer did nothing. Her hands were bound. He was the one who did it, who violated her, and then blamed her. And everyone believed him.

Carrie's heart pounded. She was panting. A little urine dribbled down the insides of her legs. Her mouth was dry. She couldn't swallow. She couldn't move. She couldn't feel her hands, couldn't feel her feet; she couldn't feel anything but the warmth of the urine on her legs. But somehow she was walking forward, right foot, left foot, right foot, left foot.

When they finally did reach home, she opened her mouth to speak. No sound came out.

Gideon sat her on the bench inside the front door. "Rest a moment, and soon you can go to bed."

Carrie grabbed his hand. "Isaac."

"Don't think of it if it upsets you. Didn't I say that. It only proves what Isaac has so often said: you know no one by their words. Only by their deeds."

She saw Running Deer's face, again, as it was in the church. Saw it again in the storm, as Isaac ripped her clothes off and pounded her head up and down. Carrie crossed her arms over her chest, leaned forward. "Running Deer. Running Deer." Her mouth formed the words, softly made the sounds, mourning her friend and what had happened to her. She started to cry.

"Carrie." Gideon patted her on the shoulder. "Come, my little Carrie." He tried to get her to stand. "Dry your eyes. It is time for bed."

"Earlier; this evening." Carrie stopped to catch her breath. Her heart still pounded. Gideon hovered over her. "Let me speak." She took another breath. "I was going to visit Rebecca—"

"Rebecca?" She nodded. "Haven't you heard the interdiction?"

"Interdiction?"

"We are to have no discourse with her. She is under

observation as a sorceress." What was he talking about? "And you were going to see her? How long has this gone on? Answer me." Carrie held up her hand. "No one is to see her. Don't you understand? The Devil takes pleasing and familiar shapes. You know this full well." He gestured toward the church.

"Isaac asked me to." Carrie spoke slowly; it took great effort to say those few words. "I have not done this in secret."

"He knew?"

Carrie nodded. "Yes." She started to cry again.

Gideon patted her hand. "My sweet wife, try not to think about it. Didn't we just agree about that."

"He did it."

"Who? Did what?

"Didn't you see?" She gestured toward the church.

"What are you talking about? Why are you not answering me? What do you do when you go to 'visit' Rebecca?"

Carrie looked at him. "Rebecca?"

"Yes, Rebecca. Why do you keep repeating what I am saying? What is wrong with you?"

Carrie shook her head, unable to speak. Inside she was crying. She felt broken in two, cleaved down the middle.

"What – do – you – do," Gideon spoke slowly, with a pause between each word, "when – you – go – to – visit – Rebecca?"

"I take her food."

"Isaac knows of this?" She nodded. "And you have not been influenced by her?"

"Influenced?"

"She has not tried to convert you to sorcery?"

Carrie shook her head. "I saw—"

Gideon's eyes were shut, his hands clasped before him, and he was praying, mouthing the same phrases over and over.

"I saw him, my brother—." Gideon opened his eyes, held a finger to his lips. "Please listen!"

"That is how evil must be dealt with. Whatever shape it takes. Are you questioning what Isaac did?"

Carrie heard a cry. In front of her she saw the vision she couldn't get out of her head: Running Deer in the compound, in the storm, Isaac tearing off more of her clothes, ripping them away, throwing her to the ground, climbing on top of her, holding her in place by the hair, bringing her head up and down on a rock, harder and harder. Thwack! She moaned. Thwack!! She moaned louder.

Carrie felt nauseous. With great effort, she stood, took a step toward the door.

Gideon looked up from the Good Book. "Where are you off to at this hour of the night? You are not trying to see the sorceress again?"

Carrie shook her head, pulled the door open, barely made it outside before she was sick.

"Oh, my sweet wife." Gideon was beside her, comforting. "Try not to think about such matters. They only upset you. Come." He led her inside, toward the bedroom. "We won't talk about it further. You need to rest."

Carrie sat on the bed. Gideon patted her hand, moved back to his place, opened the Good Book. In moments he was lost in his reading, his finger following the phrases while his lips moved.

In her head, Carrie repeated the words she desperately wanted to say: "Listen to me. Please." She saw herself in the church, interrupting Isaac and his fictions about Running Deer. She was standing by the pulpit, addressing the congregation: "What he said is not true. She was not a Devil or a licentious heathen. She did not attack him. He attacked her. He ripped her clothes off, threw her to the ground. He committed the crime too horrible to mention. And then he lied about it." She looked around at the congregation. "I knew this woman. I walked with her, in snow and rain, cold and heat, hunger, famine and feasting. I was jealous of her in the Long River, consoled her when her husband died. She was the sister of the man I love, a person, like you, or me, or any of us. And she was innocent."

They sat staring at her, their expressions unchanging. Carrie couldn't go on. They didn't believe her. None of them did. Why should they? Isaac was their Minister. He was their leader.

In the next room, Gideon's finger lifted a page, turned it.

Carrie started to cry again, not loudly but deeply, like the quiet steadiness of rain on the trees.

"Carrie." Gideon's voice came from the other room, his eyes never leaving the page. "You're not resting. What did we say about that? Be a good girl and go to sleep."

Carrie sat, not sleeping, staring in front of her at the shut door of the bedroom, up into the dark above, not seeing Many Legs, not seeing anything but Isaac with Running Deer, the flashes of lightning showing his face in the rain, his hands in the air, his fists in her hair.

The scene kept repeating over and over. With each repetition, it became more vivid and terrifying, until Carrie was shaking, uncontrollably. Lightning flashed around her; rain pelted her cheeks. It was *her* hair Isaac clenched in his fists, *her* head he banged on the ground. Thwack; thwack! Thwack!!

Carrie rocked back and forth, faster and faster, her fingers twined in her own hair, pulling it, harder and harder, trying to get the vision out of her head.

Then she was crying quietly. Slowly it grew stronger until sobs wracked and convulsed her. She hugged her pillow to her face, trying to mute the noise, while she stayed there, rocking and sobbing, rocking and sobbing.

She must have slept. She opened her eyes. It was morning. She was lying in bed. Beside her, Gideon softly snored.

Her head hurt. Her mouth was dry.

She put her hands to her temples, slid them up to the top of her head, her fingers undoing the knots in her hair. She remembered, months earlier, sitting on a rock by a pool of clear water, with a loud waterfall below. The old woman sat behind her, her fingers stroking and soothing as they pulled out the tangles, wove and braided her hair. When she was done, Carrie leaned her head back on the old woman's knee, feeling at peace.

Chapter Twenty Nine

The following morning, Isaac's serving girl came to summon Carrie. Isaac needed her. It was urgent.

Carrie was alarmed. What does he want of me? she wondered, so early in the day, and on the Sabbath too. Does he know I saw him with Running Deer?

The farther they went, the more slowly she walked. When the serving girl pushed open the door into the compound, Carrie took a few steps into it and stopped.

This is where it happened, where Isaac ravished Running Deer. There was the post he tied her to. That was where he was standing, two feet from her. And there was the rock he pounded her head on. Carrie felt sick. She swayed, held on to the post to steady herself, shut her eyes.

The serving girl tugged her sleeve. "Please, Miss Carrie. Reverend Isaac is waiting."

And then, there Isaac was, standing between the house and the church. The serving girl curtsied and left. Carrie's stomach tightened. Her ears rang. Her throat constricted.

Isaac stood, unmoving. He seemed the same as he always did, wearing his Sabbath clothes, proper and respectable, but his face was deathly pale.

Carrie stopped. She couldn't go closer to him, couldn't look at him. Her eyes darted from side to side, up and down. Goose flesh stood up along her arms, on the back of her neck. She wanted to turn, run screaming away. She couldn't move. She shut her eyes, drew in a deep breath, trying to calm herself. Slowly she exhaled, opened her eyes.

Isaac walked toward the church. Carrie followed, keeping her distance. He entered by the side door, went to the pulpit. She stopped just inside the door. Except for the two of them, the church was empty.

What now? Her breath came in quick, short gasps. Her insides were in turmoil. Her knees were weak, her face cold. She was afraid she would faint. She grabbed the railing in front of a pew, squeezed it as hard as she could.

Isaac took a step to the side, pointed behind him. At the same moment, Carrie heard a sigh, and, glancing where he pointed, saw in the shadows a shape, the back of what appeared to be a naked woman, huddled on the floor. Running Deer, she thought. No, it couldn't be. This person was alive. And her skin was pale. Isaac addressed the shape. "Here's Carrie. Will you speak to her?" The shape turned her head.

"Oh!" Carrie brought her hand to her mouth. It was Rebecca, and she was indeed naked.

Carrie removed her cape, stepped toward Rebecca, draped it over her.

Rebecca looked at Carrie a moment without any sign of recognition, then shrugged her shoulders. The cape slid off onto the floor beside her.

Carrie knelt in front of her, put her hands on either side of Rebecca's face. "I am here, sister." Carrie kissed her on the cheek. "Do you know me?" Still no response from Rebecca. With her hands, Carrie tried to lift Rebecca's face. "You can talk to me." Rebecca said nothing, did not look at her, and when Carrie's hands relaxed, turned her face away.

There was so much Carrie wanted to know. She couldn't talk about any of it with Isaac there.

Behind her Isaac was speaking. "I found her here when I came to prepare for my sermon. I don't know how she got out. She was raving all night. Perhaps in my distraction I left the door unbarred. I don't know why she is ungarbed like this." The sound of his voice curdled Carrie's stomach. She wanted to clamp her hands over her ears, shut the sound out. She couldn't. Rebecca needed her.

"I have tried reasoning with her. It is as if she doesn't hear me. She cannot remain here. The congregation will be in shortly. Wife." He looked down. "Why do you persist in this stubbornness? Have you lost your wits?" Rebecca stared at the floor. He looked at Carrie. "Can you make her leave? We have very little time."

Again Carrie soothed Rebecca's face with her hands, spoke softly, caressing with her voice, urging Rebecca to come, to walk with her back to her house. We can talk there, she thought, when we are alone. Carrie took her elbow, trying to coax her up, grasped her arm, trying to pull her along. She received no response, no movement to follow, no sign that Rebecca knew Carrie or understood where she was or why she needed to leave. "Please," Carrie pleaded.

Another shape squatted beside her. It was Isaac, speaking gently, if force would not work, trying kindness. He was talking softly, almost intimately, as a husband would to a wife he loved, with no one near to hear. He spoke about them, their past, being in England together, sailing to Boston; the life they made together; all the tribulations they had undergone. "I understand all is not as you wish, but if you come with us, now—." Rebecca did not respond.

Isaac took her hand and began again. "We can go to Boston, wife, the way you have longed for. We can leave now. Isn't that what you want? Why do you not respond? Why will you not leave?" He coaxed, he cajoled, he commanded. To all he said, Rebecca made no response, no blink, look or stare that showed she understood.

While Isaac was pleading with her, question after question ran through Carrie's mind. Did Rebecca know somehow about Isaac and Running Deer? She must, but how? They had been right outside her window. Of course. She must have heard Isaac in the storm, looked out and seen them. And then— It became clear as Carrie thought it through: Rebecca confronted him and he denied it, denied he had any concourse with Running Deer, denied her again and again as his wife.

"It is true," Carrie wanted to tell her. "You didn't imagine it. You haven't lost your wits. It really happened. I know. I saw too. He is the one who did this. He is the one who is lying." But she couldn't say it, or whisper it, or tell her by a hug, not with Isaac there. If only Rebecca would go back to the house with her.

"Won't you come with me, sister?" Carrie asked one more time, touching Rebecca's arm, and speaking as gently as she could. "Please!" Still, Rebecca did not respond.

There was no more time.

Isaac, standing above her, leaned over, took hold of Rebecca's arm, indicated for Carrie on the other side to do the same. Together, they tried to lift her. She was too heavy, and of her own did not move, but stared straight ahead into the darkness between them, her jaw set.

At the same moment, they heard voices. "It is too late." Isaac let go of her, straightened back up. His tone had changed when he spoke again. "I am sorry it has come to this. But remember, you brought it on yourself." He reached behind him, took a spread, the same one, Carrie noticed, that had covered Running Deer. He draped it over his wife, and whispered to Carrie, "Join your husband in your usual spot. You know nothing of this."

Carrie picked up her cape, sat beside Gideon in their pew, leaned forward, her head in her hands, still not wanting to believe what she had just seen. After a minute she sat back, looked forward, her hands clenched so tightly her fingernails dug into the palms.

Isaac stood beside the pulpit, nodding his greeting to the parishioners as they took their seats.

If she had not knelt beside her moments before, Carrie would not have known Rebecca was there, or that anything was amiss. As it was, she thought perhaps she imagined it, and all was as it should be. Isaac's calm demeanor seemed to support this. She hoped he would deliver his usual sermon, making no mention of his wife, and by the time it ended and everyone left, Rebecca would have returned to her senses, and would let Carrie lead her, arm in arm, back to her room.

As soon as Isaac began, Carrie knew that was not to be.

He made his text, If thine eye offend thee, pluck it out. If thy hand offend thee, cut it off.

"Here we live, my brethren," he began, "at the edge of the wilderness, where, if we are not vigilant, demons turn us into beasts and destroy us. We are none of us immune. My own wife." He pulled the cloth off. There she was, huddled and naked, at his feet.

There was a sound of surprise. The whole congregation inhaled at once, and then, "Oh, no," from one. "Rebecca?" from another. A deeper "Oh, No!" from several others. People sat at the edge of their pews. Some turned away. Others stared, wide-eyed.

Isaac waited until they were all silent and still before going on.

"In Eve's fall, we sinned all. Is this not true?" he thundered. "Here you see my own wife, who is Eve's flesh, who is virtuous, as you know, who believes, as all of you believe. If someone came to me yesterday, even this morning, and told me I would see what I see now, I would have said they were deceived, to stop spreading rumors and gossip about a member of our congregation. I would not have believed it. But now—

"Do you believe it, my brethren, what you see with your own eyes? She, this woman I have shared my bed with, and my life, and the sacred covenant of marriage, is destroyed. Why? Because, alone among the heathens, she gave in to temptation. She could not control herself. Can you? Consider her and her fate. She is the exemplum for you all, there, naked, with her belly swelling with the fruits of her evil. You know where that came from, from a virtuous daughter of Eve having concourse with the Devil."

Carrie cringed at Isaac's words, tried to shrink down lower and lower until she disappeared. She did not want to see or hear what was happening. But, do what she could, she could not shut it out. Finally she sat up straight, looked around. Here Rebecca, this sister they had all shared hopes and hardships with, was being shamed and vilified, and no one was speaking up for her. No one rose to defend her. They all sat nodding in agreement.

Carrie slid forward in the pew. Gideon put his hand on her arm. "What are you doing?" he whispered.

"I'm going to cover her with my cloak."

"You will do no such thing."

"Then I will stand in front of her."

"You will stay where you are," Gideon said, grabbing her and pulling her back.

"Here, at the edge of the wilderness, we are beset with temptations." Isaac's voice rose. It echoed off the wooden rafters. Like a stake it transfixed his parishioners. No one moved.

"They hedge us in. People all over, in other towns, in cities, in England, they do not think we are strong enough, they do not believe we are devout enough. They are waiting for us to fail, for the wilderness that surrounds us to turn us into beasts and destroy us. These are the temptations we face every day. If even my beloved Rebecca can come to this, we all may succumb. None of us are immune. None." He grew quiet. No one stirred.

"The evils of Hell. The wages of sin. They are not off in the Bible, or back in England, or even in Boston. They are here, every day, among us.

"Triumph over the heathen. That is easy, with our guns and our righteousness. Can we also triumph over ourselves, resist sin and evil, not slide back when we think no one is looking? The Lord is looking, my good people. He is always looking. Even if a woman goes on a ten-day march from here," he pointed down at Rebecca, "where none of us knows what she is doing, if she strays, He will see her. He will know. And He will punish her.

"If we go out in the wilderness, we can survive." Isaac was shouting. Sweat streamed down his face. "We can eat, kill wild beasts, make shelter, as we have shown. We have done that here, and we have prospered. Can we also survive as true, righteous believers? Can we preserve our moral spirit? or have we become like these very heathens we think we have defeated? Are they in fact defeating us?

"All of us are weak. All of us are born sinners. Even in my own family we know temptation. Even in my own family we know sin. Who among us is without sin? Who can stand up and say, 'Me, Lord! I am as innocent as Adam and Eve in the Garden?' Who?" He looked around his congregation from face to face, stared from eye to eye. "None of us!" He roared. "We are all guilty! And we also are without the strength to resist whatever temptations the Devil will bring, and rest assured, he will bring more and more until he defeats us, unless we submit to our Lord. Submit!" he screamed, holding his right hand high in the air. "Then, and only then, will we triumph. If we trust in Him." He pointed toward the heavens and paused before going on.

"If we do not, we are doomed to eternal damnation, each and every one of us." He again pointed down at his Rebecca, staring at the floor. "And, as it is here with the creature that was my wife, the promise of this new beginning, of this second Eden, is as lost to us as the first."

Chapter Thirty

Walking home, Gideon seemed agitated. He moved slowly, Carrie's arm in his. He stopped, stared at her for so long she said, "What? What is it?" He shook his head, walked a few more feet, stopped again. He took her with both hands by the shoulders and turned her toward him, examining her as if he would know what was behind the face he saw.

"Gideon, you are frightening me. What is bothering you? Tell me."

"Forgive me for asking, but the child you are carrying, is it mine?"

Carrie nodded quickly, held her breath.

"Of that there can be no doubt?"

She nodded again, more slowly.

"Why can you not say it?" Before she could answer, he went on. "I believe, my dear wife, you are a good, loyal, virtuous woman, and have been, steadfastly so, but Isaac's wife Rebecca was virtuous above reproach, and we have seen what we would not have believed had we only heard it." He paused. "I have witnessed how you, my wife, have changed. The Carrie who returned is not the one who left. I have not asked why. I have not wanted to know. It may well be from the shock of losing a child, of being away so long from those you love, of being forced to live with godless heathens with no word from us, no hope of rescue. I understand that, and can be patient until you are yourself again. But I need to know." He was breathing quickly. He looked pale. "Is the child mine?"

"Mine?" Carrie wondered, as she looked down at the toe of her black leather shoe protruding from under her dress. The way Mohee accepts Tiki, the white man's son, as his own? Or Hannah as Wren's sister? No, she thought, that is not what he was asking.

She raised her head, fixed her eyes on his, nodded.

"Why can you not say it?" He asked again.

She paused a moment, opened her mouth. "The child is my husband's."

"Of that you have no doubt?"

Carrie was sweating. "Of that I have no doubt," she said, still without averting her eyes.

"Thank the Lord! Virtue triumphs!" Gideon let out a tremendous sigh, gave Carrie a peck on the cheek, and almost skipped the rest of the way home, while Carrie stood, watching him.

She thought of all she had said or had tried to say, then, the day before, every day since her return, that he never heard or was not ready to hear, that she would not think of saying now. That this was the first time she had missed. It might be his, it might not be. In either case, it was her "husband's." She did not lie.

If she could not tell him this, if he had no interest in hearing it, everything she went through while she was gone did not matter. She was not a person all this happened to, only his house cleaner and cook, nothing more. For the period when she was not there, the hardest and happiest and unhappiest times of her life, she did not exist for him. And, she finally realized, she never had.

She had seen how her brother responded to his own wife, that he loved once as much as Gideon loved her. Carrie was mortified as he shamed Rebecca. She felt as if buckets of ice-cold water were being dumped over her. And poor Rebecca—

What he did to his wife he would surely do to his sister. Maybe worse. They were blood. He would not let her impugn his good name. And, in all that, Gideon would join him.

Her skin crawled at the thought, as if she sat down on an anthill and dozens of black ants scurried over her hands and arms and legs, biting as they went. She could not remain there, carrying a child that might be heathen.

Nothing could be clearer.

It wasn't until Carrie was kneading bread that afternoon, delighting in her changing body and in the warm rough texture of dough on her hands, that she fully believed she was going to leave, to walk out the door, down the hill, into the woods, and never come back.

A tingle went down the entire inside of her being, the way it did when Mohee made magic with his hands. Every pore was alive.

The bread was beaten two, three, four times past shaping while the thoughts crystallized in her head. It was in its pans, in the oven and baking while she worked them through. It was tender brown and ready to come out, the last bread she would bake in this house, before she knew how she would do it.

It was not about Mohee, she told herself a hundred times over, though she loved him more than she could imagine loving anyone else. If she found him, yes, a thousand times yes. That the woman captured was Running Deer, *his* sister, meant he was near, she was sure of it, so close that if she called his name he might hear and answer. Her heart leapt up at the thought.

But, she reminded herself, trying to temper her joy, she did not know if he was alive. Or, if he was, that he was here. In the time she had been back, he could have walked as far north as Canada, west to Lake Champlain, east to the ocean. She might never find him, or Tiki, or the old woman, or any that she knew. She hoped she did. She would surely try until hope was gone. But if she did not, in her time with them she had learned enough of their ways to know that, even by herself, she could survive.

It might be meager. She knew it would be difficult—fishing, hunting, trapping, skinning, gathering plants, roots, berries, nuts—but she also knew she could do it. She could keep herself and her child alive.

Whereas if she stayed, no matter how well cared for—

She took from the drawer two of the knives, tested their sharpness, dropped them into the pocket of her apron. She would be glad she had them. But, she knew, they would not be enough.

While the bread was out of its pans and cooling on the counter, she would gather a few items into a bundle, take them down into the woods, walk to the first stream, or even as far as the second, leave them not far from the path, behind a rock, where she could find them but someone else not be likely to stumble on them. Her cape she would take. The knives. Food, enough to get her through two or three days of walking: meat left over from the last night's meal. A raw potato or two. An early apple. One of the loaves of bread. And, most important of all—

Earlier she had walked through the compound, looking this way and that, thinking about Isaac and Running Deer. A few feet from the door leading out of it she found a moccasin. She almost didn't notice it, lying upside down against the fence. Her heart stopped when she saw it. It was hers. It had to be, the same shape and color. But, she realized as she picked it up, it wasn't. It was Running Deer's. She recognized the design from Quick Flashes' funeral.

Carrie was excited to see it. It was like an old acquaintance, a familiar companion. But her heart sank too. This is where it happened, this is where her friend had died. Carrie lifted the moccasin, hugged it to her chest.

She heard a noise, hid the moccasin behind her, looked around. It was nothing, the wind. No one was visible, the compound empty but for the house, the barn, the church, and her. Suppose Isaac found her there, moccasin in her hand. He would know she knew. He would lock her up too. She glanced around, eager to see if there was anything else, the other moccasin, her deerskin dress. She saw nothing. Isaac had come back, gathered Running Deer's belongings, dragged them with her out of the compound, dropping the moccasin on the way without realizing.

Carrie could not remain there any longer. She stepped outside the compound, pulled the door shut behind her, stood a moment, unsure what to do, and saw, on the ground, a few inches from the fence and several feet down the hill, toward the woods, the other moccasin. She smiled at the sight of it, bent, picked it up. Now she had a pair. She put them on her hands, held them up, clapped them together:

Patty cake, patty cake, baker's man—

She stopped in mid-clap, set them on the ground, pulled off her left shoe, raised her stockinged foot, held her breath, brought it down. Everything about her relaxed as the soft suppleness surrounded her foot. She smiled. This was a way for her to leave, a gift from Mohee's sister. "Thank you," she thought, but did not say. She started to feel deep sadness for what had happened, stopped herself. She would mourn later. She didn't have time now.

Quickly, before she got used to it, Carrie slipped the moccasin off, pushed and forced her shoe back on. She left the moccasins part way down the hill, in a small thicket, a tangle of branches. She would come back for them, hide them with the bundle at the second stream, happy to have them for her journey; and when, as she left, she stopped to put them on, she would leave in their place by the path her hard leather shoes.

As she took the bread from the oven, Carrie settled on a plan. She would stay through dinner. She would be happy, knowing how little time she had left. She might even waver in her resolve to leave. She felt sorry for Gideon, for his sorrow, his loneliness, his lack of understanding, but she knew she couldn't stay.

She reminded herself how a child would be raised there. Like Paul, not Tiki. And suppose it was a girl? Or a heathen—?

Even if she could survive somehow the death of staying, and she knew she could not, she could not perpetuate that on a child. It was about more than Mohee and Gideon, Rebecca, Running Deer, and Isaac. It was about her, and the child growing inside her. If neither of them could fully be themselves there—

She was surprised at herself for not feeling selfish.

She had heard in Isaac's sermons, she did not know how many times, how they came there to fulfill the Lord's mandate: to make a new life, do what they needed and what they were capable of, unbounded by the restraints of others. And that's what she was doing.

She decided on a time. It would be after dinner, a little before bedtime. It would already be dark. No one would suspect her of running away. They would wait until morning before searching for her.

As Gideon sat in his chair reading the Bible, his finger lifting up the next page, she would say she was going to step outside. She often did. It would not seem unusual.

Since her return, it was the one foible she was allowed. She would stand and stare at the night, seeing Mohee in it, his image formed by the green glow of fireflies, knowing he was still there.

"Don't linger," Gideon would call as she opened the door. If he was feeling jocular he might add, "And don't play the sorceress and make predictions."

No, she would not linger, not tonight, she thought as she stepped out of the cabin, pulled the door shut behind her. Overhead, hundreds of stars covered the sky. In the middle, a river of them seemed to flow from where she stood. After a moment to get used to the dark, she followed it down the hill and into the woods.

A sticky filament across the path clung to her cheek. She stopped, backed up, slid her hand up, pushed it away from her face, gently disengaged herself from Many Legs' line. She pulled her hand toward her, flicked her fingers forward. They felt free of the filament. "Come with me if you want," she thought, in her mind addressing Many Legs. "I could use a companion."

She stood a moment, to let Many Legs spin down and nestle in her clothes. Then she ducked down, proceeded past where its line had been, straightened up, settled into the familiar rhythm of walking, eager to reach the bundle at the second stream, to take off her hard leather shoes, slip on the moccasins, let her feet guide her on the paths they knew so well.

An owl hooted above her. The sound startled her.

She looked up for it, saw only darkness. It hooted again, a little in front of her. The end of the call vibrated inside her. It hooted a third time, still ahead of her, as if flying from tree to tree, leading her way.

She smiled as she went on, stepping left, stepping right. She knew hearing an owl was a good sign when beginning a journey.

Carrie needed to stop, to lie down, close her eyes. It was all she could do to keep them open. Still, on she went in the dark, left foot, right foot, left foot, right, her feet in the moccasins following the path.

For two nights and two days she hadn't slept, only napped a little here or there, all her time spent walking, stopping to drink water, eat, doze, started awake by the breeze or the call of a bird, jumping to her feet, walking again, sure Isaac on horseback was in the woods, searching for her, and in another moment would come galloping up behind her—

Her foot hit a tree root. She lunged forward, caught herself part way down, stopped, stood up straight, and, lifting her foot higher, kept going.

Maybe if she ate. Her hand went into her pocket. Its emptiness surprised her. Her fingers found one small potato at the bottom, all that remained from what she'd started with. She drew her open hand out. She would save it for later, and in the morning, in daylight, would look until she found more to eat.

On she walked, her eyes searching the darkness from side to side.

To her right she saw the outline of a boulder, large enough to sleep behind. She stepped off the path, started toward it.

A moment later she was lying on the ground. She didn't know how she'd gotten there. She didn't seem to be hurt.

She shut her eyes. She knew she should get up, go behind the boulder. She couldn't just yet. She breathed out, relaxing.

She opened her eyes. She didn't know where she was, why she was lying on the ground in the dark. Was she sick? She didn't think so, more tired and cold. She remembered, as in a dream, saying she was going to step outside to look at the stars, pulling the door shut behind her, walking as quickly as she could down the hill, into the woods, looking for Mohee, Tiki or the Old Woman. That was days ago and she still hadn't found them.

She moved her head over onto her hand, flat on the ground, shut her eyes. She would look for them later.

Carrie stirred, vaguely aware of a noise above her. Let me sleep, she thought. The noise kept repeating. In what seemed like one moment she realized what it was, opened her eyes, and was standing, fully awake, ready to move on.

She was hearing an owl and had been for a while. It was the first one she had heard since just after leaving. It sounded close enough to touch, but, looking up, she saw only darkness.

It hooted again, a little in front of her. She had not heard or seen it fly.

She tried to take a step, almost fell, tried again. She couldn't. She reached down, felt a vine around her ankle, remembered she was not on the path, but off to the side. She held the vine up, stepped away from it, backed up a few more steps until her feet felt the worn path, took a step forward.

The owl hooted ahead of her, hooted again, farther ahead. She walked after it, taking a step, looking left, looking right, taking another.

On they went, the two of them, hoot step step, step step, hoot, step step.

She smelled smoke, stopped. Her hand went to the knife in her bundle, ready to slip off the path, hide in the brush or behind a boulder.

She listened, looked around. Nothing had changed. The only noise was the constant thrumming of crickets and cicadas. A damp breeze drifted by, bringing a stronger smell of smoke.

The owl hooted in front of her. She didn't move. It hooted again.

She lifted her left foot, brought it forward, put it down, lifted her right foot. The owl moved and hooted, moved and hooted.

She came to the top of a rise, stopped. The smell of smoke was stronger.

The owl hooted a little ahead of her. Another hooted farther ahead. She looked in its direction, saw what she thought was a red glow in the woods. She must be imagining it. She looked away, shut her eyes, opened them.

The closer owl hooted, followed by the other, as if answering. She turned toward the sound, saw the same red glow. It looked like a fire. Three people stood near it.

The owl above hooted once more, followed by a quiet whoosh and a dark whir of wings as it flew off past her.

The farther owl answered. The call seemed to come not from the trees but from one of the people.

Still Carrie stood, watching and waiting.

From the direction of the fire came the sharp song of a Wren. The hair stood on end up and down her arms. Wrens don't sing at night, she thought. Could it be one of the people?

The Wren whistled again, clear and unmistakable.

Carrie started crying, her throat tight and full. There was no sound, only the silent heaving of her body.

The Wren whistled a third time.

Her heart leapt up. It was one of them! It had to be!

"Mohee? Is that you?" She asked in her head. "Or Tiki?"

There was another hoot.

After a moment, Carrie hooted back as best she could. The sound half caught in her throat. It sounded more like the croaking of a frog.

A riot of hoots and Wren whistles answered, hoot, hoot, whistle, whistle, hoot hoot hoot.

Carrie smiled, almost laughed.

She heard a quiet clicking-and-scolding noise. It went again before she realized it was a sound she knew. A Chipmunk. Her!

Chills went up and down her entire body.

She opened her mouth. No sound came out.

She heard the clicking-and-scolding again, followed by silence, and then a voice she recognized saying, “Chipmunk?”

She bit her lip, smiling and crying at the same time. As quickly as she could, she started forward. After a few steps, she stumbled off the path into a patch of brambles. They latched onto her dress, stuck into the backs of her hands. She stopped, pulled the prickers out, backed up onto the path, looked ahead.

The people seemed to be coming toward her.

Holding her breath and walking more slowly, Carrie moved toward them.

About The Author

Jonathan Gillman is the director of *Looking In Theatre*, a teen interactive social issue theater group in existence for over forty years. It was the recent recipient from the State of Connecticut of the Katharine Hepburn Award for Using the Arts as a Platform for Social Change.

My Father, Humming, published by Antrim House Books, was a finalist for the 2014 Paterson Poetry Prize.

For over thirty years, Jonathan was also the head of the theater department at the Greater Hartford Academy of the Arts, a public magnet high school.

Captivity is his first novel.

Other Books by Jonathan Gillman

Looking In

My Father, Humming

Grasslands

The Magic Ring

Made in the USA
Monee, IL
12 February 2020